FREE FALL

By Glenna Jarvis

Other novels by Glenna Jarvis
Sandmann 2011

In loving memory of my sweet aunt
Lena Marie Price Modin
You were my friend and I miss you terribly.

And in memory of a big wall climbing legend:

"When I touched the rock, it had in turn touched my spirit, awakening an ineffable longing, as if I had stirred a hidden memory of a previous existence, a happier one. While I was climbing, it was glorious to be alive." – Royal Robbins

Acknowledgements

First, a huge thank you to the members of my critique group, The Writerie: Rocky Hatley, Jane Ostrander, Kathleen House, Wyatt Trost, and Miguel Nolasco. Your support, encouragement and comments helped me get where I am.

Former member of The Writerie and my mentor, Kathy "Kat" Goldring, whose critique and editing skills are top-notch and I wouldn't dare send out a manuscript without them.

Nellie Serna and Annie Rodriguez at the Chowchilla branch of the Madera County Library. The small conference room houses my muse.

My reviewers who read and offer insight: Larry Patten, Roy Sollenburger, retired criminal investigator Detective Robert Salas, big wall climber and County Supervisor David Rogers (my real-job boss), his climbing buddy Assistant Chief of Corrections Gerald King, Kathy Goldring, Bradley Phillips, Tanna Boyd and Rocky Hatley.

National Park Service public information officer, Jamie Richards who was kind enough to answer a string of questions about law enforcement, climbing accidents and investigations.

My coworker Brittany Dyer who put me in contact with Jamie Richards. Thank you for helping me with the information I needed to keep my story real.

Penny Lane, the best Border collie and companion I've ever had. Her spirit will stay alive in these pages.

And my family, who have always offered their encouragement and support: my son Aaron Sanders and fiancé Cassie Berquist, son Adam Sanders, daughter in law Hannah Whatley-Sanders, grandbabies Tristan and the princess Crimson Olivia, my brother Robert Jarvis and family, and my sisters; Rena, Donna Holly and Tracy.

Chapter 1

Crisp September air laced with scents of pine filled my senses. I breathed deeply and scanned the soaring, jagged cliffs on the south side of Yosemite Valley. Above those peaks, the sun lightened the sky to shades of violet. From my perch five-hundred feet above the valley floor, towering ponderosa pine, incense cedar and white fir which grew to more than two hundred feet, spread out below like shag carpet. Evidence of the ongoing drought speckled that carpet with brown, visible signs of death from years of bark beetles boring holes into the trees. The insects weren't new to California, but their populations exploded due to the lack of water and warmer temperatures than the Sierra Nevada usually experienced.

My glasses slipped. I poked them into place. Overdue for a new pair, I posted a mental sticky note to see the ophthalmologist. My temples throbbed with a hangover. Not bad, but enough to leave a steady thumping.

Again I breathed deeply, savoring the sense of cold. Beside me, Diane Spinelli sipped from her travel mug and set it aside. The sun inched higher, its rays outlining the mammoth rocks with a golden halo that stretched out and touched the tops of the trees.

I tugged the edge of my knit cap over my ears to cut back the chill. The mile and a half hike to the base of The Nose in darkness, the rugged, rock strewn trail lit only by flashlight, had been worth the trek just to see the spectacular sunrise.

"Beautiful, isn't it Hannah?" Diane hugged her knees to her chest.

I nodded. "More coffee?"

I offered her the thermos. She shook her head. I filled my mug and used my finger to fish out a few grounds. Sipping the tepid coffee, I peered up at the granite monolith beside me, but we were still cast in shadow. My boyfriend, Quint Rydell, and his climbing buddies had begun their ascent five hours ago. By now they were likely a quarter of the way up El Capitan. Even if I could've spotted them, they'd be no more than tiny stick figures on a vast canvas of stone.

My palms sweat at the thought of scaling a three thousand foot granite rock with nothing more than rope and cams, spring-loaded metal devices wedged into cracks. I couldn't get close to the edge before me without being overcome by vertigo. I hated heights. But Quint loves climbing and I love him so I tagged along whenever he invited me. This spot, on a ledge high above the valley, was worth the trip.

I'd done some research when Quint said he was a junkie for the sport. John Muir had been the first to climb Yosemite's big walls. In 1869 Muir climbed Cathedral Peak, what is now a class four crack. Muir did it all without a rope. Today, most climbers used ropes, Quint had told me. In 1958, it took a group of men twelve days to reach El Cap's summit. Quint and his companions intended to reach it by nightfall.

Cams and caribiners, locking devices used to attach the harness to the rope. No way, not me. They could keep their gear. I'm fine on a ledge or below with good old Mother Earth beneath my feet.

I also came with Quint because it was a relaxing break from my job as crime reporter for the Borden Gazette, a daily newspaper in a small town nestled in California's San Joaquin Valley.

"Quint's new book came out," I said, referring to the enormous volume containing his photographs of the national park's big walls, *Faces of Yosemite*.

"I'll get a copy," Diane said.

"Let me give you one," I suggested. "They retail for fifty bucks. Ready to head back?"

"A few more minutes." Concern creased her forehead.

Sunlight brightened the shadow over us to an ash gray. As was our routine when we accompanied Quint and Diane's husband, Grady Spinelli, on their excursions, we often waited until the sun had fully risen.

Cold bit my cheeks. My head ached from too many beers the night before. I had hoped the coffee would ease that pain a bit, but it hadn't. I'd have to wait until Quint returned. As required, we'd locked everything food related (and yes, he considered pain reliever close enough to food to count) in the bear-proof containers and I couldn't remember where he'd left the key.

"You don't have any Advil, do you?" I asked.

"Back at camp." She continued staring across the valley. Something in her demeanor wasn't right. I'd known her about a year now and she was normally upbeat. The lines in her forehead deepened.

"Everything okay?"

"No." She lowered her gaze, picked at a rough spot on her nail, usually manicured to perfection.

My own were ragged from the bad habit of biting them. I turtled them into my coat sleeves. "I'm a decent listener."

"I don't know what it is," she said. "Does Grady seem distant to you?"

I shrugged. "Hadn't noticed."

"There's something going on at work. He won't talk about it."

He was one of Madera County's supervisors, a decorated war veteran and the front-runner in November's congressional race. As a reporter, I knew how politicians often got a bad rap. Everything they did was scrutinized, as though they were bacteria studied beneath a high-powered microscope.

She looked at me, her blue eyes moist with the anguish she felt. They'd been married fifteen years. Although I wasn't married and wouldn't pretend to understand how she felt, I knew she loved him deeply and therefore the pain was just as deep.

"His position requires he maintains confidentiality," I said.

"It's not that. I think—" She breathed deeply. Tears rolled down her cold-reddened cheeks. "I think he might be seeing someone."

"Grady?" I scoffed and then realized my insensitivity. "Sorry, but there's no way. He loves you. He'd never do anything to harm your relationship."

"He's edgy," she said. "This morning, he almost backed out of the climb."

"Why didn't he?"

Pebbles and a rock the size of a quarter rained onto the ledge a few feet away. I gazed up the monolithic prow. Although I couldn't make out individuals, I detected shapes the size of cockroaches move slowly over the cliff's face, which had lightened to a pale shade of gray.

"The new climbers," she said with a wistful smile. "He didn't want to disappoint them."

Quint and Grady often climbed together, usually by themselves. But they'd met four others who wanted to try scaling El Cap and offered to help them out. They'd planned this trip, the Nose In A Day or *NIAD*, for about a week. I could understand why Grady wouldn't bail.

I touched her arm, a feeble attempt to offer comfort. I've never been good at the shoulder-to-cry-on routine. I'd been raised to bottle my feelings as though letting them escape would somehow brand me as weak. But over the past few years, I've grown to realize that emotion in the form of compassion wasn't weakness. A touch on the arm was miles from where I'd started.

"He'll talk when he's ready," I said, trying to offer reassurance.

She nodded and smiled, then peered out over the treetops. I followed her gaze just as sunlight crept around The Nose, touched my face with its warm amber hues.

Above, someone shouted—*"Oh shit."*

Shock froze me, left me acutely aware of what those words meant: One of the men was in trouble. I scrambled to my feet.

Just as I looked up a man cried out, his voice thin from the distance. He leaned back, the rope he'd been secured to flapped against the stone. Then he fell.

Instinctively, I reached out the way a mother would extend her arm to protect her child upon slamming the breaks. I wanted to stop him.

"No," I breathed, unable to speak beyond the horror that gripped me.

The body struck the mountain, bounced, struck again. He careened toward us, crashed onto the corner of the ledge with a bone-crunching slap. Pink mist bloomed in the air around him. He tumbled over and continued his hundred-mile-an-hour decent. Red rained over us.

I stared at my jeans, speckled with blood, and screamed.

Chapter 2

My body trembled. My throat burned. The screams ripping from my lips echoed in the valley below. At some point—I had no idea when—I'd grown quiet, yet the sounds continued to pierce my head. Everything became vivid, sharp, and brighter and I realized where the sound came from.

"*Grady*," Diane shrieked and scrambled toward the ledge's bloodied edge.

"*No*," I shouted, snagged the hem of her coat and yanked her back. She sprawled over my legs. I clutched her quivering body and held her, wanting to take away her pain, wanting to comfort her, wanting to change reality and return to the peaceful morning we'd enjoyed moments before.

Using my coat sleeve I tried to wipe blood from her cheeks, but I still shook too badly. Tears flooded Diane's eyes. She struggled to speak, as though she didn't have the strength to breathe. She pulled away and rose to her knees. I half expected her to bolt for the cliff again, so I held onto her arms.

Slowly, with a look that revealed disbelief, she shook her head.

"Grady." She doubled over and wailed in such deep anguish she sounded like a tortured animal. "Oh, God—Hannah, it's *Grady*."

A nauseating blend of relief and guilt filled me. Quint hadn't died. That overwhelming fear that I'd lost him faded, replaced with an emotion I couldn't define. Diane's husband was dead.

"Come on," I said, still shaky. "We've got to get back to camp."

She nodded mutely. I stood, helped her to her feet and wrapped my arm around her waist, letting her lean against me for support. When we both felt steady enough to walk, we left the ledge that had, only moments before, offered such peace and serenity. Now, it had turned ugly, morphed into a terrifying place I would never visit again.

The path, steep and rocky at first, gradually became less severe. Once below the tree line, birds took flight, loosening dew from overhead boughs. In my mind, those virgin drops turned red. I cringed, half expecting them to rain on me as Grady's blood had.

Squirrels scurried across granite that had long ago tumbled from the side of El Capitan. The image of Grady tumbling filled my mind. I shuddered and forced myself to focus on the trail, one that could become my deathbed if I wasn't careful.

Because the path was narrow, Diane hiked behind me. I periodically stopped to make sure she continued to walk. In shock, she moved like a robot, as though not knowing or caring where I led her. I'd get her to the clinic as quickly as possible. I felt sick, but could only imagine what she was going through and mentally asked the creator of all life to keep Quint safe. My stomach knotted at the thought of seeing his broken body.

The scent of pine, no longer refreshing, clogged my nostrils and I drew short, shallow breaths. Again I glanced over my shoulder. Diane stopped and sank to a boulder.

I knelt beside her and tucked her blond hair behind her ear. Blood had turned some of the strands red. Breathing deeply, I forced a smile I didn't feel.

"Come on," I said, hoping my tone sounded encouraging. "Not much farther."

"I can't." Tears streamed down her face. A drop glistened on her chin, fell and dampened her down jacket, turning it the sooty shade of El Cap before sunrise.

"You can." I didn't know what to say. "There's a clinic in the valley. They can help."

"No one can," she said, her voice barely a whisper. "I want Grady."

"I know." Sitting, I drew her into my arms and let her weep against my shoulder. I wanted to wake her from the stupor she'd fallen into, but I didn't know how. At the same time I wanted to berate myself for thinking thoughts so calloused. Instead, I held her more tightly. "I know, Diane. I know."

I couldn't tell her Grady was never coming back. If he had been alive when he struck the ledge, he wasn't any more. The spray of blood, the snapping of bone—no one could have lived through such physical torture.

The cold wind, once soothing, now grated my cheeks like sandpaper. Two climbers approached us, one of them carrying a haul pack on his shoulder, the other his harness and specially designed shoes. They slowed as they drew closer and, apparently seeing the blood on Diane and me, stopped. First one, then the other, shed their gear and moved closer, with deliberate caution, as though we were wounded animals.

"Are you okay?" he asked. Dark hair and a French accent. The other, blond, said something I didn't understand, apparently not knowing or understanding English.

"The blood isn't ours," I whispered, unable to summon the ability to speak louder.

"It is a climber?" he asked. The men exchanged uneasy glances.

Diane's shoulders trembled. She hid her face in her hands. I tightened my arms around her and nodded.

"Alexis, Peut-etre nous ne devrions pas monter," the non-English speaker said, and I got the feeling they were canceling their date with the big wall.

"Peut-etre vous avez raison," Alexis said. To me, he asked, "The ledge. That is where you were?"

Again I nodded, not wanting to speak. My throat felt tight, and although I tried to assume my reporter's persona—distance myself from what happened—this time, it wasn't that easy, this time I wore the blood of the victim.

"Come," he said, and motioned us to stand. "We will assist you back to the road. Are you staying in Camp Four?"

Another nod. Another constricted sob. Another heavy sigh. My chest cramped, my breath became short and labored. Fresh tears scraped my face every bit as harshly as the wind.

I peered up, but from our position on the trail I could no longer see the rock formation where Quint and the others still climbed. El Capitan was now hidden behind the two-hundred-foot trees.

I don't know how long we sat there on the cold stone before she recovered enough to dry her eyes and nod her willingness to continue. I helped her to her feet and, keeping her hand firmly in mine, followed Alexis back to the trailhead. The other walked behind us, helping Diane over the craggy boulders.

The cold morning air, no longer invigorating, seemed to seep into my very core as though wanting to freeze my blood and numb my brain. My world threatened to stop—God how it wanted to stop—but not yet. I had to get Diane to the clinic. Her skin had gone pale. Her eyes were wide and vacant with dilated pupils. I wasn't a doctor, but even I knew that if she didn't get help soon she'd likely be in danger of something brought on by shock. Hypothermia? I didn't know, and not knowing scared me.

By the time we reached Camp Four, climbers had gathered in a silent vigil near the rocky incline at the base of El Cap. In hushed tones, they exchanged what little information they had. Higher up, among the boulders, Yosemite Search and Rescue—YOSAR—had already arrived. Grady's body lay hidden beneath yellow tarp. His fall onto the rock's knife-like edges had severed one of his legs, which lay a couple yards away, his bloodied climbing shoe was partially exposed beneath tarp.

My stomach knotted. Pressing the back of my hand to my mouth, I closed my eyes and again summoned my reporter persona. When I didn't know how to deal with situations, I distanced myself and focused on work, a survival trait acquired over the years.

"Vous serez d'accord?" He closed his eyes, shook his head and regarded Alexis.

"He wants to know if you will be okay," he said. "Do you have someone? Perhaps someone we can call for you?"

"No," I said, and again glanced up at the monolith. "I'll find help to get her to the clinic. Thank you."

"Etre bien, Mlle," Alexis said. "Be well, Miss."

They joined their fellow climbers. I regarded Diane, her profound look of loss breaking my heart.

News reporter. Stiffen the spine, girl. Focus on the job. Soon media vans would clog Northside Drive just outside of camp. Word would spread that a member of the county Board of Supervisors had fallen to his death. A channel 31 news van was already there, probably covering the upset after a new vendor won the contract to run the park and the old vender insisted names of places within Yosemite were intellectual property.

A brunette I recognized sat on a bumper and traded her heels for sneakers. Morning dew had dampened the hems of her slacks. She had the milk and honey complexion that seemed to be a prerequisite in television.

Houston. I couldn't recall her first name. She spotted us, waved and headed over.

"Oh, no," Diane said, backing away from the approaching reporter. "I can't—Hannah, I can't talk."

"Of course you can't." I gripped Diane's hand and tried to veer her in the opposite direction, but she was sluggish and stumbled over some pine cones.

The cameraman, his San Francisco Giants ball cap backward so it wouldn't interfere with the hunk of equipment on his shoulder, moved in. He crouched, and I knew he was filming. I stepped between him and Diane, although my height wasn't enough to block her completely.

"Mrs. Spinelli," Houston shouted, and the other reporters headed for us. I had to get Diane out of the media circus and to a clinic. "Mrs. Spinelli, did you see your husband fall?"

Insensitive bitch. Such language doesn't often worm into my mind, but just then I couldn't think of a more appropriate term.

"Do they know what happened to make him fall?" she asked over the onslaught of words and questions bulleted our way. "What happens now? What happens to his seat on the Board?"

"Not now," I said, and wanted to add, not ever. How would Houston feel if it had been her husband who had plummeted to his death? "Please, show some respect."

"That's funny coming from a reporter." Houston stopped, hand on hip, and smirked. "Going for an exclusive?"

"Back off," I shouted. "I'm her friend."

"Uh-huh." That smirk again.

Peering around, I recognized one of the rangers, an NPS public information officer. I'd met him about a year ago when covering a story of a local climber who had gotten caught off guard when a storm no one expected moved in and quickly turned to snow. YOSAR had waited until the storm passed in order to help the climber into a wire carrier hung from a helicopter.

The NPS ranger had been great about giving me the story. Maybe he'd fill me in on what they'd learned in the hour it had taken us to hike back from the ledge.

First, Diane needed medical attention. I waved toward the ranger— Xavier, if I remembered correctly. A tall man, he reminded me of an NFL linebacker: thick-necked, broad shoulders and someone you'd want on your side should you ever meet a shady character in a dark alley. He trotted over, glanced at Diane and paled.

"Mrs. Spinelli?" he asked.

"Yeah." I met Xavier's gaze. "We saw . . ." I swallowed hard.

"Right." He waved toward another ranger. To him, Xavier said, "she's in shock. Get her to the clinic. A-SAP," he added, as though it wasn't an acronym but a word.

The ranger, Wade according to his brass nameplate, led Diane to his Expedition, helped her inside and headed east toward the village. She looked back at me with a vacant expression as though she'd already checked out and now just waited to join Grady in whatever realm he'd gone to.

This story would fall on my plate. I not only covered the crime beat, but also county government when we were short staffed. Which was most of the time. I had no desire to do so, but resigned myself to becoming the detached reporter and focused on getting the details of the rangers' investigation. What had happened to make Grady Spinelli fall?

Diane said he'd been preoccupied. Had he made a fatal error?

Grady wasn't the first experienced climber to fall from El Cap or any other big wall. Sometimes, Quint had explained, people became too comfortable, the climb too routine, giving them a false sense of security. They didn't set a second rope, or didn't add that extra cam for protection. They became like children, who believed themselves invincible, like they couldn't die.

A helicopter thumped overhead, near the face of El Cap, its occupants probably checking the condition of the remaining climbers. The copter tilted near the cliff face, righted and flew off.

Shading my eyes, I peered up and spotted Quint and the others, nothing more than specks against the gray stone. I imagined Quint trying to reassure the others, not an easy task given the fact one of their experienced comrades had died.

Please be safe. The thought of Quint up there, dealing with the devastating loss of his friend, twisted my gut. *Please be careful and make it back.*

Grady had been on the Madera County Board of Supervisors less than six years and had led the race for Congress last June. A rancher by trade, he lived in Coarsegold, a small community in the Sierra foothills. He and Quint were like brothers. They were very strict when it came to safety. Although no one could guarantee perfect climbs, they took every precaution.

Knowing this only increased my anxiety. Quint had once told me that it was too dangerous to rappel down from an ascent because of the length of their ropes and number of pitches—places where they'd have to hook cams into cracks. He and the other climbers had no choice but to continue upward. If Quint's calculations were accurate, they would reach the summit by nightfall.

Xavier leaned against the trunk of a giant pine and watched the other rangers as they took photos, measurements, and penciled notes.

Although I wanted to collapse and cry, I couldn't. Not yet. Take care of business first, break down later. I drew a deep, long, cleansing breath and slowly exhaled, willing the action to settle my nerves enough to do the job.

"I have to cover this," I said. The last thing I wanted to deal with was writing a story. I'd filter out what I'd witnessed and focus on the facts. Cut and dry. No emotion and that would be the easiest part. The horror of seeing a body slam against the granite ledge, getting sprayed with blood, would haunt me the rest of my life.

Xavier nodded, an over-emphasized motion that seemed to tell me he understood my dilemma.

"I need paper," I said. "And a pen."

Xavier handed me a gnawed pencil and a report he'd gotten that morning that ended up innocuous.

I scratched a line in one corner as if it were a pen, testing its ability to write.

"Who called this in?" I asked.

"Half a dozen people." Xavier gestured toward the scatter of domed and peaked tents. "Several climbers. A visitor saw the fall from across the Merced River."

I jotted it down. "Your men have been looking at this for about an hour now, right?"

He nodded.

"Any idea what happened?"

"Preliminary report only," Xavier said and crinkled his brow. "It appears as though some of the cam's we recovered from Grady's belt were compromised."

"They used Quint's equipment. He's meticulous about his gear. He checked everything yesterday when preparing for the climb. He would never use a damaged cam."

"The cam. Black Diamond brand. Odd," Xavier added. "I've never known a Black Diamond cam to fail."

That's because they didn't. I knew the brand. Quint wouldn't trust his life to anything but the best.

He'd examined everything last night. Had he checked again this morning?

Had someone intentionally damaged the gear? If so, could Quint now be using equipment that could pose a risk to his life?

Chapter 3

That someone could have intentionally damaged Quint's climbing gear chilled my blood. My body trembled again, this time from fear. Although I wanted to collapse, I couldn't. I had to do my job. I had to get the story.

"Diane said something had been going on with Grady at work," I said, only barely aware I'd spoken aloud.

"How's that?" Xavier asked.

"She said he'd been distracted, and this morning had almost bailed on the climb."

I didn't add that she was worried enough to question his fidelity.

"You think someone wanted Grady dead?"

"I don't know what to think," I said, and an icy finger trailed my spine. I shivered.

Xavier removed his Smokey Bear hat and scratched his graying hair. "That's a far stretch. He was from Madera County, not San Francisco or Los Angeles. You don't have much controversy, and what you do have isn't worth killing over."

Unless there was something going on in District Five I wasn't aware of.

What did I know? Only what Diane had said, and the look of anguish she'd exhibited had been enough to convince me. Besides, if Diane felt something was going on, I'd bet a week's pay she was right.

And the damaged climbing gear. I didn't have an overactive imagination. What I do have is a keen sense of reporter's intuition. My gut told me that, somewhere, there was motive for Grady's death. The dread that filled me settled like a dark cloak attempting to smother reason. I shook it off, gripped the pencil and jotted a note to check into issues facing constituents in District Five.

Several rangers were scattered about camp.

"What are they doing?" I asked.

"Talking to anyone who may have seen something." Xavier regarded me. "Mind if I ask you a few questions? Part of the job."

I wanted to shower, get out of the clothes that were speckled with blood that had turned the color of rust.

"It won't take long," he added.

"I didn't see anything," I said, and the image of Grady falling, striking, tumbling filled my head. I closed my eyes. "Except the fall."

"You and Quint stayed here last night?"

I nodded.

"See anything suspicious?"

"Nothing." I looked up at Xavier. "I'm a reporter, and naturally suspicious. I didn't detect anything out of the ordinary."

He made some notes of his own. After compiling the little information Xavier could offer on an ongoing investigation, I retreated to the tent I shared with Quint, found clean clothes and made use of the showers in the restroom facilities. Then I started packing. Although we'd planned on staying another night, and heading back to the San Joaquin Valley early tomorrow, I didn't feel like camping any more. I doubted Quint would, either.

By nine the sun had warmed the air to a comfortable degree. I traded my Anorak coat for a hoodie softened by age and bearing the park's logo. I needed a distraction, but all I could think about was Quint. I wished they could have shortened the climb. It would be well after dark when he returned.

At ten, I walked to Yosemite Lodge's food court, hoping to find coffee and Advil. My head still ached, now worse than before. Maybe Snickers, too, get some sugar in my bloodstream. Shaken, worried and hung over. Bad combination.

Between the lodge and food court stood The Nature Shop. In the window, prominently displayed, was Quint's *Faces of Yosemite*, the cover photo showing Grady climbing Arrowhead Spire, one of several other formations that drew sports people from all over the world.

Grady. Smiling. Alive. Forever captured on the glossy page of the oversized coffee table book. Diane had wanted a copy. I wasn't sure that was a good idea after this morning.

A sense of panic weighed on me, as though that book was all I had left of Quint, and I resisted the urge to duck inside, grab it and clutch it close. He'd be okay. And with those words firm in my mind, I stomped down that fear.

The concessionaire nodded as I stepped inside the gift shop. After a bit of hunting, I found the Advil, bottled water and Snickers. I paid, tucked the candy bar into the kangaroo pouch on the front of my hoodie and returned to the outdoors. Too early for lunch, the air hadn't yet taken on the scents of grilled beef and greasy fries, yet a faint scent of those clung to the wooden structures and tables. Otherwise, the air was crisp and clean and heavily perfumed with pine.

After swallowing two Advil with a swig of water, I recapped the bottle and headed back for camp. Men and women in the latest North Face and Paramount clothing, one wearing a tee shirt in blue and brown with mountain peaks, pines, a camp fire, the slogan "Look deep into nature and you will understand everything better." Words of a tree hugger, which most of us were.

Acquaintances we'd met on prior trips to Camp Four stopped by, offered their assurances that Quint would be fine, and left trinkets and bouquets near the heap of boulders where, higher up the avalanche of rocks, Grady's body had landed.

Time passed painfully slow. The sun sent shadows shortening, then lengthening across the meadow and darkening the heavily wooded campgrounds. Night had brought an inky black that left it hard to detect movement. If all went well, Quint should return soon.

If. All. Went. Well. Words that bred pain and fear in my heart.

I nibbled my thumbnail. From the blackness came whispers of wind through pine boughs. An owl hooted. A twig snapped. Hikers moved between their tents and the restroom facilities.

Campfires dotted the darkness, casting warm glows over faces of climbers gathered in somber silence. Word had spread quickly. One of their own was dead.

Twisting my Celtic knot ring on my middle finger, I sat on the felled tree near the fire pit, from which flames licked the cold, damp air, and I could almost hear it sizzle.

Headlights pierced the night. A jeep hummed along the two-lane road. Another set glowed, the vehicle slowed and parked. Squinting, I tried to make out what type of car. The door opened and the overhead light spilled over Quint in the driver's seat.

Relief flooded me, making me weak. I breathed deeply, perhaps the only deep breath I'd drawn since watching Grady fall. Tears stung my eyes from the overwhelming release of stress. I strode toward the Land Rover.

While the other men climbed from the four-wheel drive, Quint leaned his head back and ran his fingers through his blond hair. He must have been exhausted.

To look at him one would never know he was an artist. Cameras and lens, photo paper and old-fashioned darkroom developing were his canvas and brush. We were both musicians: he on guitar, me on drums.

One would know he had discipline that went deeper than being true to his craft: Strong bodied, he had the lean physique of a SEAL. Although he'd left the team almost a year ago, he still worked out every day, ran six miles—three more than my morning routine. He could tote an MK-11 sniper rifle in one hand, a bouquet of daisies in the other. Not in a passive-aggressive way, but a balance between justice and peace.

As I approached, he scrubbed his hands over his face and peered through the bug-spattered windshield. He locked his gaze on me and a subtle hint of relief registered in his face. He slid out of the car, closed the door with a soft click and leaned against it. He reached toward me, wiggling his fingers as though doing so would hurry my pace. I clasped his hand and pulled it behind me, rested against his chest, closed my eyes and drew strength from the sound of his heartbeat.

Alive. Thank the creator of all living things. Its life coursed through Quint and allowed me to hold him, him to hold me. Alive.

I realized my cheeks were wet and sobs tugged me like hiccups. Quint wrapped me in his arms, held me almost painfully tight. Thoughts raced through my mind. I wanted to beg him to never climb again, but at the same time knew I'd never voice those words. We had an unspoken rule: Never attempt to control what the other did. Respect each other's intelligence and freedoms.

I slid my arms around his waist, held him as tight as he held me. Then I leaned back and looked up at him. Moisture glimmered in his hazel eyes.

"Why didn't you call?" I asked.

"Sorry, Babe. I dropped my cell. Rangers met us at the summit and separated us for questioning."

"What did you tell them?"

"Nothing. I have no clue why Grady . . ." He cleared his throat, kissed my forehead, and offered me a pained grin. "Where's Diane?"

"A ranger took her to the clinic." I swiped moisture from my face. "I went over there around noon and gave them contact information for her brother."

"He came for her?"

"He said he'd take her to Borden Community," I said, referring to the hospital in our Central Valley hometown. "Xavier said the investigation will probably take a couple weeks but the preliminary report shows faulty equipment. Quint, that's not possible."

His spine went rigid. "No, it's not. We used my pro. I never—"

"I know. They found some cams on Grady's harness that were damaged."

"They could have gotten damaged in the fall."

"The ranger seemed to think otherwise."

Quint shook his head. "That's bullshit."

"Let's wait for their final report," I suggested, knowing it wouldn't placate Quint. "They might find something totally different that could have caused the accident."

If, in fact, it had been an accident. Call it reporter's intuition, gut instinct or just plain old suspicion, but something wasn't right about Grady's death or the rangers' preliminary findings. I knew Quint. He was almost OCD when it came to checking his equipment. He tossed anything that appeared even remotely compromised.

"If that's their finding," Quint said, "and they issue a report saying my pro was faulty . . ."

His reputation as a climber, as a person other climbers could trust, would be just as compromised.

"I'll be known as the idiot who killed my climbing partner," Quint said, and his Adam's apple bobbed. He turned away, raised his arm and swiped it across his eyes. "No way," he muttered. "I didn't kill Grady."

"I know," I said.

"You know, I know, but they—" he jabbed a finger toward Yosemite Valley behind us, swallowed by the inky night. "*They* don't know."

A breeze raked over me, chilling me. Hairs at the nape of my neck prickled. I touched my finger to his lips.

"We will prove that it wasn't your fault," I said, hoping I had the know-how and resources to support my promise.

"Okay. We'll prove it." He tilted his head. "How are we going to do that?"

How? I shrugged. I hadn't quite worked out the details. But we would prove it hadn't been Quint's equipment that led to Grady's death.

I studied the group of men and women who had gathered around a campfire near our tent. One of them cradled a Bible. His lips moved as though reciting scripture.

He had been on the climb with Grady and Quint as had three others, all of whom stood at the group's outer edge. I didn't know their names, but I'd make a point to find out. If Quint was right, and he was always right about such matters as preparing for a climb, maybe one of the others had . . .

"Had what?" I said, barely aware I spoke aloud.

"Hannah?" Quint waved his hand before my face. "Had what?"

"Switched camelots? Cut the rope?" I said.

"They would've had to during the climb," Quint said. "I led. I wouldn't have seen anything."

"Who cleaned?" I asked, recalling the process Quint had described where one of the others used a special tool to remove the gear from the cracks.

"It's always the last climber," Quint said. "Grady cleaned. Until . . ."

I cupped Quint's cheek, lifted onto my toes and kissed him. "We'll figure this out."

And that was a promise I intended to keep.

Chapter 4

Now that I knew Quint was safe, fury simmered just below my boiling point. I didn't anger easily, but the thought that one of the other four climbers could have killed Grady and laid the blame on Quint heated me to my core.

My notepad and pen were next to my canvas suitcase. I picked them up and toyed with the pen's cap. Questions filled my head like a pack of dogs begging for scraps. But the scraps I wanted were answers. Who were these other climbers? How long had Quint known them? They were inexperienced, so why had they taken on the most difficult big wall in Yosemite? Where did they come from? Did they live in Madera County? In District Five?

I tucked the pen and notebook into my coat pocket. Later. The last thing I needed was to make Quint feel like the subject of an interrogation, and after covering the crime beat for more than nine years I had a bad habit of adopting the calloused attitude of a cop.

I ducked into the round, four-person tent that never housed more than us two. Quint had already rolled his sleeping bag and went to work on mine. His fingers had scratches and cuts, evidence of his recent climb. Beside his North Face jacket, I found the neatly folded nylon sack and crammed it over the sausage-like bag.

Heat rose in my face. Perspiration dampened my hairline despite the cold. I drew several deep, calming breaths. I wanted to voice my anger, but Quint was dealing with his own mix of emotions. He didn't show it, but I knew him well enough to know a storm brewed beneath his calm façade.

I'd packed most of my belongings earlier, an idle task I'd hoped would help keep my mind off of Grady's death. Now, I balled up the shirt I'd worn that morning and shoved it into my case. Then I reached for my jeans and stopped. The legs were speckled with rust splotches. Grady's blood. I picked up the pants by a belt loop and dropped them into the trash we'd haul out.

Someone cleared his throat. "Excuse me?"

"Yes?"

The tent flap opened. A park ranger, Jon Cosyns, squatted outside and peered through. An expert climber, he, Grady and Quint had often scaled the walls together.

Crossing my arms, I clenched my teeth to lock in words of annoyance. I wanted to pack and go home, take a shower and crawl into bed. I hadn't climbed, yet I was physically and emotionally exhausted. If I felt this way, I could only imagine how Quint felt.

An unspoken condolence made its way into Cosyns' pale gray eyes. Tall, lean, he too, had the scratches on the pads of his fingers that were common among big wall enthusiasts. "I'd like to talk about what happened to Grady Spinelli."

"In a minute. Need to finish packing." Quint folded the green plaid sleeper in half lengthwise, gripped one end of the sleeping bag, tucked it tightly over. His knuckles whitened as he rolled, as did the line of his jaw. He collected the tin coffee pot and tucked it into the plastic box among metal plates and tableware. He lifted the solar-powered Coleman lamp and added it to the implements in the box.

I touched the back of his hand. He looked up, met my gaze and gave me a pained grimace. An ache settled in my heart. He shouldn't have to deal with questions. Not yet. But he would, because he was just as eager as I was to find out what had gone horribly wrong. I slid the slipcover over the bag and pulled the drawstring.

He ducked out of the tent and stood. I slipped out behind him. If they were going to talk, I wanted to hear.

He settled on a felled tree that served as a bench beside our campfire. Within the flames, burning wood smoldered and glowed orange. I sat beside him, reached for his hand and he locked his with mine.

The air, still damp and cold, carried scents of wood ash. A breeze shivered through the trees overhead, their branches bowing in an almost reverent manner as if they, too, mourned the dead.

The fire's golden glow cast shadows over his face, lending him a ghostly look—hollow around his eyes, dark creases at his brow. He breathed deeply and shifted his gaze toward Cosyns, who sank onto a nearby boulder and pulled a small notepad and pencil from his jacket pocket.

"You're working this case?" Quint asked.

Cosyns nodded.

"The other ranger already questioned me."

"I know. And I'll likely ask some of the same," Cosyns said. "You and Grady—I'm going to make damn sure we know what happened on that wall."

"I'm not sure what more I can tell you." Quint raked his fingers through his hair. "I don't know what happened any more than you do."

"Who led the climb?" Cosyns picked up a pine cone, pulled off dead needles that had caught beneath some scales and tossed them into the fire. They sizzled and were quickly consumed.

Quint's spine stiffened. "I did."

"Whose gear?"

"Mine." Again he raked his fingers through his hair and narrowed his eyes. "Hannah said you found some that had been damaged. I checked everything yesterday."

Cosyns nodded, sending his hat tilting. He removed it and set it on the stone beside him. On the hat's rim, he set the pad and pencil. "I know you and Grady were like brothers. Sorry for your loss," he added, almost as an afterthought. "But the others. How well do you know them? You're SEAL, right?"

Quint glanced at me and shifted slightly. "I was."

"Did you serve with Pratt?"

"No. I just met him a couple weeks ago." Quint's bicep tightened in a subtle movement only I noticed. I stroked his arm. "Grady and I had just climbed Wawona Dome. We met Pratt on the Chilnualna Falls Road."

"He climbed with you guys?"

"No, he was on his way. We'd just finished," Quint said. "He mentioned that he'd never climbed El Cap, said he had some friends who wanted to and we made plans for this trip."

"Do you usually climb with people you just met?" Cosyns tapped the cone against the rock, pried back one scale and shook a couple pine nuts into his palm. He must have been a rookie. Yes, pine nuts are expensive, and harvesting them is easier on the pocketbook. But this was a national park, where nothing was supposed to leave, not a rock, twig or cone. Those seeds were future trees.

"You're a climber," Quint said, not defensively but as though speaking to a brother, two men bonded through their passion for the sport. "We trust each other."

"You said you met Pratt on CFR," Cosyns said. "Had he ever climbed the Dome before?"

Quint shook his head. "He asked us about its difficulty and I told him he needed a lot of runners."

Cosyns tucked the pine nuts into his breast pocket, beneath his badge. "Three of the five pitches are long." He pried off another pedal-like scale and found two more nuts. "Extra runners help reduce rope drag."

"He didn't have number three cams, either." Quint furrowed his brow. "He wasn't equipped for the climb."

Several tents away, a boisterous group enjoying their post-climb beers hollered and whooped, darted after each other like children on a playground. Only these children were in their thirties and halfway to tomorrow's hangover.

The log in the fire pit crackled and spit orange into the air. The night had grown cold, and the fingers of my free hand were numb. I reached toward the flames and let the warmth seep in and chase the chill away.

Pratt wasn't equipped for the climb. I don't indulge in the sport, but even I know of the numerous Web sites that map out the different routes up the big walls, detail what gear would be needed and how long the climb should take. If Pratt was a serious climber, why hadn't he done his research?

The notebook weighted my coat pocket. My fingers twitched, itching to retrieve the tools of my trade, jot down the tidbits of information. I flexed my hand, as though working out stiffness.

"I ended up giving him some of my pro," Quint said, pulling me back to the conversation.

Cosyns pocketed more seeds and continued deflowering the cone. He glanced up, caught my scowl and shook his head.

"Regrowth project," he explained. "My wife is heading the effort to replant once all the dead trees are removed. She's growing them in a greenhouse and later, we'll plant the seedlings."

Made sense.

To Quint, he asked, "And the others? What do you know about them?" He picked up his notepad and one-handedly thumbed through the pages until he found what he'd been looking for. "Bob Roberts and Antoine Yates."

"I've seen them on the walls before, Higher Cathedral Spire, Glacier Point. Not together." Quint frowned, as though searching his memory for information that eluded him. He shook his head. "Seems like I'd seen one of them with Pratt, but I can't be sure. I'd never met them. The only one of the climbers I know, and not well," Quint added, leaning slightly forward as though to get his point across, "is Wickham. He's the priest at the Catholic church in Oakhurst."

A priest on the wall. His God obviously wasn't capable of protecting them. I slipped my hand into my coat's deep pocket, touched the spiral of the notepad, found the pen and twisted its cap.

"You attend church in Oakhurst?"

"No, but Grady did until about a month ago."

"How well did he know the others? Pratt, Roberts and Yates?" Cosyns had found more pine nuts and dropped them into his pocket with the others. I'd lost count as to how many he'd collected.

"He'd climbed with Wickham."

Behind us, voices rose in anger. Quint stood and squinted toward the commotion. He let go of my hand and strode toward the sounds.

With him distracted, I retrieved the pen and narrow reporter's notepad. After jotting down the information he'd given Cosyns, I turned sideways on the log, opting to remain close to the fire's warmth.

Cosyns pocketed the last of the pine nuts, stood and followed Quint.

A group of climbers had gathered near another, larger fire. Two of the men who had been with Quint and Grady were locked in a brawl, punching, pushing and pulling as though engaged in morbid ballet.

Chapter 5

Cosyns and Quint strode toward the men locked in battle. They each grabbed a man by his arms and forced them apart. To one, Quint said, "Yates—What the hell's going on?"

"Dude," said a tall man with narrow, rat-like features and pinched lips. Antsy, pumped on adrenaline, he danced a little jig. "The dumb shit, accused me of killing that guy."

"Roberts?" Quint asked, assuming the role of parent trying to get to the bottom of his siblings' dispute.

"I didn't say you killed him," Roberts said, leaning around Quint to shout at Yates, who turned and flicked his gaze across the fire's orange flames at the men on the far side. I tried to figure out who he was attempting to make eye contact with, but was too far away.

"I just said you were next to last on the rope," Roberts said. "You were closer than any of us."

Quint gripped Yates' elbow and led him toward our campground. Good. With any luck, I'd hear what they had to say. I swung my legs to the other side of the makeshift bench, the fire warming my back, and poised my pen over page.

I could wander closer, but night had brought near freezing temperatures. Instead, I stayed near the warmth of the glowering coals, hot orange with fire snakes twisting among the ruins of wood. Staying in the background, watching body language, often told me more than any confession. Yates seemed nervous. Like any animal backed into a corner, he seemed to be searching for means to escape. Only, what he might be attempting to escape could amount to murder.

I'd recently read a true crime book written by an attorney. I'd found it fascinating, as I did with anything that gave insight into crime scenes and the criminal element. In the book, he'd written about consciousness of guilt, actions by the accused that implied guilt such as fleeing the scene or resisting arrest. More interestingly, he'd turned that theory to consider actions that could reveal consciousness of innocence. Same with circumstantial evidence, this has come to mean guilt. What about innocence?

Yates' hands trembled. He wiped sweat from his upper lip and rubbed his nose against his jacket sleeve. "Never seen anything like that. Don't ever want to again. Man," he said, and again rubbed his nose. "Oh, man."

"We're all shaken." Quint clamped Yates' shoulder. "We may never know what happened today."

Maybe they wouldn't, but I would. Quint had once likened me to a pit bull: When I sank my journalistic fangs into a story, I never let go.

Yates' actions appeared to show lack of guilt. But what if this was a planned display? Maybe he had intentionally tried to garner sympathy to hide his involvement.

Glancing at Quint, making sure he wasn't watching, I scribbled notes.

"It's going to take all of us time to move past this. If you need to talk, give me a call." Quint fished his wallet from his back pocket, found a business card and handed it over.

Yates turned the card over, peered up at Quint and shifted his attention to me. "You're reporters?"

"She is," Quint said, tilting his head toward me. "I'm a photographer."

"No shit?" Yates stared at me. "No fuckin' shit? You're Hannah Monakee, aren't you? *Fuckin' shit,*" he added, and I couldn't tell if he was impressed or disgusted.

"Guilty as charged," I said, considered standing and offering my hand, and decided against it. This guy might prove to be a suspect and something about him unnerved me.

He backed away, keeping his gaze locked on me, and a slight grin lifted one corner of his lips. That small gesture sent fingers of panic playing upon my spine.

At the fire's far side, in the center of the group, stood Wickham, the priest. In tight climbing pants, matching long sleeve shirt, I found it hard to imagine he led a congregation of Catholics. He had the boyish good looks of a young Brad Pitt, back in his Thelma and Louise days. He cradled his Bible in his hands. His rosary swayed from his fingers. He read with such reverence I found it odd, as if he were afraid to be judged.

"Grady died doing something he loved," Wickham said. "I will always be grateful that he cared enough to share his passion for climbing. He literally taught me the ropes. He was a dear friend to many of us and he will be missed."

He switched to Latin, a prayer I assumed by the manner in which several men and women bowed their heads. When Wickham finished, Quint crossed himself in the Catholic fashion. Everyone else muttered, "Amen."

I closed my eyes in a moment of silence. I didn't clutch a rosary, nor did I try to figure out what God thinks or feels. I believe everyone and everything returns to the power that created all things, so I knew Grady was now part of the breeze that washed over me, the trees that embraced that breeze and swayed in the darkness above me.

Wickham seemed comfortable among the other men and women who had come to the Valley seeking thrills only climbing could provide. Just because he was a man of the cloth didn't exempt him in my book. He'd seen enough grief and loss through his position he may have developed mannerisms to mask what he really felt.

Or what he had done?

He didn't seem rattled at all. In fact, he seemed perfectly calm. That, too, I found odd, unless his demeanor was typical of clergy.

I peered around for the former SEAL, Pratt. A Matthew McConaughey look alike with one very disturbing difference: his eyes were like twin windows to a cold, lifeless void.

He had broken away from the mourners and now knelt beside one of the plastic storage containers next to Quint's Rover. He caught my gaze, worked the laces on his boot and stood. He strode across the campgrounds toward the parking lot. He'd already gathered his belongings, his backpack rested on the Mitsubishi's trunk. He tossed the luggage inside, slid into the driver's seat and sped off with a roar of the car's engine.

I returned my attention to Quint. He'd gotten the two men to shake hands. Anger gone, peace reigns and the problems were over?

I didn't think so.

No, this was just the beginning.

Chapter 6

As Quint drove, I peered through the passenger window. Battery-powered flood lamps illuminated the underside of the grand pines in a surreal manner as broadcast media continued their coverage. I had my notes and Xavier said he'd fax their findings, once the investigation was complete. He expected it would be about a week. I knew what their findings would show: an accident due to faulty equipment. I had until then to scare up evidence that would clear Quint and point to the person who had sabotaged his gear.

Only a week to save the reputation of the dearest one in my life. Tears dampened my lashes. I brushed them away and breathed deeply.

The road out of Yosemite on state Route 140 looked glassy in the Rover's headlights. Warm air seeped from vents beneath the dashboard, heat that rose in gentle waves and chased away the chill. But it couldn't thaw the cold that had settled deep inside me, and I wondered if anything would. Sleep, perhaps, and I held onto the thought of curling up in my bed, closing my eyes, blocking out the images that stained my memory.

The gentle glow from the dashboard was enough to reveal Quint's white-knuckled grip on the steering wheel. The tight line of his jaw and the way he bit his lower lip, as though trapping words he wasn't ready to speak, created an awkward silence between us. Although I wanted to talk about what had happened, I'd wait. He would break that silence when he was ready.

Wiper blades slid across the glass, clearing what had become a sprinkle. We wouldn't see any of this in the Valley, where drought conditions had gripped the farmland the past five years. We hadn't had rain since winter, and those showers had been short-lived bursts that dried as quickly as it had fallen. In the San Joaquin Valley, cooler days would kill off the summer heat and bring at least the hope for rain.

I pried off my hiking boots, dropped them onto the floorboard and drew my legs onto the seat. Exhaustion ached in my muscles. I wanted to sleep, but my mind was still wired from the day's events.

I returned my attention to the night. Overhead, beyond the flicker of trees, stars grazed on the field of black sky. Suddenly I felt small and insignificant.

I focused on what I believed to be murder.

Strong word. The intentional killing of another person. I shivered. Hair on my arms prickled, and I rubbed them through my jacket's sleeves.

"Cold?" Quint cranked up the car's heater.

I offered a smile, hoping his single word would evolve into conversation.

He returned his attention to the road. We passed the small huts marking the exit from the park. Soon Merced River, reduced to a trickle, ran along the left side of the road. The clouds dispersed, the three-quarter moon shone a nicotine-yellow, spilling its faint light onto smooth stones that normally would have been buried under swift rapids.

To unburden myself of the weight of silence, I returned my thoughts to the murder.

Such an ugly word, but one I've dealt with for years. Under other circumstances, such as covering a trial or breaking news events at two in the morning, I was able to detach myself from the emotional impact of such crimes. Now, I had to view Grady's death as any other, but every time I closed my eyes I saw his body strike the face of El Capitan, the ledge and heard the bone-crunching slap.

Again I shivered, and pulled my coat tightly around me.

Quint reached for the thermostat. I touched his fingers, hoping the simple gesture would let him know that I was warm enough. He drew his hand away.

My purse, an oversized bag with pockets and zippers, but in which I still managed to lose almost everything, lay on the floorboard next to my boots. I pulled it into my lap, dug around and found a narrow, spiral notebook. I'd clipped pens inside one of the sewn-in pockets and now tugged one free.

If the NPS determined Grady's death an accident, how would I prove otherwise? I glanced at Quint, his intense stare at the road was his attempt to escape, for a little while, the horror of the day. He would help. He had his reputation to protect, if nothing else, and Grady had been a close friend.

But how would he feel about my prying into Grady's background? Uncovering any skeletons in his closet?

Everyone had them. Grady was no exception. During his campaign, word got out that he'd experimented with marijuana while in high school. Who hadn't? Instead of using the Clinton defense—*I never inhaled*—Grady admitted that he'd been a stoner as a teen. As it turned out, the attempt to discredit him backfired. He'd won reelection by an overwhelming eighty-seven percent of the votes.

"Those gears are grinding." Quint glanced at me and back to the road, visible only by the Rover's headlamps. "Come up with a plan yet?"

"No." I returned my attention to the darkness.

I made a mental list of questions I'd ask once Quint was ready to provide answers: Was Grady having an affair? Did he have enemies? How was he this morning while hiking to the base of the Nose? Had he been seen with someone he didn't normally associate with? How were things between the six of them before the climb?

Had there been any tension during the Supervisors' meetings? Quint shot photos any time a controversial issue came before the board. Had he seen or heard anything?

Grady had been well known, not only in District Five but throughout Madera County. In the back of my mind, where my lust for criminal investigations dwelled like a troll beneath a bridge waiting for the Billy Goats Gruff like in the morbid children's story, I began compiling a list of names. At the top were Wickham, Pratt, Roberts and Yates. To those I added the other County Supervisors. One of them may know something. I had a good relationship with one, he'd been my contact with the sheriff's department before retiring and running for Supervisor. A retired cop always had gut instincts I might be able to glean from.

Two hours later, we entered Borden from its north side by way of state Route 99, the main artery that ran through Madera County, and gently slid into the small city.

In 1892, the town had been built near the railroad tracks, which now separated the east and west sides. Before the streets had been paved and concrete sidewalks installed, Borden had an opera house, mercantile, stables and brothel.

Over the years, the east side, where we now exited the highway, had fallen to decay. Gang-related graffiti marked most of the fences and trashcans that had been left in the gutters overflowed. I didn't know this side of town so much by street names, but by crimes and where they'd been committed. Mostly drive-by shootings, gang retaliation and domestic violence. Drugs. Rape. Murder. I'd become numb to the sensations of disgust and fear when covering trials and had, over the years, come to view crime as one would an amoeba: with curiosity.

Beyond the tracks, a new world opened up, one of modest middle class. Farther to the west, high-end homes stood in gated communities. I lived in the middle-leaning-toward-east, but far enough away from the nightly shootings to faintly hear the pop of gunfire and therefore felt relatively safe.

Quint pulled into the driveway of my rented duplex, shifted into park and left the car's engine idling. He climbed out, pulled my canvas case from the cargo, came to the passenger side and opened the door.

I slid out, my stocking feet immediately chilling as they touched concrete. Tucking my notepad and pen into my purse, I gathered my boots and stepped past him. As always, he walked me to the door and waited until I'd found my keys—front left pocket in my oversized bag—and unlocked.

He reached past me, opened the door and set my suitcase inside.

I slid my hands to the back of his neck, spread my fingers through his hair and met his gaze. The pain I saw gripped my heart as if someone had clenched it in a vise.

"You're welcome to stay," I whispered, hoping he'd accept, let me hold him during the night and offer the comfort of my body against his.

"Tempting." He bent close, brushed his lips against mine, straightened and let go a long breath. Then he clutched me almost painfully tight as he had when he'd returned from the climb to find me waiting, needing to find him alive and safe. "Not tonight."

"Okay," I said, and stroked my finger against his cheek. "If you change your mind I'm a phone call away."

He nodded, kissed me hard as though needing to pull from me the strength he couldn't find within himself. Planted his lips against my forehead and let me go.

I stood on the porch until he'd climbed into the Rover and drove away. Then I stepped inside, closed the door and flipped the deadbolt. If he changed his mind, he knew I always kept a spare key duct-taped beneath the porch railing.

All the lights except that beneath the stove vent and one upstairs in the hall were extinguished. My roommate had gone to Fresno to take in a play. Excuse me, a *performance* at a theater in Fresno.

In the scant glow, I found the bookcase at the bottom of the stairs and deposited my purse. Leaving the suitcase in the entryway, I climbed to the second story and into my bedroom.

Queen bed with rumpled sheets as I'd left it Friday before leaving for Yosemite. The overstuffed green chair by the window which held the clothes I'd stripped off Thursday night. The laundry basket overflowing with wash I'd neglected more than a week. All the familiar surroundings left me feeling cold and empty inside. My entire world had changed in the course of a day.

I stripped out of my coat, jeans and flannel shirt. Too exhausted to rummage through the dresser for shorts and tank to sleep in, I crawled onto the bed, rested my head on the pillow and pulled the sheet over me. Although I'd been tired—I never slept well when camping—all I did was doze.

Shortly after five I gave up, donned yoga pants and sports bra, running shoes and pulled my hair into a ponytail. Still cold at this early hour, I added a hoodie sweat jacket and headed out for my morning run.

The streets were empty of traffic. We'd gotten a sprinkling during the night, just enough to draw gray tendrils of fog from the earth. Those tendrils first curled and then split in gentle waves as my feet pounded the sidewalk.

Usually I headed for the river, where the asphalt bike trail led to the Catholic Church. Instead, I turned left toward the residential neighborhood. I needed a change of pace. I needed to clear my head. I needed to outdistance the images that continued to fill my mind.

The four-four beat of my shoes striking asphalt created a rhythm in my mind, one that accompanied images of Grady tumbling, the bloody mist, the crack of bone. The thoughts disrupted my stride, tripped me up and I stumbled to the sidewalk.

Bending over, I gripped my knees and drew several deep breaths. I could let Grady's death distort my life, or I could shove it behind me and focus on here and now. Choosing the here and now, I continued my run, cleared my mind and listened to the sound of blood pulsing in my temples.

I'd reached south Sycamore, which didn't have trees of its namesake but rather Oak and Mulberry. Beneath trees old enough to have reached across the roadway and clasp branches as though shaking hands stood homes as vintage as the town. Some structures were shabby, some had been restored and others served as multi-family apartments. They resembled San Francisco's Painted Ladies, only their colors less bright, the gingerbread trim more brittle.

At the end of Sycamore stood the house built by the town's founder, Franklin Borden. A three-story gothic Victorian with witch's hat turret and wrought iron widow's walk, it held all the charm old man Borden had tried to instill into his namesake's community. At one time, he'd succeeded. Today, he'd die of heart failure if he hadn't been dead already.

In the front yard, a for sale placard had a *SOLD* sticker plastered over it. Someone had purchased the house five months earlier and only now were there signs of activity. I had attempted to get a promotion in hopes of buying the house. In the end I'd lost both.

I sighed and continued my run. Distancing myself from the distraction of the house left my mind open to the elements of Grady's death: the damaged cams. The altercation between Roberts and Yates. Wickham's prayer that, to me, seemed more a plea for redemption. And Pratt's departure as though something had angered him. What had taken place while Quint and I spoke with the NPS ranger?

I'd probably never know. One of them held close a secret that had resulted in Grady's death. Unless I could figure out which one, they'd walk and the tragedy would be forever considered an unfortunate accident.

I again focused on the rhythm of my pace, the cold air biting my cheeks. After three miles, I returned to my duplex, sprinted across the lawn and pushed past the door with the mauve flowered Welcome wreath I detested but had gotten used to. My roommate had replaced my sign threatening criminal prosecution for disturbing me. As long as he answered the door and dealt with solicitors, I didn't care.

With two goals in mind, a shower and coffee at Starbucks, I headed upstairs. Even though it was Sunday, I needed to get to the office. I'd oversee production of tomorrow's edition of the Borden Gazette since our managing editor refused to work weekends.

Upstairs, I turned on the shower's hot tap, stripped out of the running clothes and tossed them into the laundry basket.

I returned to the bathroom, expecting to see steam floating and the mirror fogged over. No hot water and it was Sunday morning, which meant I'd have to do without until Monday when I could get hold of the landlord.

After a cold shower, I dressed, got my triple Grande caramel macchiato at Starbucks and drove to the office. Humid air streamed in through the Corsica's partially opened windows. Storm-laden clouds that held the promise of rain were expected to skim over the valley and drop their precious load on the Sierra's highest peaks. But here, on the Valley floor, where we desperately needed the moisture, nothing.

I parked next to the pox-marked, tan building that housed the Borden Gazette. Its splotches, where graffiti had been painted over in a shade three times darker, made the structure look as though it suffered from a skin disease, like an inert form of psoriasis. New slogans, those of opposing criminal street gangs, had been sprayed on the side of the building. I'd call the graffiti task force and ask that they work us into their busy schedule.

I keyed my way through the heavy steel door that led to the composing room, defunct in this age of digital pagination. Light tables dark, the waxer cold, blue pencils and Exacto knives sporting a layer of dust. A slight hint of cleaning solvent still clung to the wood and glass prompting memories of years before when I'd pasted the pages by hand.

I crossed to an inner door that opened to the newsroom. A skeleton crew consisting of our sports reporter, an intern, and Quint busied themselves writing stories, composing the community calendar, and adjusting color on photos. Here, the composing room scents carried through and mingled with those of ink and paper.

Pausing between Quint's and my cubicles, I lightly knocked on the metal frame. He looked like he hadn't slept any better than I had.

"How're you doing?" I reached for him, stopped and curled my fingers against my palm. While our coworkers would have to be blind not to know Quint and I were an item, rules prohibited relationships between those working in the same department.

He turned in the swivel chair and attempted a crooked grin, his way of trying to reassure me. Only the expression was anything but reassuring. A haunted look had taken up residence in his hazel eyes, which were ringed in a smoky shade. Instead of his work week attire, he wore jeans, boots and a gray, collarless, button-up tee with three-quarter sleeves that looked more fitting for a hike in the woods, which is probably where he'd rather be. Me, too, for that matter.

"That good, huh?" I settled in the metal chair beside his desk. On his computer screen was a photograph of him climbing Half Dome.

"Didn't sleep at all. Got a SAR call," he said, referring to the county's Search and Rescue team. "We found the guy. After that, I kept thinking about Grady. Do you know what it takes to ruin a cam? It's not easy." He leaned back and peered at me. "I don't want to sound paranoid, but someone had to work hard to damage it."

"So," I said, and set the sheet of paper aside. Intuition had always served me well, and this time was no different. If I'd been uncertain before, I wasn't now. "Someone wanted Grady dead."

Chapter 7

The criminal element with its various bits of evidence could develop into a multitude of possibilities and was, to me, like meth to a tweaker. Once in my head, a portion of my brain became obsessed with solving the problem, linking together each piece of a case as one would a puzzle until the whole picture emerged. This one would be difficult since there wasn't a crime scene, just damaged cams. I'd have to figure out motive, and to do that I'd need to carefully examine every aspect of Grady's life.

What did I know about him? I set my tools of the trade on the corner of Quint's desk and jotted notes. The ink faded to gray. I tossed it into the wire wastebasket.

"Those gears of yours are grinding." Quint returned to adjusting the contrast in a photo of heat shimmering above a road while the sun blasted down on Borden. We would use the image on the weather page. "Figure out how we're going to prove I didn't kill Grady?"

"Working on it." Setting my coffee on the bookshelf where he kept copies of Shutterfly and Outdoor Photographer, I shifted in the hard metal chair and bit my thumbnail. Then I reached toward Quint, wiggled my fingers, willing him to hand me a fresh pen. He passed me a Paper Mate. "Grady was a County supervisor," I muttered, and scribbled it down. "Married, no children," I added the information to my list. "Did he serve in the military?"

"Air Force," Quint said. "Earned the Cross for extraordinary heroism. Why?"

"Getting a feel for who he was," I explained, although I wasn't sure how I'd use the information. "Was he active in American Legion?"

"VFW." Quint finished adjusting the photo, saved it into the folder marked Weather and turned toward me. "He chaired the committee who brought the traveling wall to Courthouse Park last spring, cooks for Thursday night spaghetti dinners, so yeah, he was active."

"Service clubs?"

"Rotary. Lyons."

I tapped out a beat against my jeans while *Tom Petty* sang in my head "Running Down a Dream." I needed a good workout on my drum kit. Nothing better than pounding my Ludwig to clear my mind. But I had stories to write and a paper to get onto the presses.

"I need to look into the issues of District Five." Scratching out another note, I sighed. "That could take a while."

Quint pulled a legal pad from the black file holder and a pencil from the cup, where all the writing instruments matched. Same brand, same color. His degree of neatness unnerved me, although he could find what he needed and I had to hunt.

"Your gears grinding now?" I asked.

"Must be contagious," he muttered. "Thought I'd list everyone who had access to my equipment. Wickham, but I think we can rule out."

"Why?"

"He's a priest."

"So?" I sipped my Starbucks, cooled enough so it didn't burn the roof of my mouth.

"I'm not accusing a priest," Quint said with a tone of alarm, as though to negate any wrath God might dish out for even considering a priest could kill. "Pratt, Roberts and Yates."

"What do you know about them?"

Quint shifted his weight. The chair, probably as old as the building, creaked in protest. "Not sure about Roberts. Yates, he lives in the Bay Area. That's it."

"Doesn't Grady have an assistant?" I asked, searching my mind for a name. "Eva Mobly? Something like that?"

"Ava," Quint said. "You guys were in the same class in high school."

"Don't remember her."

"You wouldn't. She was the studious type."

I opened my mouth to speak, realized he'd unintentionally slammed me, and shook my head. "If there was something going on, she might know, right?"

"Probably." He pulled up the County Web page and searched for legislative aids. Ava Moaler. She was assigned to District Five. Below was her direct phone line. Even though it was Sunday, I jotted it down, retrieved my caramel macchiato and headed for my cubicle. If I couldn't reach her at home, I'd wait until morning and try the office.

My newspaper world wasn't orderly like Quint's, but I knew where everything was. For the most part. Balled-up papers lay on the low-pile carpet near the wastebasket. Stacks of old editions of the

Gazette and Computer Aided Dispatch sheets that were now obsolete gave the impression of working in a paper fort. My penholder, a coffee mug, held different colors and brands. While I'd used blue pencils back when we still pasted up pages on grid sheets—we'd been the last in Central California to go digital—I now used red when editing my coworkers' copy. Housed with the pens were yellow and pink highlight markers.

Shoving aside a stack of CADs I'd gotten from the police department on Friday, I set my coffee on the blotter already stained with rings and showing July although the month had passed. Then I pulled the phone book from the shelf above my desk and flipped to the M section. Moaler, A, 555-8719.

It being Sunday, I hesitated a moment before disrupting Ava's weekend with not only the news of her boss' death, but questions on what could have led to his demise. She answered on the third ring.

I introduced myself, and asked, "Has anyone contacted you about your boss?"

"Yes," she said, and I detected a hint of grief. But only a hint. "Dangerous sport, climbing."

"It is. Grady was a good man."

"What do you want?"

Wow. Direct and to the point. Okay, I'll play by her rules. "Do you know if he was having trouble with anyone?"

"He was a politician," she said. "Some people didn't like the way he handled certain issues. Why are you asking?"

"Curious."

"They said it was an accident. It was, right?" Short pause followed by a deep sigh. "I know you. I remember how snoopy you were, always trying to prove something isn't what it appears to be."

Now I remembered her. She didn't like me then and it sounded like she still didn't. Odd that she spoke present tense. Was she referring to her boss' death? I'd take a closer look at her, too, although she didn't have access to Quint's gear.

"Like I said. Curious. So?" I prompted. "Was he involved in something that could have upset someone?"

"Plenty, but that's confidential," she said, and I could almost see her smug expression. She'd been a diminutive girl, had a habitual squint and tight, thin lips that made her look as if she was always angry. For all I knew, maybe she was. "Don't call my home anymore."

She hung up. The steady hum of the dial tone filled my head as though mocking my attempt to garner information. I set the receiver in its cradle and leaned back in my wobbly chair. She had been borderline hostile, but why? I hadn't asked anything out of line. The activities of an elected official were public, so why get offended?

How was I going to figure out what Grady had been doing prior to this weekend?

Diane had expressed suspicion that he may have had an affair. I'd take a look at who he hung out with, other that Quint. She and Grady had never had children. I didn't know of any siblings, but if he had any they would be easy enough to track down. He belonged to a number of community service organizations. Maybe his fellow Rotarians or Lyons knew what he'd been working on.

He'd become very vocal about his opposition to a proposed Indian casino project along state Route 99 just north of Borden. Maybe one of them decided to silence him? But no one on the climb was Native American.

I would need to write an article for tomorrow's paper. The image of Grady's broken body was too fresh in my mind, and I almost wanted to hunt down our intern and get her to handle the story. Instead, I'd research deaths from falling off Yosemite's big walls to support my article.

I launched a search, mentally thanking the powers that be for Google. I couldn't imagine what reporters did BC—*Before Computers*.

Climbing safety. More than a hundred climbing accidents occurred in Yosemite every year. Between 1970 and 1990, fifty-one climbers died from traumatic injuries. Yep, I'd say falling off the face of a cliff would be traumatic. At least fifty climbers suffered survivable injuries, anything from fractured skulls to broken legs.

Statistics. Loved them. They make an interesting addition to any story and gave credibility to the article. Most climbing related injuries occurred during leader falls, whatever that means. They accounted for twenty five percent of the fatal and near fatal injuries.

"Quint?" I called out.

"Yeah?" He folded his arms on top of the blue, cloth-covered partition that separated his cubicle from mine.

"What's a leader fall?"

"Research?"

I nodded. "Much as I hate to. Grigsby," I said, referring to our managing editor, "will want a story for tomorrow's paper."

"I can find art," Quint said, and his eyes adopted a vacant look. Haunted, yet reserved. "I've taken hundreds of photos of El Cap."

It would take a long time, perhaps years, for him to adjust to the loss of his friend and I wondered if he'd ever climb again. He probably would, but not anytime in the near future.

"Leader falls," he said, bringing me back to my question. "The guy leading the climb. If he falls, the stress on the rope can bring down the others."

I imagined the movie, *Vertical Limit*, where the rookies fell, caught the rope of a family of climbers and the son, who in my mental version was Quint, had to cut his father loose to save himself and his sister. Shivers worked my spine. I closed my eyes.

"It happens. That's why the most experienced lead."

Small comfort, in my opinion, but I'd never climbed. Never would. Especially after watching Grady fall.

"Anything else?" Quint asked.

I shook my head. He sank back beyond the partition.

I resumed my research, jotting notes on the information I'd use in my story. About ten percent of deaths resulted from falling rocks, twenty-five from climbing without ropes, forty from simple mistakes with gear.

Damaged gear? I shivered, sat back and rubbed my arms.

"Why would anyone do this to themselves?" I muttered.

"Do what?" Quint asked, his voice trailing over the cubicle.

"Experienced climbers, those who have participated in the sport three or more years, at least fifty suffer fractures. How many fractures have you had?" I asked.

"None." He came around the partition and settled in the chrome and plastic chair beside my desk. Then he angled my computer monitor to see what I'd been reading. "A person can climb all their lives and never get hurt. Someone can be on their first climb and break a hip and probably never climb again. That's why I'm so particular with my gear. Decrease the odds by taking care of what needs to take care of me—ropes and cams. Which," he added, "is why I'm positive someone deliberately compromised my gear and Grady died because of it."

"I'm not arguing," I said, "I just don't understand why someone would risk their lives to climb a rock."

"Personal challenge. Any leads?"

"A lot people to speak with, but no leads."

Were he and Grady close enough to confide in each other about an affair? I bit my lip and studied him. If so, would he tell me? Maybe. Maybe not. I'd never know if I didn't ask.

"How well did you know Grady?"

Chapter 8

To approach the question of Grady's fidelity directly was my manner when working on a story, but now it seemed calloused, even insensitive. I wasn't dealing with a gang member or politician, someone from whom I'd gained insight from shock value. This was Quint. He'd just lost his friend. His world had to be spinning out of kilter.

A couple more reporters, those who hadn't finished their assignments before leaving Saturday, drifted in. Hums as computers booted up, clack of fingers on keyboards, added to the drone of the monster air conditioning unit that oozed tepid air. Scents of ink drifted in from the press housed behind the newsroom. I loved that scent, it seeped through my skin and into my blood, gave me a solid sense of where I belong in the grand scheme of life. Here was my sanctuary. And in that sanctuary, I gained strength from that ink and clack of keyboards. Here, questions were necessary, never frivolous and I breathed deeply, rounded the wall between cubicles and returned to the uncomfortable metal chair beside Quint's desk.

"I've been thinking about something Diane said."

"I called her brother." Quint sat at this desk and picked up the Nikon's telescopic lens he'd been cleaning. "He's taken her to his place in Elk Grove so she won't be alone. He said he'd call when they arranged the service."

Sometimes silence is the best way to get the story. Only, that wasn't what I intended. Maybe, finally, he just needed to talk.

He wiped the lens, stopped and rolled one corner of the cloth between thumb and finger. Frowning, he returned to cleaning.

"I know this isn't our jurisdiction, but I really need to know what happened." He met my gaze. "Not just to restore my reputation, but . . . Diane needs closure. So do I. We can do that, can't we?"

There was the heavily weighted question, one that seemed to thicken the air between us. While I wanted answers just as much as he did, just as much as Diane deserved, and I knew, while I wouldn't quit until I'd followed every lead—once we uncovered them—I couldn't give Quint false hope.

"I won't stop until we do," I finally said, and folded my leg onto the chair's seat. The question swelled in my mind, prompting a pain in my temples. I opened my mouth. Closed it. Tried again, and the words gushed out: "Was Grady having an affair?"

Quint stopped cleaning the lens. He breathed deeply, tilted his head and looked at me with a dumbfounded expression as though the words had struck him like a ladle full of cold syrup. Heat flushed my cheeks. Part of me wished I could take the question back, erase it from the universe. But another part of me knew I couldn't and wouldn't. I needed to know.

"Just between us—off the record," I added, as though interviewing a valued source, "it's a concern Diane mentioned."

Quint set the lens and cloth aside, laced his fingers and let them droop between his knees. Head bowed, he appeared to study the faded and threadbare carpet.

I shifted uncomfortably. Not just because the chair was cold and hard, but also because I'd asked for the ultimate breach to the sacred male-bonding union, one I felt was just as strong as that between a married man and woman.

He breathed deeply, the effort causing his shoulders to slowly rise and fall. "I wish I could say no. Truth is I'm not sure."

I let my foot drop from the chair and leaned forward, closing the gap between us. Sliding my hand over both of his, I struggled to quell the excitement that bubbled up within me. Finally, a lead, and while my reporter/crime scene junkie wanted to do the happy dance, my human side warned me to tread lightly, take this slowly, use the compassion that I knew I possessed but that the junkie in me tried to suppress.

"I don't have any details, if that's what you want," he said, a note of harshness in his tone.

"What makes you think he may have been seeing someone?" I tightened my hand over his.

"Something he said the other night. We were having drinks at The Dock and he said he may have made a huge mistake." Quint straightened, drawing his hands from beneath mine. He picked up the lens and cloth and resumed cleaning. "That can be taken so many ways I hadn't considered an affair until now."

Quint was right. Making a huge mistake didn't constitute infidelity. But it did testify to the weight he'd felt, for whatever reason.

Dead end? Not necessarily. I now knew that something had been going on.

"Grady told Diane he wanted to bail on the climb," I said.

"He was really quiet that morning. Distant. He should have trusted his gut and stayed off the wall."

This was bigger than my crime-junkie mind could handle. I needed backup, the big guns, and resources my job as reporter didn't have access to.

"I'm going to go see Morales," I said, referring to Borden's detective sergeant and my police contact. I'd been meaning to stop by and check on him. "If nothing else, he can get into Grady's office. We might find something."

"Good idea." Quint set the cloth aside and tucked the lens into a pocket in his canvas case. "What about Ava?"

"She's not talking." I bit my thumbnail. "But," I mumbled and tucked my thumb against my palm. "She said something was going on, only it's confidential."

"That's a lead, right?" he asked, his voice tinged with hope.

"It's a start. If it wasn't something at work, we'll have to talk to Diane," I said, "and I really don't want to upset her."

Quint nodded. "Let me know what the Sergeant says."

Since Sergeant Dan Morales had been placed on administrative leave, he tended to ignore his phone. Every time I'd called his cell it went straight to voicemail, which was full and couldn't take any more messages.

The drive to Borden's west side depressed me. Lack of rain had taken its toll in town as it had in the hills. Because of the state's regulation that everyone, excluding farmers, reduced their water usage by twenty-five percent, brown was the new green: once lush lawns had given way to drought tolerant weeds, and they were few.

While most of the yards were still manicured, albeit dead with the exception of trees and shrubs, Morales' house looked like an abandoned property. Since his wife had left three years earlier, he'd lost interest in upkeep. The shrubs had died and became a fire hazard so he'd pulled them out.

He answered in a sleeveless undershirt and sweats, barefoot and clutching a mug of steaming coffee. Weeks-old beard darkened his olive skin. Black disheveled hair. Eyes dark and piercing, he fixed me with a glare as hard as obsidian. Although he wasn't in his signature black jeans and tee shirt with his Glock holstered to his side, he still had the cocky attitude of a cop who packed a gun and wasn't afraid to use it.

"What the fuck?" he asked.

"Don't take it out on me." I motioned at his mug. "Got an extra cup?"

"Pot's in the kitchen." He stepped aside and I ducked past him.

He'd been forced to take time off following a shooting that had been determined to be suicide by cop. Although Morales hailed from East L.A., and had fired his service weapon numerous times, this recent incident had been his first since returning to Borden seven years ago.

I headed for the kitchen at the end of the entryway next to the breakfast nook. Stacks of unopened mail and files from cases he'd been working littered the table. Dishes had taken up residence on the counters, and the trash canister overflowed with beer bottles. A trail of ants marked a line between the trash and the baseboard.

One thing was missing: there were no Three Musketeers wrappers. Had he gotten so depressed he wouldn't indulge in his candy addiction?

"How can you live like this?" I found a mug among the dishes, squirted Dawn onto a paper towel and twisted the tap. Once the water heated, I scrubbed the cup clean and helped myself to the coffee.

"Don't know what to do. Used to working." He sat at the country-style dinette. I had a feeling he'd spent a lot of time there. "This is bullshit. Chief wants me to talk to a shrink. No fuckin' way I'm talking to a shrink."

"They won't let you come back until you do. Isn't that how it works?"

"The guy had a gun," Morales said, slamming his cup to the table. "He fired first. What the fuck did they expect?"

"You did what you had to, I get that." I settled across from him and sipped the overcooked coffee. Not quite as bad as the sludge from the vending machine at the newspaper, but not Starbuck's, either. "This is a small town. It's rare you guys shoot anyone. The chief wants to make sure you're mentally stable before returning."

Morales glared at me. "Fuck mentally stable. I'm as stable as any cop. Whose side you on, anyway?"

Shaking my head, I sat back and closed my eyes. "I'm not taking sides."

He scratched his chest and peered through the dingy glass doors to the patio, littered with dead leaves. In the back yard, the grass had grown tall then died from lack of water and I couldn't help but think of the fire hazard he'd created there, too.

"Maybe I should apply with Fresno PD."

"You can't leave Borden—you're my best source," I said, and offered a smile. He was more than a source, he'd once been a lover and even after I broke it off we'd remained friends. "Besides, Fresno would make you see a shrink under these circumstances, too."

"Not just that." He returned his attention to me, and there was a tormented look to his dark eyes. "We got the fuckin best closed case rate in the state. We do well and they pat us on the back. Screw up once and they want to cuff me to a desk or assign me to patrol. It's bullshit."

Shifting uncomfortably, I thought not only of his disappointment but my loss of a great contact. Not many cops trusted reporters enough to talk shop, even with off-the-record information. I didn't want to lose that trust. Selfish? A little.

"They can't put you back on patrol," I said.

"Chief's considering taking me out of criminal investigations, sonofabitch," he said, as though the words numbed him. Taking Morales from the detective's unit would be like cutting out his heart and soul. He was every bit the crime scene junkie I was.

No wonder his house was worse than usual. If my managing editor took me off the crime beat, I'd hole up in my bedroom for a month. Depression can drag a person down pretty deep. Maybe Grady's' accident, which I believed to be murder, would cheer Morales up.

As I told him what I knew, that I strongly believed someone had damaged the climbing gear in order to kill Grady, Morales seemed to sit a bit straighter. The forlorn look faded, replaced by the hardened cop I knew him to be. When I told him they'd used Quint's climbing gear, Morales beamed, and I inwardly cringed. He'd love in the idea that Quint had contributed to Grady's death. To say Quint and Morales weren't friends was a gross understatement.

"We don't have Grady's harness or cams," I said.

Morales picked up the phone and punched in a number. "Deb? Morales. Good, you?" He fiddled with a file from the stack on the table. "That climbing accident yesterday. Who's the lead on that?" He looked at me, nodded, and continued. "I need to talk with him. He in today?" Again he nodded, hung up, grinned broadly and laced his fingers behind his head. Stretching, he stood. "Looks like I'm driving to the park. Wanna tag along?"

"I'd love to, but I've got tons of work." I trusted him. He was detail oriented and more of a crime-scene junkie than I am.

"Gonna shower and change, talk to Chang and meet you at the Gazette."

"Awesome." Finally, we'd gotten a break. A small one. Might be insignificant. But it was more than we'd had. I only hoped it would give us a clue as to how Grady had died.

Chapter 9

While Morales drove to Yosemite, I returned to the Gazette and worked on the feature that would accompany an update on Grady's death. Details always fascinated me. Google was my best friend when hunting tidbits I could use to inform the public. But informing them about climbing would be difficult. I was only interested because of Quint. I didn't even like heights.

I pulled up the NPS website and found their statistics page. As many as fifty thousand climbers used Yosemite National Park on an annual basis. I also found that two-point-five died per year, on average. I've always found it almost comical that they use the one half people as if two completely died and one only partially. The bit of humor faded when I imagined Quint in a wheelchair because he'd broken his back. I shivered at the thought. I just didn't understand the attraction.

Yosemite filled my computer screen. Even as a digital picture its massive granite walls were startling. I've always felt dwarfed among them, felt the power of something vaster than this world and everything in it. I understood why Quint loved the park. While I'd never share his passion for the sport, I did love Yosemite.

In the latter half of the eighteen hundreds, the first climbers drilled holes and fixed bolts, some of which are still in the face of Half Dome and El Capitan. After John Muir, a guy named Anderson set several firsts in big wall history. Five years after the geological survey had claimed Half Dome un-climbable. Anderson drilled holes and ascended the distinctive monolith at the Valley's eastern end. He was probably the first guide in Yosemite to teach others the ropes. It wasn't until 1953 that the initial route was established on the flanks of El Capitan. Now, climbers flock from all over for the thrill of challenging some of the most famous rocks in the world.

I had five pages of notes, plenty for the feature. I wanted to get it knocked out before working on the follow-up which would include Grady's history in Borden. He'd played high school football with Quint and my deceased brother and later was an alumni of Fresno State. After serving in the military, he gave to the community through public service on school boards in Eastern Madera County, and a list of other positions dealing with water and forestry issues. Most recent was his job as County Supervisor, elected to District Five.

The front office staff had let Morales into the Gazette, and he now leaned against the metal frame of my cubicle. So much for working on the feature. He wore his signature black Wranglers and tee, and a windbreaker that had the faint outline of the word *Police* on the front left side. While his hair was still disheveled, at least it was clean.

He toyed with his cell phone, turned the screen toward me and showed me digital photos of the cams in gallon-sized Zip-locks. Rust colored flakes had settled in the bags' lowest corners.

Dried blood. Grady's blood. The image of red spatter on my jeans filled my head and I mentally shook it off. With a wistful glance at the computer screen, now filled with a page holding a headline—*History of Climbing in Yosemite*—and a byline, I swiveled in the chair and offered Morales a half-hearted smile.

"Back already?"

"No traffic now that the casino's shut down."

"What's happening with that?" I asked, thankful for the change of subject even for a brief time.

Morales shrugged. "Two factions claiming to be the tribal council left. Others gave it up."

"Which two?" It would be another story I'd write before leaving. I'd covered the discourse at the Chukchansi casino since its closure about a year earlier.

"Most reasonable group and the assholes," Morales said, and grinned. "Assholes behind the disenrollment, reasonable ones trying to make peace with the County Supervisors. The assholes are facing charges for raiding the place."

"Trying to make peace with the supervisors?" Had he stumbled on a lead that could explain who killed Grady? I made notes in the pad I'd been using, hoping I didn't lose the information among statistics of climbing Yosemite.

He ran his hand over the pocket of his black jacket, probably searching for a candy bar. I opened the pencil drawer of my desk, pulled out a Three Musketeers and tossed it to him. I usually kept a couple in case he stopped by and went into withdrawals.

"Goddess," he muttered and ripped the silver wrapper.

"I wouldn't go that far." I stood and slipped past him. Quint's cubicle adjoined mine. I ducked into his pristine space and sat on the metal chair.

Morales joined us. He glared at Quint, seated at his desk. His computer screen showed an image of El Capitan at sunrise, the same time I'd been there, on the ledge, with Diana, waiting for the sun to chase away the shadows.

Quint looked up. The presence of Morales registered in his features as if he'd just tasted something foul. He combed his fingers through his hair.

"Sergeant."

"Rydell." Morales plucked the chocolate end from the candy bar and popped it into his mouth. His eyes narrowed slightly. The corner of his mouth twitched, and I knew a nasty remark wiggled in his mind. Knowing Morales, it was something like, *Kill any friends lately?*

Not for the first time, I couldn't help but notice the drastic contrast between them. Morales in black, the badass cop. Quint the nature lover, ready for a hike.

Morales stripped more of the Three Musketeers coating, glanced at the power bar Quint had been eating, and scoffed.

"Health nut? Thought you smoked."

"Quit," Quint said. "Never smoked much and I prefer to take care of myself. Unlike," he added, and gestured toward the candy bar.

"Let's get to work, okay?" I asked.

"Don't know what you're missing," Morales said around a mouthful of chocolate.

"Yeah, I do. That stuff will kill you."

"Death by chocolate?" Morales chuckled. "Worse ways to go."

"Let's use the conference room," I suggested. The cubicles were tight quarters and Quint had only one extra chair. Besides, the conference room would be neutral ground.

I led the way down the threadbare carpet that separated the news reporters from the minimal sports staff, only one of which—the sports editor—was in. At the back of the newsroom sat an eight by fifteen rectangular space with glass-topped table and faux leather and chrome chairs.

Getting Morales and Quint at the same table hadn't happened since last winter during a fundraising event, and that had been very uncomfortable. There was a rivalry between them. I had dated Quint in high school, Morales years later—which had lasted a whole seven months—and now dated Quint.

I sat at one end of the table. Before Quint settled beside me, he and Morales studied each other. Morales retreated to the other side, pulled out a chair, flipped it backward and straddled its seat. He rested his arms on the back.

He brought up the images on his cell, turned the glass toward Quint.

Quint leaned over the table and touched the screen to enlarge the photo. Then he breathed deeply and sighed.

The sadness in eyes tightened my chest. I stroked his arm.

"Can you email those to me?" Quint asked Morales. "I'd like to print them, get a better idea of how they might have been damaged."

"Sure. Who had access to your equipment?"

"Everyone who climbed. The six of us. We set some pitches the evening before to give us an early start the next morning."

"What the fuck's a pitch?"

"The space between belay stations." Apparently reading the confusion in Morales' expression—drawn brows, twisted lips—Quint added, "belay stations are where, when I lead a climb, I place gear. The cams. Then I climb the pitch—the space between stations—to the next and place more gear."

"So, between stations, you're just . . . climbing? What the fuck do you hold onto?"

"The wall," Quint said, and showed Morales his scraped up fingers.

"Don't get it. Why the fuck would anyone climb?"

"Personal challenge."

"It's a rock," Morales said, and scoffed. "There's no challenge in a rock."

"What are you doing here, anyway?" Quint stood and leaned over the table, the dominant male claiming his territory. "I thought you were on leave."

"Am," Morales said, calm and not the least bit intimidated. "Friend asked for my help. I don't turn my back on friends."

"Too bad," Quint muttered.

"How's that?"

"Truce, okay? Let's be civil," I said.

"Yeah, I can do civil." Morales flashed a cold smile. This "itching, climbing shit. Something you two do together?" He gestured between Quint and me.

Quint chuckled. "Hell no. She's afraid of heights. Can't even get her to hike to the summit."

"That's not fair," I injected. "I hike—"

"Gets all woozy. I'm surprised she can handle the ledge at the base of the nose."

"The ledge doesn't bother me. It's not like hanging from a wall of granite."

"Seems like you guys got nothing in common," Morales said.

"We've got the band," I said, which was true but weak in comparison to big wall climbing.

Morales shot me a grin. He liked getting me riled up, derived some sick sort of satisfaction from it. "This equipment or pro or gear, whatever you call it—someone could have messed with it. Right?"

Quint shifted uncomfortably, picked up a paperclip left from some prior meeting and toyed with it. "Disturbing to know someone deliberately damaged my gear."

"Only reason to do that is to kill someone," I added, solidifying what we all were thinking—this wasn't an accident but a homicide. "Why would someone want Grady dead?"

"Guy's a politician." Morales shrugged. "Run for office, you make enemies."

"That *guy*," Quint said, "was Grady Spinelli."

"Yeah, yeah," Morales said with a wave. "You guys were friends. I get it. Meant no disrespect." Morales studied the remains of his Three Musketeers, bit into the lighter filling, rested his chin on his arms and closed his eyes. "What about this secretary?"

"Legislative Assistant," I corrected him. "Ava Moaler. I tried to find out what he'd been involved with, but she isn't talking."

"How well to you know the other supervisors?" Morales asked.

"One of them used to be my contact at the sheriff's department," I said.

"Maybe he'll know?"

"Worth a try." I hesitated and studied Quint then Morales. Leaving them alone might not be a good idea. The last thing I wanted to return to was a bloodbath, another crime scene I'd have to decipher. "You guys behave yourselves, okay?"

They both rewarded me with blank looks, as though they had no idea what I meant.

I retreated to my workstation. Wiggling my mouse, I brought the computer out of its slumber. My Tom Petty and the Heartbreakers screen saver came up—images of the band brightening, fading, reemerging with a new photo. In my Outlook contacts I found Carmello's cell number, called and left a message for him to get in touch with me. He never answered his cell, but always returned calls as soon as he saw them.

Then I googled Grady's' name. More than seven hundred hits, but that wasn't surprising. He'd been a supervisor for four years. Links to video-streamed board meetings and agendas filled the first couple of pages, then mentions of him in news articles, some of which ran in the Gazette. Those would be easy enough to find. We kept a morgue, or library as non-newspaper people would call it, full of large, bound volumes dating back more than one hundred years. Each volume was marked with the dates the newspapers inside had been published.

I jotted the articles that Grady's' name had appeared in for the Gazette, then Fresno's paper and the smaller publications in Chowchilla, Oakhurst, Coarsegold, the Ranchos and Raymond.

District Five included every other town except Chowchilla and the Ranchos, so I crossed out those newspapers. Chances were good that whoever had wanted him dead came from his own jurisdiction. The situations in eastern Madera County were complex. One of the gateways to Yosemite National Park, it housed the Devil's Postpile, Bass Lake, and several small communities. Numerous environmental issues. Several developments had been proposed and were currently in the appeals process.

Taking my list, I headed for the morgue next to the conference room. Floor to ceiling bookshelves filled all four walls. Behind the cupboard doors were the broadsheet editions, which made for very large volumes. Each held two to three months' worth of papers.

This was one of my favorite places, other than the old composing room. Dark enough to keep the editions from yellowing, cooler than any other place in the building and always quiet. Sometimes I came in here to gather my thoughts. Very few people used the room, other than the community news reporter, Vi, who collected old stories for her *Remember When* column.

Earthy scents of paper and ink hovered in the air. I set my list on the solid wood, badly scarred table in the center of the room, opened the cabinet holding the most recent editions and decided to work my way back in time.

Five minutes later, after I'd gone through a month's worth of papers without finding a single story on Grady, Quint and Morales joined me.

"What'd you find?" Morales balled up the Three Musketeers wrapper and tossed it toward a gray steel wastebasket. The silver wad bounced off the rim and landed on the floor.

Quint picked it up and set it in the basket.

"I've got a list," I said, and tapped my pen against the legal pad. "Articles. Thought I'd start here and save the others for tonight. I can research them at home."

They consulted my list and pulled corresponding books from the shelves. We settled into hard wooden chairs and worked in silence. Although it was a long shot, a trace of excitement worked my mind. A clue. That was all I wanted. Something that would lead to answers.

"Got something to write on?" Morales raised a brow at Quint.

"Sure. Notebooks." His jawline tightened. He left and returned a moment later with two more canary-yellow pads. He tossed one onto the table near Morales.

"This guy's involved in everything," Morales said. "Sits on state boards and commissions. Could have been something he did in Sacramento."

"I'll search the Sacramento Bee's website." I scratched notes beside other newspapers I would research online.

"Were these the only references you found?" Quint asked.

I shook my head and bit the cap of my pen. "Meeting videos, agendas, and a bunch of reports by the grand jury."

Morales raised a brow. "Oh?"

"Grand jury looks into all kinds of things," I said. "They inspect the county jail and write their findings. They do the same with the two prisons near Chowchilla."

"They take complaints," Quint added, "and investigate. Maybe someone logged a complaint about Grady?"

"Maybe what we're looking for is in one of those reports," Morales suggested.

I made another note: pull every grand jury finding with Grady's name. "Quint?"

He peered at me from across the table.

"The other four guys. Do you know how to get a hold of them?"

"I can track them down."

"One of them did this," I said.

"Or someone else in the area." Morales stretched. His spine responded with a muted crack. "Where'd you stash your gear?" he asked Quint.

"Inside the Land Rover. Which," he added, "is kept locked."

Morales pushed the bound volume aside, leaned back and laced his fingers behind his head. "You said something about pitches the night before?"

"Yeah," Quint shrugged. "We usually set some to give us an edge in the morning."

"Leave any gear?"

Quint shook his head. "Just the cams . . ." He frowned.

I straightened. "What if the damaged cam was one of those first pieces of protection? They were left in the wall overnight. Two sets of three climbers, with Grady at the end of the second—"

"He removed the pro and, sometime further up, used it for some reason?" Quint shook his head and raked his fingers through his hair. "I use two, sometimes three depending on the needs of the belay station. Additional pro wouldn't have been necessary."

"Maybe someone else removed your cams and replaced them with the damaged gear?" Morales jotted notes, the beginning of a case he wasn't supposed to be working on. "If you can track down the other climbers, I'll see what I can do about getting them in for an interview."

"You're on administrative leave," I reminded him. "They can refuse and there's nothing you can do."

"Realize that," he grumbled and shot me a dark glare. "They don't have to know I'm on admin leave."

"The NPS is still investigating. Once they reach a determination, we'll know. But that could be weeks. I want this cleared up as soon as possible." I glanced at Quint, leaned my elbow on the table and tapped out a four-four beat against the legal pad with the tip of my Papermate. "I think we should conduct our own parallel investigation. Whatever we find, we'll share with the NPS."

"Yeah." Morales tossed his pen onto the table. It rolled near the far edge and stopped. "I'll coordinate. Rydell, track down those other climbers. I'll get one of my guys to help run reports, but I can't risk using them too much. Hannah, research online and see what those grand jury reports show. I'll keep reading these," he said, waving at the stacks of bound newspapers on the table. "We'll meet tomorrow."

"My place, five thirty," I said. "I'll even provide dinner."

Morales blanched. Quint grimaced. A twinge of anger started to heat my face, but I breathed deeply and shook my head.

"Don't worry. Sandwiches. I can make sandwiches. Or," I said, and hoped my roommate wouldn't mind me volunteering his services. "Oz might cook."

"Oz," Morales said, too quickly.

"Yeah, Oz." Quint grinned. "That guy can cook."

Chapter 10

Time slipped by while in the morgue, and I'd stayed too long looking at the old editions of the Borden Gazette. I didn't get back to my desk until after four, and at a quarter of five, I moved the sidebar story into the edit folder and started hammering out the follow up on Grady's death. If I didn't get this story in the digital queue by five the managing editor would be on my case. The last thing I needed was an alcohol-fueled lecture on meeting deadlines.

I gathered my notes, opened a new Word document and bit my thumbnail. The lead was always the hardest to write and although I'd known Grady, this time was no different. In fact, I found it more difficult. My words would forever dictate how people who didn't know him would remember him.

"Got another Musketeers?"

I spun my chair and found Morales in my cubicle doorway.

"No." I returned my attention to the computer, the glaring white page that seemed to mock my efforts. "Try the vending machine."

Pause. Then, "Got any change?"

"No." I shot him a scowl that I hoped was half as effective as his flint-like glare. "What I do have is thirteen minutes to write this story. So if you'll excuse me?"

He raised his hands in the all-too-familiar surrender motion and backed out of my workstation. Moments later, from Quint's station:

"Got any change?"

Sounds of coin rattling in a jar jangled my nerves. I breathed deeply, tried to quell the hint of panic that threatened to rise and focused on the story. I'd written follow ups in less time. I could do this.

It scratched my moral fiber to state his death as an accident when I was thoroughly convinced it hadn't been. But like any other news report, I'd need to state only the facts as law enforcement saw them. Regardless. No exceptions.

After falling to his death in what National Park Service officers believe to be an accident . . .

That worked. Unless the managing editor changed it, and that depended on how much bourbon he'd consumed. I finished the sentence and launched into Grady's history in public service. At five thirteen, I ended with *Services are pending*, and saved the story—ten column inches was all I could produce where I usually wrote thirteen—into the folder.

Quiet had fallen over the newsroom, with the exception of the press's low rumble as it printed an insert for tomorrow's edition. A yellow Post-It had been stuck to the metal framing the entrance to my cubicle with a message from Quint: He was on his way to check on Diane. Apparently, Morales had reached his goal of finding his fix and had left as well.

I shoved the notepad with the list of research I'd do at home into my purse and headed out of the now-empty newsroom. The only light that glowed, other than the dim overhead fluorescents, was that in the editor's office, a box with windows on three sides that we called the Fishbowl.

I headed in the opposite direction, hoping he hadn't gotten to my stories. If he had, he'd probably berate me for such a short piece.

Outside, hot air pressed over me, provoking a sticky layer of perspiration. I'd forgotten to call the landlord and leave a message about the lack of hot water, but with these temperatures a cold shower sounded invigorating. Home, shower, research. In that order.

I crossed the pothole-riddled parking lot and climbed into my used Corsica. Inside, the air was even hotter and I sat with the door open while I started the car and lowered the windows. The air conditioner had gone out, as had almost every part on the car since I'd bought it five years ago. I kept telling myself, after the new starter, catalytic converter, fuel and water pumps, radiator and battery, that I couldn't afford a new car. Every penny I'd saved toward a better ride got sucked up by this wreck.

I wound my hair into a sloppy ponytail and secured it with a Scrunchie, although it didn't stop the wind blasting into the car from tossing the strands across my face. Even the mulberry trees that lined Yosemite Drive seemed to shrink in on themselves as though attempting to escape the scorching sun. Hard-pack dirt below the trees had cracked and what little grass that remained had gone brown. The city had stopped watering in light of the drought.

I turned onto Mariposa, also lined with trees that had gone brittle from lack of water. Not for the first time, I wondered if they would uproot themselves, crash onto the road. My cell phone chimed announcing a text and I groaned. I hated texting. I dug it out of my purse and glanced at the number. My managing editor. I set the phone into a cup holder. It could wait until I reached home.

Oz's lipstick red Dodge Neon was in the driveway. The two-story tan stucco duplex, half of which I rented, had heat rippling from its roof regardless of the steady hum of the air conditioner. The forecast called for cooler weather. It couldn't come soon enough.

I parked, grabbed the cell and jogged up the sidewalk lined with basil, oregano and rosemary growing in terracotta pots. The frilly wreath, with *Welcome* now in rhinestones since Oz picked up the old art of *Beadazzling*, swung as I opened the door and stepped inside.

Scents of onion and garlic greeted me as I stepped inside and set my purse on the bookcase at the foot of the stairs. In the kitchen, Oz hummed a tune I couldn't decipher as he measured some spice in the palm of his hand and tossed it into a pot of bubbling sauce. He wore a *Kiss the Cook* apron, also in rhinestones and trimmed in pink satin, over neon green shirt and skinny jeans that made him look like an anorexic teen. He'd gotten a haircut, and his usual short spikes tipped in pink were now all black. The bangs flipped upward an inch. The rest was combed toward his face.

"Hey, Girlfriend. Like the new doo?" He touched his fingertips to his head. "That new stylist at *Hair to Dye For* is a true artist. Don't you think?"

"Yeah," I said, and resisted the urge to cross my fingers behind my back. "What's for dinner?"

"Asparagus in white wine sauce over fettuccine with red chili flakes for a little heat," he added with a swing of his hips. "I am an artist with the ladle. The rest of the bottle is in the fridge, should you want a glass of white." He stirred the pasta, fished out a noodle and ran it under cold water. Then he taste tested. "Perfect."

I slid my cell on the table, sat and considered my options. I could pretend I never saw the text—driving with the windows down created a lot of noise. I could drop it into the black hole that had taken up residence inside my purse. Or I could dunk it into a glass of wine, but that would ruin the phone and Quint was adamant that I kept it with me. Charged and working.

I read the text. Grigsby's lingo wasn't quite as bad as Oz's, but I still had trouble.

"Oz? What's AW, CYE, IMO your story's NM?"

"Must be from Grigsby." Oz poured the pasta into the sieve and joined me at the table. "Apparently, he's at work, wants you to check your email, and he doesn't think much of your story."

Great. Too short. I knew that when I'd saved it into the queue. While Oz rinsed the pasta, I sprinted upstairs and booted up the computer.

Nothing. Checked the connections, and tried again. Still no Internet.

Anger heated my cheeks. I gripped the mouse, rolled it over the pad, willing the aged computer to life as Dr. Frankenstein had his creature. Both were constructed of leftovers.

"Seriously?" I had a ton of research I needed to do before tomorrow. And, because I couldn't *CME*, I'd have to call Grigsby.

"If you're trying to use the computer," Oz called from downstairs, apparently having heard my comment, "forget it. System's been down all afternoon. I called it in, and it's the provider's problem not ours. So," he added in his singsong manner, "nothing we can do."

Those words sent needles stabbing my brain. I could go back to the office, but already it was getting dark and I hated that building in the dark. It creaked and groaned. The AC actually *moaned* when it came on.

And I didn't want to be there with Grigsby. I grabbed the cordless receiver from the nightstand next to my rumpled queen-sized bed, sat on the mattress and punched in his direct line.

He answered on the second ring. "I said check your email."

"Can't. Internet's down." I drew my knees onto the bed and leaned against the pillow. "What's going on?"

"Your story."

I cringed and gripped the phone. "What about it?"

"I thought the NPS said this was an accident. Want to explain your lead?"

Good. He wasn't angry about the length. I wouldn't have to go back to the office.

"They did." I bit my thumbnail, searched my mind for an excuse he would buy, couldn't find one. "I'm not convinced it was. Neither is Quint."

I neglected mentioning Morales. He was on administrative leave, and Grigsby was tennis buddies with the chief.

"I'm listening."

I gave Grigsby the tidbits of information we had, and added, "You know Quint. He's meticulous."

"He's OCD," Grigsby said, and chuckled at his joke. "I'll leave it as written. But we get any phone calls—"

"I'll handle them," I finished for him.

Grigsby hung up. I returned the phone and bounded downstairs, relief giving me a boost of adrenaline. I still had the problem of researching without online access.

I retrieved my cell and punched in Quint's number. If he wasn't busy I could drive over after dinner and use his laptop. He answered on the third ring, the background filled with rumbles and static.

"You're on the road, aren't you?" I asked, my hopes of research deflated like a balloon that had been poked with a knife.

"I'm on my way to Elk Grove to check on Diane. What's up?"

"When do you think you'll be back?"

"Not until late."

I thanked him and hung up. He wouldn't care if I went over and used the computer anyway, but I didn't feel right invading his privacy.

I called Morales next.

"I don't have a computer," he said, and moaned. Most likely his dinner consisted of a Three Musketeers.

"Seriously? Who doesn't own a computer these days?" Frustration tapped on my nerves. "How do you get by without a computer?"

"Just fine," he said. "Need to search something I go to the department."

"But you're on leave."

"Yeah. So I get you to look stuff up."

Wonderful. I signed off, returned to the kitchen where Oz had just mixed linguini with sauce and placed the bowl on the table. Then he added matching dishes, wine glasses and cloth napkins. Although I preferred paper, he washed the napkins along with his laundry so I didn't complain. He said he wanted to go green, reduce his carbon footprint and add less to the landfill.

"How was the show last night?" I held my bowl so he could heap on the pasta.

"Oh, Girlfriend," he said, and went about serving himself. "It wasn't Broadway, or even off Broadway for that matter, but for a Central Valley production it wasn't half bad."

"Then you enjoyed it?" I twirled noodles on my fork, blew on them and ate. The wine complimented the pepper flakes and garlic to perfection. "Oh, God, this is awesome."

"Glad you like it." Oz smiled. "The acting troupe and I had a lot of fun. Oh, we critiqued the beejesus out of their performances. I mean, they're not anywhere as polished as we are." He looked up and smiled, excitement glimmering in his eyes. "Did I tell you what we decided to do for our fall production? *Singing in the Rain*. Oh Girlfriend, it's going to be fantastic. Only, there's no rain, but we thought it might be nice, you know, to shower people with hope."

As long as they didn't use real water, I didn't care.

"Tomorrow night, Morales and Quint are coming for dinner if that's okay."

Oz set the serving utensils aside and stared at me. His hand fluttered to his throat.

"Quint *and* Morales? At the same time?" Oz fanned himself as though he might faint. "They will be on their best behavior, right?"

"I promise. No brawls." Not that they'd ever had. They were less than friendly, but never violent. So far.

"How about a stir fry?" Oz suggested. "I bought a new wok and bamboo utensils. It'll give me a chance to find out if it's as good as the advertisements said."

I nodded. "That'll work. We're researching the county supervisor's death."

"Oh, dear," Oz said, and again the hand went fluttering. "I heard about that on the news. Dreadful sport, in my opinion. But, sweetie, they said it was an accident."

"I'm not convinced. Neither is Quint. Morales finally saw it our way."

"Morales is back at work?"

I shook my head, ate, and closed my eyes. It's a wonder I didn't weigh more than I do. Running. If I didn't get up every morning and run, I'd make the Goodyear blimp look sleek.

The cats joined us. Flapping his napkin, Oz shooed them from the kitchen. They retreated to the living room and curled up on the lavender La-Z-Boy. I hadn't been fond of animals in the house, but when Oz discovered the wayward couple on the patio in the only rainstorm we'd had this year, I relented. As I always did when it came to what Oz wanted. As a joke, I'd called them Bonnie and Clyde. Oz loved it, and the names stuck. He'd even gotten them matching handgun nametags. They were a couple of criminals, always stealing sandwiches left unprotected a few moments or jumping onto the counter to rip apart a loaf of bread. He decided to purchase top-of-the-line cat food. His pocketbook, not mine. I didn't complain because they'd stopped stealing my lunches off the table.

"Oh, almost forgot—you got a letter yesterday. The postmark is from Texas, but there's no return address. On the bookcase," Oz added, and gave his fork a dainty wave. "It was sent overnight express."

I'd get it after dinner. Most likely, the correspondence was from my mother, who I referred to as Ruth. Everyone else I knew used email. She and I weren't close, and she'd never send a letter just to keep in touch. She probably had news I wouldn't like. I'd eat first so she couldn't ruin this awesome meal.

After I scraped the last of the sauce with the side of my fork, I rinsed my dishes and set them into the dishwasher. Then I picked up the letter, returned to the table, sat and pulled my foot onto the seat. Using the butter knife I hadn't used during dinner (but that Oz insisted on placing on the table with all the other tableware we didn't use), I slit open the envelope and tugged out the single sheet of stationary.

I regret to inform you that your grandfather has passed away. I have enclosed the obituary that ran in the Dallas newspaper. You are expected to attend the funeral.

Ruth

Nothing like breaking the news gently. My throat constricted. Tears stung my eyes. Breathing deeply, I flung the letter onto the table.

"Damn her."

Chapter 11

Oz hummed as he washed the dishes with a pink sponge on the end of a wand. Hitching sounds of my sobs must have caught his attention; his humming drew down to silence, followed by a sharp intake of breath. I looked up, unable to hold back tears and warm trails wove down my cheeks. Forehead creased in concern, he dropped the sponge, wiped away suds on his apron and hurried toward me. He clasped both my hands as he sank to a crouch before me.

"Oh, sweetie," he said, a hint of fear in his tone. "What's wrong?"

I motioned toward the letter. He picked it up and read, looked over the obituary, then pulled me close, hugged me, stroked my head as he would one of the cats. "What an awful woman. Sorry, Girlfriend, but she is," he added, pulling away and using the apron's satin edge to dry my face. "A considerate person would have called, would have shown some compassion, after all this isn't like the neighbor's dog died."

"Ruth doesn't call anyone." I sniffled and looked around for a tissue. He handed me a cloth napkin. No way would I blow my nose on a cloth napkin. I'd once seen a woman do just that in a restaurant, and I've never used them in public since. I used Ruth's note, instead, which scratched the tender flesh.

Since my brother, Richard, had died more than thirteen years ago, she didn't exert her energy on caring about anyone, especially me. But that wasn't fair. She'd wanted nothing to do with me for as long as I could remember. Richard and I used to call her Mrs. Spock behind her back. Later, that nickname had turned to Ice Queen. She was as cold as the glaciers that had formed Yosemite Valley.

I'd been close to my grandfather, as much as possible from three states away. He and Grandmother had visited at least once a year and, when I was a child, Richard and I accompanied Ruth to Texas every summer. In between those visits, we spoke on the phone at least once a month. I'd continued those calls after Richard died and I'd moved out on my own. The last time I'd spoken to my grandfather was three weeks ago.

I swiped at a tear that trickled down my face. Oz retreated to the living room and returned with a box of Kleenex.

I pulled two free and again blew my nose. Picking up the neatly cut strip from the Dallas paper, I dabbed my eyes again, readjusted my glasses and stared at the photo of my grandfather, Alford Ronald Bogette. He'd been eighty-three years old, but acted more like sixty. Good health, very active, he should have seen another ten years at least.

Just like that. A once alive, vibrant, fun-and-life-loving man gone, leaving a vast hole in the lives of everyone who had known and loved him.

Wiping my eyes with the heel of one hand, I set the obituary aside. Between now and the funeral, in order to squeeze out the pain of loss, I'd throw myself heart and soul into figuring out what had really caused Grady's death.

Since the computer couldn't aid me in research, and I didn't feel up to staring mindlessly at the television, I took a cold shower and went to bed. Sleep was just as elusive as it had been the night before.

By the time bruised shades of dawn seeped through the sheer curtains, casting the room in a purplish wash, I gave up trying to sleep. The ceiling fan hummed, its scant breeze doing little to cool the room. The air conditioner had kicked on around three AM. Tepid air seeped through the vent. I'd call the landlord about the water and the AC. Maybe getting it serviced would allow it to blow a little cooler.

While the meteorologist said there was a good chance for an El Niño weather system, its strongest point wouldn't be until winter. I had hoped that the little bugger would sneak in early, bring temperatures in the seventies and, maybe, a couple of showers.

The air was dry and already in the upper seventies when I set out for my run. The sounds of my shoes slapping the sidewalk tapped out a tune that consisted of two words: Grady and Grandpa. Grady, Grandpa. Grady Grandpa.

No matter how fast I sprinted, I couldn't outdistance myself from the grief I'd tossed and turned all night dealing with. I would call my aunt, also in Texas, and ask if I could stay with her if I decided to wait until Friday to return to California. I needed to make flight arrangements and would once I reached the office.

I had no destination in mind, just that I'd hoped to go an extra mile. After breaking my leg last winter, and the several months it took to heal, I'd been working my way back to five miles. Three had become easy. It was time to leave my comfort zone.

Again I found myself outside the Borden House. Workers on scaffolds scraped paint from the eves and gables. They had replaced most of the gingerbread trim, which was a good sign. At the very least, maybe they would preserve the façade while they butchered the inside, carved out cramped apartments.

Stopping briefly, I guzzled half the bottle of water I carried. Perspiration streaked down from my hairline. I swiped the moisture with my arm to keep the drops from stinging my eyes. Resuming my run, I circled around and came to the river trail.

Quint, dressed in snug-fitting shorts and sweat-drenched wife beater, had just entered the strip of asphalt that wound beside the now dry river. My pedometer already showed two point seven miles. I caught up with him and we headed for the Catholic Church, an additional mile away.

"Get the research done?" he asked, and I mentally cursed him for not sounding winded. My heart pounded. My breath came in deep and harsh.

"Computer's . . . down," I managed.

"Might want to slow your pace, Babe."

I knew the rule. If you couldn't carry on a conversation while running, you were outpacing yourself. I slowed to a steady gait. He matched my stride, which wasn't much of a workout for him, but I was grateful for the company.

"You sure . . . that c-cam is . . . yours?" Extra mile. I had to hold out for that extra mile.

He uncapped his water bottle and drank, a talent I have yet to master while running. "It's mine. Like I told Super Cop, I mark my cams."

"Do you . . . remember . . . placing it?" The pathway curved, as did the reverbed with its wilted Cottonwoods, silver-dollar sized leaves brown on their edges.

He recapped his water without missing a beat. "No telling. I use different-sized cams depending on the size of the crack in the wall."

Fiery pain erupted in my leg. I groaned through clenched teeth, tried to slow but stumbled and crashed to one knee. My palms scraped the asphalt, bits of grit embedded in the pads of my hands. My water bottle bounced, just as Grady's body had, and rolled toward a clump of dead grass. I hunched over, rocked back and sat on the pathway.

The impact on my tailbone sent jolts up my spine. Drawing harsh, ragged breaths, I drew my knees to my chest and rested my chin. *"Damn-it!"*

Quint knelt beside me, twisted the cap on his Aarrowhead and handed it to me. Nodding my thanks, I took the water and drank. It wasn't ice cold, but enough to chase the heat from my body.

I started to give him the bottle and push up from the road. He rested his hand on my shoulder, a silent urge for me to stay. Not a bad idea. My body felt wrecked from the fall.

"You're pushing too hard, Babe," he said, his tone soft to take away the sting of stating the obvious. "We both have demons chasing us right now. You can't outrun them, and I don't want you injuring yourself trying."

He sat beside me, slid one arm sticky with sweat around me and kissed my forehead. I relaxed against him and closed my eyes. I wanted to tell him about Grandpa, but the loss of his friend—*our* friend—was still too fresh.

"You're not fooling me, Monkey," he whispered, his breath soft against my face. "Talk to me. No secrets, remember?" He gave me a tight squeeze, silent encouragement that I talk, tell him what I still couldn't emotionally absorb. That Grandpa had died.

Died. Dead. I'd grown to hate those words.

Tell him, part of me insisted. Another part didn't want to cause him further pain, and the two sparred inside me, leaving my head aching and my chest heavy.

Tears blurred my vision. I told him about Grandpa, and the weight of the loss shook my shoulders, wracked my body.

"Babe," Quint said. "I'm so sorry."

A couple of runners in high-dollar Under-Armor passed us, their pace that of a couple of corgis. For some, it wasn't about getting healthy but looking good while fooling themselves that they would drop that extra pound when what they really needed to drop was the wannabe attitude.

That wasn't fair. My leg hurt, I'd crashed and burned and my pride had taken a bruising. My attitude had turned foul.

How long we sat there, on the hard, sun-baked trail that framed the dry riverbed, I wasn't sure. That I'd finally given in to not just the grief over Grandpa but the horror of watching Grady die, the heartbreak I felt for Diane, the pain I knew Quint must feel, was strangely comforting. By the time the hitching sobs subsided I felt in one way empty, in another somehow renewed. I could move forward now with a more clear sense of direction, not only on the trail but also in my investigation into who had damaged Quint's equipment.

Quint cupped my face in his hands. Then he kissed me, not with passion but reassurance and tenderness.

"I know what he means to you. I'll take care of flight arrangements as soon as I get to the office. We'll be there for your grandmother."

"You'll come with me?" I don't know why, but the thought struck me as odd. I knew I'd be there for him in a similar situation. Why his offer shocked me, I didn't know.

"I'm not going to leave you to deal with Ruth alone," he said, half muttering but loud enough so I heard. "That would be . . ."

"Cruel and unusual punishment?" I asked.

"Yeah. First degree . . . *something*," he said, and offered a reassuring grin.

He leaned away and gingerly touched the calf on my right leg. Then he massaged it, gently and, at the same time, I knew he checked for an injury.

"Does it hurt?" he asked.

I wanted to shout *Yes*, but didn't want to make an even bigger deal of my crash and burn so I said, "No."

"You're a rotten liar, Monkey." He stood, grasped my upper arm and helped me stand. "I'll walk you home."

Testing my weight, the pain had almost subsided, I shook my head. "I can make it."

"I know you can." He looped his arm around my waist and matched my crippled pace.

Grateful for his support, I walked, slowly at first then, as the pain ebbed from my calf, at a more normal gait. Ten minutes later, we reached my duplex.

He left me on the porch and sprinted across Norton toward the Save Mart shopping center. He'd probably continue to the church, cross over and head home.

Inside, I collapsed onto the lavender La-Z-Boy in the living room. My leg still ached, as did my lungs, but I felt alive with all the endorphins flooding my bloodstream.

I recovered quickly, zipped through getting ready for work, drove to Starbucks drive-up window for a triple-shot Grande and arrived at work five minutes late.

Unlike yesterday, the newsroom was alive with noise. The television suspended from the ceiling on a shelf had been turned to CNN, the low rumble of the press in back printing the special Fall Gardening section that would accompany tomorrow's edition. The section would be worthless without rain, that El Niño event that would bring enough water to drink, shower and flush toilets. Oz had been so freaked over the possibility of not being able to flush he'd been rinsing out every orange juice bottle, filling and stashing them throughout the duplex. My bedroom closet now housed twenty, one-gallon jugs.

After setting my bag next to the stained desk blotter, I regarded the calendar and considered updating to the current month. Not that it mattered. I'd been using the Outlook calendar now that Quint had shown me, which made the blotter-style obsolete.

I sank onto the wobbly chair and sipped my coffee, now cooled to a pleasant temperature. Closing my eyes, I savored the brew lightly sweetened with caramel and coconut milk. Savored the scents of ink and dusty paper. Savored, too, the quasi solitude of my cubicle. Too much had crowded my life lately, the deaths of Grady and Grandpa at the forefront. I needed a moment to gather my thoughts and prepare for the day. The cops and courts beat always offered the unexpected. My life wasn't structured or organized, which is probably why I was so well suited to covering crime. That, and the fact I was a junkie for the tidbits brought to me by homicides, shootings, burglaries, thefts and anything under the definition of breaking news.

At least I'd be able to conduct the research my dead computer stole from me last night. I launched the web browser. On the shelf above my computer, the police scanner emitted static, brief interruptions, then dispatch calling a Ten-Fifty—fire alarm.

God, I love this job. While I'd have to postpone the search, the endorphins that had flooded my bloodstream that morning returned. While I silently asked the powers that be no one had been injured, the thought of a structure fire, the heat and the flames and the flurry of activity, made my pulse quicken.

Chapter 12

While I needed to conduct research, breaking news was part of my job and a story on a fire with art on the front page would empty racks all over town. High sales volumes made the advertisers happy, and they were the lifeblood of any newspaper. Before I could call out to see if Quint had made it to work, he ducked into my cubicle with his camera case's strap draped over one shoulder.

"Apartment fire," he said. "Three units involved."

"You driving?"

He grinned. "Yeah. I'd like to make it there with my limbs intact."

"Smart ass." I grabbed pen and notepad and brought my coffee.

It was no secret that my driving scared him. Scared everyone in the newsroom. And I was the only one with a perfect driving record. Go figure.

He opened the passenger door, hurried around the Rover's hood and climbed in. Grabbing the dashboard, I pulled myself into the seat. One reason I liked my Corsica, despite its ailing condition, was the fact I didn't feel like I needed a stepladder.

Quint propped his hand-held police scanner in the drink holder. Verbal traffic between dispatch, the fire chief and his men had been switched to a secure channel, but Quint had gotten the location before they'd changed and now headed down the redwood-lined Yosemite Drive.

"How's your leg?" He tapped the blinker and prepared to turn.

"Fine. And no," I added, knowing what he would suggest. We'd known each other since we were kids, and it wasn't unusual for either of us to dip into the others stream of thought. "Not going to the doctor. It's healed. I just need to quit pushing it, that's all."

"Like that'll happen," he muttered, and his lips twitched with a suppressed grin.

Ahead, black smoke billowed into the air. Behind us, sirens wailed. He eased to the curb, let an engine pass and pulled back onto the road.

I found a clean page in my reporter's notepad, a long narrow pad that fit nicely across my palm, and tested a pen. I hated when, while taking notes, I ran out of ink. I never used pencils, like some reporters, because I had a habit of pressing too hard and snapping its tip. That was worse than a pen running dry, unless I carried a sharpener and that took precious time I didn't have. Once cops, firemen or attorneys started talking they got on a roll and a snapped pencil could cost me good quotes.

Although some reporters used recording devices, I didn't trust them. Electronics had a way of garbling voices and losing battery strength. Pen and paper. There wasn't anything better.

Quint had turned on the air conditioner, which blew icy cold. I closed my eyes and enjoyed the blast, a luxury absent in my lemon of a car. His had the earthy scent of new leather and an underlying odor of fresh paint. Satellite stereo. Heated seats, which would come in handy this winter. All the luxuries of a top-of-the-line vehicle. Room to haul his gear, whether climbing or camping. I'd been curious after he'd purchased the car and did some research. Not that it had been any of my business, but that had never stopped me. This was the Range Rover edition, fully equipped, which meant it carried a six-figure price tag. How he managed on a photographer's salary, I didn't know. Although his coffee-table books were popular.

He'd once said he'd made investments that had done well. Yet he lived with our bass player, when he could afford a house of his own. But knowing our bass player as I did, I understood Quint's hesitation in moving out.

Ahead, plumes of black smoke rose like an inverted tornado. I wanted to tell Quint to stomp on the gas, get us to the site of the fire. Instead, I bit my thumbnail. He always drove the limit.

He parked half a block from the multi-unit complex. The front building was almost completely engulfed in flames.

Cutting the engine, he stared through the windshield that, unlike mine, was clean and free of insect particles.

Letting one of his hands stray from the two-o'clock position on the steering wheel, he clasped my hand.

"Sure you're up to this?" he asked, tilting his head toward the inferno raging across the street.

"It's the only thing that keeps me sane." I kissed him, gathered my notepad and pen and slid out of the car.

Before I'd gotten halfway across the street, intense heat struck me. The flames, more than thirty feet away, felt as though they were close enough to melt my flesh. My cheeks burned. The air was filled with a crackle that reminded me of static electricity, only louder.

Borden Fire Department's chief, Dell Hodgekin, looked less like a fireman and more like the host of children's television shows; kind eyes and smile, all-American, apple pie, cliché as hell. Until he spoke. Where one would expect a gentle voice, he barked orders better than a carnie. The microphone tethered to his handheld radio was clipped to the strap on top of the shoulder of his uniform shirt. He lifted the plastic device, bringing it closer to his mouth, tilted the small square with slats that captured his voice and relayed it to his fire crew, scattered in a tactical manner behind and to both sides of the four-unit complex.

He glanced my way, finished giving orders and flashed a smile.

"Hey Hannah. Glad they sent you. That stringer? J.D. Ecker? Real bitch, that one. I refused to give her info on an investigation we're working on, and she tried to go over my head. Bitch! And guess what? I'm the boss. Not too bright, that one."

J.D. filled in on weekends so, occasionally, I'd get a break. Dell's sentiments were not unique. I'd gotten the same from the police and sheriff's departments.

"Good to see you, too," I said, and tilted my head toward a girl who appeared to be no older than twenty with three children, the youngest a newborn cradled in her arms. They stood beside the playground, which consisted of a slide with rusted bolts, three swings and sand in a concrete square. The complex had been built in the sixties and hadn't seen upgrades beyond a paint job since. "Victims?"

Dell nodded. "One of three families who lost their home. Fire started in a bottom unit."

I jotted down the information and kept my pen poised over the long, narrow notepad.

"It appears the lower unit resident was smoking in bed," Dell said, his voice deep and gruff. "Cigarette probably smoldered most of the night. That's him," Dell added, motioning toward an ambulance, its back doors open. "Second and third degree burns. They'll probably take him to Community Regional in Fresno."

Borden Community was capable of handling traffic collision patients, but CRF, south of Borden, had one of the best burn units in the Valley.

"Who was in the third unit?" I asked.

"An elderly woman who lived alone. Well, with a dog. That's it there," he said, and lifted his chin toward a black and white Border collie. "The kids say the dog's name is Baby. It was all the woman had."

"Had?" I swallowed hard, my own grief still too fresh in my heart.

"She died of smoke inhalation. The flames went up inside the inner wall, burned through the floor of her unit and left a hole big enough to let smoke in. The kids, they said the dog barked her head off. That's how they knew what was happening. It was probably trying to wake the old lady, but we found several empty wine bottles in the kitchen and figure she was inebriated beyond the ability to respond." Dell shook his head, as if berating the woman even in death. "None of them had working fire alarms. Fire Marshall inspected these buildings just last week. The owners were cited. We're going to inspect each unit once we're finished here."

I scratched pen to paper until I'd caught up with his monologue. Then I regarded the dog, sitting patiently, whimpering and starting to bolt toward the burning building whenever a fireman extinguished flames only to have them reignite.

"What's going to happen to the dog?" I hated the thought of any pet going to an already overcrowded shelter. I would take her, but I had a small place and two cats.

"We'll contact animal control." Dell tilted his microphone close to his lips and shouted, "Let's move to the sides and work on the front of the structure."

Two of his guys nodded in unison and dragged a heavy hose around the building. Quint strode into the street, where the front of the building sported yellow-orange flames that spit black smoke. The road had been blocked off, so he jogged to the center, raised his camera and snapped off several shots. Then he wandered over to the children with their mother, said something to her. She nodded, pulled first one then the other child close to her legs and continued watching the fire.

I'd gotten all the information Dell had to give, thanked him and tagged along with Quint until the fire was out. The dog shadowed his movements. He noticed, too, and finally stopped to scratch the collie's ears. She looked up and wagged her tail.

"Her owner's deceased," I said. "Dell's going to call animal control."

"Then she'll go to the shelter?" Quint shook his head. "What a shame. Good dog."

The collie whimpered, looked up at Quint, raised a paw and tapped his leg. He reached down and again scratched her ears. He glanced up, caught my grin and stopped.

"What?"

"Never thought you'd be a dog person," I said, and bit the cap of my pen. "You've never had a pet, have you?"

Looked like the dog wouldn't be going to the shelter, after all. Not I could help it.

"I really don't care for animals," he said, although his fingers played the top of the collie's head. "Not that I dislike them," he added, as though undoing some wrong he'd confessed to. "Have to admit, she's got something about her that I haven't seen in a dog before."

"Why don't you take her?" I suggested.

He furrowed his brows. "I don't know. I'm still living with Robin," he said, referring to the bass player for our classic rock band, Miles Creek. "Not sure he'll like me bringing home a dog."

"Are you kidding? He'll love it. When he comes over, he never greets me first. He goes straight for the cats. Take this girl home. Trust me."

"Guess I could." He glanced at the car, and back at the dog. "She'll get hair all over the seats."

"Have you unpacked from the weekend?"

He smirked. "Everything except my gear and our change of clothes, I keep those containers locked in back."

We loved spontaneous trips to the mountains or the coast, and kept clothes to accommodate each in his Rover. Jeans, jackets, shirts and boots for the mountains. Swim suits, towels, flip-flops and sunscreen for the beach. Nothing of which I'd want to use to cover the seat to save it from dog hair.

"Vacuum later. A little dog hair won't hurt anything."

"Guess you're right." He shrugged, strode to the car across the street and let Baby into the back seat. Almost as an afterthought, he rolled the window down four inches and closed the door. Baby poked her snout through the gap, sniffed and whined.

"Might want to turn on the AC," I suggested.

"Leave the car running?"

"The dog's going to bake in there."

He glanced at the Rover, returned to the far side of the street, got in, started the car and used the key remote to lock the doors. AC blasting, Baby's fur was blown backward like a model in a photo shoot. I'd swear she smiled.

Then she tucked her snout through the gap again, panted, tongue lolling. She watched us as we watched her.

"Really?" Quint stalked back to the Rover and motioned toward the glass. "She's slobbering all over the place."

"It'll clean." I bit my lip and turned away, trapping a giggle in my throat. I swallowed it back although it felt good to want to laugh again. For a moment, life felt normal, and I sorely missed normal—or what passed for normal in my life.

"I'll get it detailed," he muttered. "You finished?"

"I've got what I need. You?"

He raised the Nikon and nodded.

"Let's get back to the office." Careful not to let Baby out— although in the back, she tucked her nose in the narrow space beside the door as though trying to squeeze through—I slid into the passenger seat, buckled up and retrieved my coffee that I'd left in the cup holder. Lukewarm, but sweet and strong and containing three shots of caffeine.

"Sorry to bring this up, but you said your grandfather's funeral is Thursday?" Quint asked. I nodded. "I want to get tickets as soon as we get back to the office."

"Sure you want to come with me?" He and my mother, Ruth, didn't get along and that was an understatement. It wasn't that he wasn't good enough for me. In Ruth's opinion, no one was good enough, me included.

My mood darkened. As if he sensed this, Quint lifted my hand and kissed my palm. I offered him a smile, weak but genuine. I loved the way he always tried to lift my spirits, even when he struggled with the death of his friend and not for the first time I wondered what I'd done right in life to deserve such a caring man, such a devoted companion, as Quint.

Angels sitting on my shoulder, Grandpa used to say. Now he was my angel. My throat constricted with the threat of tears, but I breathed deeply, forced them to dissipate. I'd cried enough for one day. Save the tears for Thursday, when I'd attend Grandpa's funeral.

Quint didn't answer, didn't need to. He'd never offer if he hadn't intended to come to Texas with me. His presence would provide a measure of strength that would help me get through the service, the memorial, the burial. Quint could be, as the saying went, my rock.

He parked in the pothole-riddled lot beside the chain-link fence, beyond which stood the dumpster where pressmen had found a body last winter. I shivered at the thought; the madman who had discarded the woman had later come after me, the result of which had left the madman dead and me with a broken leg, the same injury that had sent me skidding in the dirt earlier. I glanced at the scrapes in my palms and shivered.

Shoving the memories aside, I cupped Quint's cheek, leaned close and kissed him. His lips were soft and tasted of coffee.

We returned to the newsroom, the body of the paper that has its metaphorical thumb on the pulse of the community. We were the first to know what happened in Borden, how its residents felt, and relayed this information to the population by way of a daily newspaper dropped on their doorsteps.

Although he didn't have a leash, Quint led Baby into his workstation. She complied as though she knew exactly what he expected. Smart dog.

I took refuge in my cubicle. I would write up the story on the fire and then research Grady's grand jury connections. I had to find something that pointed a finger at Roberts, Yates, Pratt or, yes, Mr. Catholic Priest Wickham. I didn't care how close he was to God. A son of God's first humans, Cain, proved capable of murder. Why should I rule out a man of the cloth? Sounded like the perfect camouflage to me.

I posted a mental sticky note to take a closer look at Wickham.

Chapter 13

While the newsroom buzzed and clicked around me, I wrote fifteen column inches on the apartment fire, I saved my story in the electronic folder for front page and opened Explorer. Although Quint and Morales would expect something on the grand jury reports, the need to research Wickham gnawed at me like a gnat buzzing in my ear. Maybe there would be something. Maybe nothing. But I couldn't ignore that buzzing so in the Google search bar I typed *Wickham* and *Priest Oakhurst*.

I neglected to tell Quint that I suspected Wickham. While he held his Catholic faith close to his eternal soul, and knew priests were capable of sin, he'd already mentioned eliminating Wickham from our list. I respected his choice of religious beliefs with its punishments and purgatory, but I didn't share those beliefs. Product of a Baptist father, Mormon mother and exposed to my uncle's commune of Latter Day Saint fundamentalists, my religious background was pretty screwed up. Therefore, my politically correct filter was disengaged, which afforded me the luxury of seeking the truth without fear of burning in the fires of Hell.

Okay. Focus. The Google search. In less than three seconds, more than a hundred responses came up. Including—and the crime reporter in me felt both guilt and joy—Wickham's relocation from a parish in San Diego.

Questionable conduct with altar boys? Children who had attended the Catholic school? I wouldn't find solid evidence of criminal activity, not online because there hadn't been charges filed and therefore no criminal proceedings. But reporter's intuition told me something had happened. Otherwise, why remove him and stash him in Oakhurst? Take him from a city with more than three million people and drop him in an unincorporated town of barely three thousand? Wickham-man-of-the-cloth may not be as clean as Quint assumed.

De-frocking a priest left a nasty taste in my mouth, but not so repulsive that I wouldn't continue the search. The reporter in me demanded facts. Quint's reputation was on the line and I intended to salvage what respect in the climbing world he still had.

In order to do so, I needed to find a connection between Grady and one of the other climbers. Quint had said Grady used to attend the Catholic Church in Oakhurst, but had stopped about a month ago. Why? I scratched down a note to ask Wickham, who I fully intended to interview.

Setting aside the look into Wickham's past, I consulted the list I'd made the day before that I would have researched if my computer at home had worked. The grand jury's website listed the current members and the presiding judge next to links to each year's reports. I choose the most recent and decided to search backward.

The phone rang. I trapped the receiver between shoulder and ear.

"Newsroom. Monakee speaking."

"Any luck?" Morales must have been bored, which meant he probably hadn't gotten anywhere with the National Park Service. His voice was almost lost in the sound of wind. Which meant he'd called from the car. I crossed my fingers and hoped he wasn't on his way here. I didn't need to lose any more time.

"Just starting the search," I said.

"What about last night?" he asked, as though I'd been slacking on the job.

"My home computer was down. This is the first chance I've had. You?"

"I got nothing."

"I'll let you know if I uncover something." I hung up without waiting for a reply.

Shoving aside the life-crippling events of the last couple days, I returned to the reports, listed in the order they had been released. I started at the bottom and worked my way up.

"Any luck?" Quint asked.

Seriously? What were he and Morales doing, parroting each other? Sighing, I glanced at Quint. He'd folded his arms on top of the cubicle wall. If he and Morales would leave me alone, I just might find something.

I shook my head. "You?"

He sat in the hard plastic chair designed for backyards, not offices. Baby followed and curled up beside his feet. She appeared to smile, as though she'd adapted to her new life and approved of the changes. Something about her drew my affection. I'd never had pets growing up, except a kitten that had clawed me, and didn't know how to interact. Besides, with my schedule, I wouldn't trust myself with an air plant.

"I tracked down Yates," Quint said. "He'll be passing through town at three and agreed to meet us at Books and Bagels."

"I'll let Morales know." I reached for the phone. Before I could dial, Morales strode up the hall and into the newsroom. I'd left word with the front office staff that he would be coming by to help with some research. Great. I peered at the reports online, resisted the urge to grind my teeth, and turned to face them.

"Let me know what?" He scratched the Collie's ears. I told him about Yates. "We'll all go. Until then, I'll be in the—what did you call it? Morgue. Kind of like that. I'll be in the morgue." He motioned at Baby. "Nice dog."

"You want her?" Quint asked.

"You kidding? I'd forget to feed her, she'd die. I'm not responsible enough." He retreated to the room in back.

Quint left to take Baby home before our boss ventured out of his office and found the dog in the newsroom. I tried to give the report on the computer screen my full attention.

The grand jury had written about their visit to the county jail. Their recommendations included building on to the existing facility to accommodate the influx of prisoners that would no longer be shipped off to the state prisons. A couple years earlier, a three-judge panel found that overcrowded prisons resulted in lack of proper medical care for the inmates, and that was unconstitutional. Several nonviolent, non-sexual related crimes were reclassified from felonies to misdemeanors, and the time served reduced to three years or less. Those criteria mandated they now served their sentences in county jails.

I moved on to the next. According to this report, they had visited the two women's prisons near Chowchilla, one of which now housed men for the same reason our jail was overcrowded. I scanned the report, didn't find anything worth killing someone over, closed that window and opened the next.

Municipal airport. Findings were suggestions on educating the public. Nothing there, either.

Over the course of the next year, they'd written about the county's clerk-recorder's department, probation, treasurer-tax collector, and auditor, all based on complaints from apparently disgruntled employees. Nothing dealing with Grady.

My heart felt like it shrank three sizes. I scrubbed my hands over my face. "There's got to be a lead in here somewhere."

By 2:30 I'd read more than a years' worth of reports. I'd also worked through lunch and decided I'd get a salad and coffee at Books and Bagels. After printing the remaining reports, about fifty pages total, I bound with a binder clip and tucked them into my purse.

While Quint drove across town, opting to use state Route 99 instead of weaving through the business district, I returned my attention to the grand jury's findings. Traffic consisted of a tractor-trailer rig, a blue Saturn with primer spots and a classic Nineteen-Fifty-something coup. Two things those in the Central Valley love; classic cars and classic rock.

Even here the evidence of drought was apparent in the closely-cropped barrier of oleanders between north and southbound lanes. Although still clinging to a hint of green, between those leaves were dry, brown twigs that I couldn't help but see as a fire hazard.

"I spoke with Diane's brother." Quint tapped the turn signal, glanced over his shoulder and eased into the left lane to pass the big rig. "He said he'll let me know when they schedule Grady's services."

"How's she doing?" Dumb question, but it was the only one I could think to ask. How would I be if I'd seen my life partner fall to his death? Not good. No, not good at all.

Quint shrugged as he eased the car back into the driving lane. "Doctor gave her something to help her cope."

"Think she ever will?" I asked, mostly to myself. I'm not sure I'd ever be able to cope if it had been Quint who had struck that granite ledge with the crack that almost sounded like gunfire.

Quint reached out and stroked my cheek with the back of his finger. "She's pretty messed up. What did she see?"

"You don't want to know," I said, and although I tried to block the image from filling my mind, the burst of pink that stained the dawn filled my head anyway. Staring out the window, I let the fuzzy images of buildings and trees we passed provide a backdrop, a blank screen that I filled with a void, one that replaced the image of Grady falling with streaks of tan, brown, gray. I couldn't focus on the past. If I did, I could be just as zoned out as Diane had become.

The job. The pending interview with Yates. That was my safety net, my climbing harness, my means to rise above the scenes of death and maintain my hold on life.

Quint drove down the ramp to the Sycamore-lined street and parked next to the coffee shop. Sunlight seemed to wilt what foliage that hadn't died. Heat rippled the air above the asphalt around the dozen cars parked outside. Flower beds where miniature rose bushes had once thrived were now filled with crushed rock, intensifying the heat.

Aromas of freshly-brewed coffee and the spicy scent of sausage greeted us. Yates hadn't arrived, so I hunted for a salad in the cooler that held water, sandwiches, fruit trays, but no salad. They did have Greek yogurt with honey and granola, so I chose one of those and a triple-shot cappuccino.

Quint got a cup of espresso and joined me at a tall round table near the entrance. Beyond the large window, Morales parked his silver Bronco. He stepped inside, letting in the heat and cutting off its invasion as the door swung closed behind him. He strode past us, coffee'd up and joined us.

Morales tugged a paper napkin from a dispenser, clicked ready a pen and studied Quint. A twinge of fear snuggled uneasily in my stomach, one that warned me Morales was in the mood to rattle cages. I'd known him since I began working for the Gazette almost ten years ago, and had seen him rattle a lot of cages. It always began with the narrowing of his eyes, an intense gaze that, I'd swear, held a flicker of red, the slight upturn to one side of his lips. He was moving into interrogation mode, and Yates hadn't yet arrived.

"Could anyone have gotten into your car? Accessed your ropes and shit?" Morales set aside the pen and dumped three packets of sugar into his cup.

"I lock the car, but I guess it's possible." Quint toyed with the empty paper packets Morales had tossed onto the table, rolling one into a long, thin tube, then folded it over and set it in the table's center. "I'm not overly cautious in Camp Four. It's an unspoken rule among climbers. Respect everyone else's property, privacy and personal space."

"Can't trust anyone," Morales said. "You served in Afghanistan, and you haven't figured that out?"

"Yosemite isn't Afghanistan." Quint tapped his fingers against the table. "If I can't trust people, can't enjoy a sport like climbing without fear that someone would kill someone else, would sabotage . . ." He raked his fingers through his hair. "What's the point? What did I fight for, what did my SEAL team fight for?"

"World's full of low life criminals," Morales said. "People don't base their worth on morals any more. It's all about greed, power and a perverse definition of respect."

"Okay," I said, and held up my hands. "Let's focus on Grady's death."

Quint shot Morales a glare. "I'm not going to claim I've seen the worst a human can do, but I've seen my share. You have, too. Still, I'm not going to live my life afraid to trust people."

Morales slid his hand down his side. I figured he was searching for his gun.

"Enough," I said. "We're not here to battle among ourselves, but figure out what really happened to Grady. Let's focus, guys."

Quint leaned back, stretched out his legs and folded his arms over his chest.

Morales, simultaneously, did almost the exact same thing, and they stayed that way, glaring at each other.

The door opened. The tall man with narrow face and pinched lips that I'd met in Yosemite two days ago stepped inside. He was lean like most climbers and wore a gold chain that, in my book, marked him as a lounge lizard. The diamond on his pinkie was worth a chunk of change. He was from the Bay Area, Silicon Valley, the land of Facebook and Google, and he dressed the part. Even his jeans were top dollar, Naked and Famous brand denim which sold for about a hundred and fifty on sale.

Quint waved him over. Yates dragged a chair to the table and sat.

"Thanks for coming," Quint said.

"No problem, it's on the way to Fresno. Not sure why you want to meet, though." Yates shifted his gaze from Quint to Morales, me, and back to Quint. "Is there something going on?"

"It's about Grady," Quint said. "How well did you know him?"

"I've seen him in the park several times. We both climbed the Merced River canyon one day. That's when I met him." Yates shifted uncomfortably. "Why?"

Morales flipped his chair around, sat and rested his arms on the chair's back. He poised his pen over the napkin. I found a notepad and replaced it for the napkin. He acknowledged the gesture with a slight nod, and returned his attention to Yates. "We're not convinced this was an accident."

"Yeah it was. The cam," Yates said. "It was flawed. That's what the NPS said."

Quint shook his head. "It was in perfect condition when we started the climb."

Yates paled. His features slackened. Then he sat up straight and leaned toward Quint. "Are you telling me someone deliberately killed him?"

"That's what the evidence suggests," Morales said. "You get along with Grady?"

"Whoa," Yates said, and pushed away from the table. "You don't think I had anything to do with this. Do you?"

"We're talking to everyone on that climb, and anyone we can track down who stayed at Base Camp, anyone who may have seen something." Quint finished the espresso, dropped Morales' empty sugar packets into the cup, gathered my discarded yogurt container and tossed them into a nearby waste can. "I always check the gear before packing it after a climb. If anything's compromised, I toss it and replace it. I don't take chances on the wall. You and Roberts were on the line with Grady."

"So you just assume it had to be me?" Yates stood. "Fuck off, dude. I didn't kill *anyone*."

Morales stood and widened his stance as though squaring off with someone who was a potential flight risk. "We're not accusing. Just want to talk."

"What are you, a cop?" Yates scoffed.

"Yeah, asshole." Morales reached for his badge, apparently realized he didn't have it and let his hand fall to his side. "Sonofabitch. Left my badge. But yeah asshole, I'm a cop."

He hadn't left it at home, but on his chief's desk along with this 40-caliber Glock and his pride. Administrative leave had stripped him of everything except his clothes.

"Look," Yates said, and waved his arms. "I ran into the dude in the park a few times. We climbed the same walls twice, just happened to be there at the same time. That's it."

"So you didn't know him," Morales said.

"Sort of—not really."

"So you did?" Morales shook his head. "Which is it? Either you knew Grady, or you didn't. It's not complicated. Yes or no."

"Okay, I knew him," Yates said, his face red. "What do you want from me?" He paced the tight space between the table and condiment bar.

"Enough," I said, falling into the good-cop role. No one but Morales could play bad cop. He came by it naturally. I held my palm toward him, and shifted my attention to Yates, whose pinched face seemed even more rat like. "Look," I said, focusing on Yates. "I've forgotten I knew someone. If you don't see them often, or talk often, it's easy to forget. Everyone does it."

"Yeah," he said, nodding.

"It's no big deal." As I'd hoped, he relaxed a bit, evident in the way his pacing slowed.

"That's right," he said, and settled back into the chair.

"We just want to talk," I said in as soothing a manner as I could manage. To Morales, I added, "Save Mart's a few stores down. Bet they've got Three Musketeers."

In other words, get out of here and let me give it a shot. If Yates wouldn't speak with Morales, maybe he'd talk to me.

Chapter 14

While Morales headed for the store a few doors down from Books and Bagels, I volleyed questions in my head—how well did Yates know Grady? Why was Yates lying about it? Biting my thumbnail, I studied the wisp of a man in the chair across the table. If I could get him to trip up on his story, contradict himself, even display body language that would lean toward deception, I'd at least know where to start digging. If Yates was innocent of any involvement in Grady's death, I could cross him off my list.

"Is he really a cop?" Yates asked, thumbing toward the door.

"He is." I pulled out a notepad and pen. "You don't mind if I take notes, do you?"

"Why're you taking notes?" Yates narrowed his eyes. "That's right. You're that reporter, the one from the Gazette."

I nodded.

"You're working on a story?"

Again I nodded, although I hadn't considered a feature on the other climbers. Good cover, if nothing else. I jotted the date at the top of a clean sheet of paper and returned my attention to Yates.

"You don't live here," I said, stating the obvious. "Did you grow up in Madera County?"

"Yeah, Oakhurst. I live in the San Francisco Bay Area now." He glanced at the barista behind the counter, produced a wallet from his blazer's pocket. "Just a minute." He headed for the counter, paused, and turned toward Quint and me. "You guys want anything?"

I motioned to the cup in front of me. Quint shook his head.

Once he ordered, Yates returned to the table. "I've been in the bay area a while now. Still have family in Oakhurst, usually stay with them when I'm visiting the park and climbing, unless I get a spot in Camp Four."

"Did you camp when you guys climbed?"

"No." He glanced at the half-moon counter where the workers set orders upon completion. While he yearned for the coffee, I rifled through mental files trying to remember if he'd camped or not. I jotted—stayed with family—and added a sloppy asterisk, my private question mark.

"Bay area's nice," Quint said. "We try to get over there a couple times a month in the summer. You live near the coast?"

"Near Montara, north of there, close to Santa Cruz," he said.

Expensive area, million dollar homes, nice clothes. This time my note taking was mental, an imagined Post-it tacked to my inner bulletin board.

"What do you do for a living?" I already knew, and the job didn't pay enough to live near Montara.

"Engineer," he said, and again glanced for his coffee. "I used to work for San Mateo County."

"And now?"

"I got hired on with the high speed rail project."

"They must pay pretty well," Quint said, and shot me a sideways glance as though to say, *something fishy this way comes*.

I peered at Yates' hands, taking note of the fact he wore no wedding ring, didn't even have a pale line where one would have been. Two incomes might—and that was a very tenuous *might*—provide for such upscale living.

As if snagging my thread of thought, he raised one hand, palm toward himself as though to pat his chest, and added, "Small house, two bedrooms, one that I rent out. Only way I could buy a place near the ocean."

More scribbles, another asterisk—who was his roommate?

"You said you worked for the county," I said, staring at the pages as though consulting my notes. "Is that how you met Grady? I know counties have conferences," I added, giving him a lead. "Do you go to any of those?"

"Oh, yeah, CSAC has one every year. I'd seen Grady last year in Monterey."

"So you did know him," I said, reinstating the fact.

"Yeah, I mean, hey, I know a lot of people." He stretched out his arms and laced his fingers. "Slipped my mind until you mentioned the conference. Yeah, I knew him."

"The night before the climb, maybe that morning, did you see anyone around Quint's equipment? Anyone at all?" I asked.

Yates shifted, flicked his gaze at Quint and appeared to study the table between us. "I've been thinking about that, the equipment," he said, and pulled his feet beneath his chair. "Could have mistaken gear that someone else left in the wall as Quint's gear. Maybe it was left by another climber, someone who was on the wall the day before our climb. I really can't say."

"How well do you know the other climbers? Those on the wall with you and Grady?" I leaned forward slightly, not enough to make him feel trapped but just so he would feel I was interested in what he had to say, let him think I was buying into his suggestion. Which I wasn't. Everything about him, his posture, his gestures, the alternate scenarios he offered were all signs of deception. He knew something, I'd bet a week's pay he did.

"We're all climbers," he said. "We've seen each other, I know some better than others." He shrugged.

"You were on the rope with Grady, right?"

Yates nodded.

"Did you lead? Or were you in the middle?"

He folded his arms over his chest and although he leaned back, the muscles in his neck tightened. "I don't know. I don't recall—I think I led. Yeah. I led, but we used the cams Quint placed during his climb."

It hadn't been so long ago he'd forget where he was on the rope. If he had led, who had been between Yates and Grady?

Roberts was on the same rope, above Grady and in the perfect position to remove or add cams. Yates had blamed him, publicly, the night following the climb. Had he seen something?

"What made you implicate Roberts?" I asked.

"I didn't say anything like that," Yates insisted. "Just said he was the middle man. So yeah, definitely, I led."

"One last question." I sipped my coffee and set the cup aside. "Do you have any idea why the grand jury would have investigated Grady?"

Yates' eyes widened slightly, one side of his mouth curved down. Then he tilted his head and shrugged. "I didn't know him well enough to talk about anything like that. Maybe he was doing something he shouldn't have, like misusing county funds or something. I really can't say."

The barista, a young man with pocked face and looking all of sixteen, approached our table. He grinned at Yates and handed him the coffee.

"When I heard triple-grande, caramel macchiato I knew it had to be you," the kid said. His smile faded, his features became grim. "Sorry about your friend, man."

A loud crack issued from the refrigerated unit beside the cash register. A spasm gripped me, my chest tightened and I spun toward the sound.

"What was that?"

Beside the cooler, a young woman yanked her child, a tow-headed boy, away and shielded him with her body just as the glass shelf tilted and smashed over bottles of water, cans of berry refreshers. Fragments shot outward like buckshot made of diamond dust, most of which landed on the woman's bare legs just below her shorts. Blood oozed from several cuts, grew into rivulets that trickled down her pale flesh.

The barista pulled his cell from his pocket and thumbed in three numbers. Quint sprinted toward the woman. He'd had field training while in the Navy and could offer aid until help arrived.

As though the sound were a jolt of electricity, Yates sprang to his feet. But he didn't move toward the commotion. Instead, he glanced through the wall of windows toward the parking lot.

"Hey, I gotta go," he said, and stepped toward the door. "Gotta be in Fresno. You have my number. Anything I can do let me know."

I nodded absently, more concerned about the woman whose legs were bleeding. Quint had gotten a clean cloth from one of the workers and now applied pressure to a particularly bad wound just above the back of the lady's knee.

I grabbed a chair and slid it toward them. She couldn't sit, but at least she could grasp onto it to steady herself. Tears in her eyes, she nodded silent thanks. The boy, probably three years old, cried, his bottom lip trembling, snot glistening above his upper lip. If nothing else, I could keep him company until helped arrived.

I pulled some napkins from the stack near the condiment bar and gently wiped the child's nose. Grasping his hand, I urged him to step away from his mother so Quint had room to work. He went limp, arched his back and let loose a wail that pierced my brain.

"Okay," I said, letting him go.

He tried to move back toward his mother, but she held out her hand.

"Stay back," she said.

"What's your name?" Quint asked.

"Loretta," she said, and sucked in a ragged breath.

The child kicked at the chair's legs. It rocked back. I caught it before it could tumble over.

I understood that the boy was upset. What child wouldn't be? But his behavior bordered on brat.

"She's going to be fine," I said. "Sit so she knows you're safe, okay?"

He looked up at me through tear-dampened lashes. Regarded the chair. Climbed onto the seat and swung his feet, a foot off the floor.

Quint had managed to slow the bleeding by the time the paramedics arrived. Once he handed over both his patient and the child, he headed for the men's room to scrub up.

Yeah, I had Yates' number. Heartless type, didn't even wait to make sure the lady was okay. Maybe not heartless. Maybe by design.

Maybe he'd used the distraction to slip away before we could ask any more questions.

Chapter 15

While I waited at the table in Books and Bagels for Quint to return from the men's room, and Morales from his quest for a Three Musketeers, I added to the notes I'd already taken and mulled over my talk with Yates. Something twisted lazily in the fog of my memory, something I'd missed, an indistinct shape that, although I couldn't recall, I knew was important.

The barista who had brought Yates his coffee now swept broken glass into a pile that glistened beneath the shop's subtle lighting. He filled a dustpan, dumped it into a hard plastic bucket, the pieces clinking as they formed a pile in the pail.

I wanted to spend the remainder of the day making a list of the boards and commissions Grady had been assigned to, including those that met in Sacramento: Rural Counties and the San Joaquin Rail. Provided the internet had been reinstated, I would google the Sacramento Bee newspaper from home.

Fifteen minutes later, I stepped into my duplex. Aromas of garlic, onion and braised beef filled the house. Awesome. Not stir fry, which was fine. Oz made a wicked good pot roast.

Sunlight slanted through the vertical blinds, cutting bars across the newly-installed linoleum. Oz insisted on replacing the floor himself. The old one had cracked and curled around the baseboards. While not top dollar—Oz couldn't see paying big bucks when in a rental—the beige, sage green and earthen flooring was a tremendous improvement. The color scheme matched my Fifties-style dinette. Well, table. I didn't have the original chairs, and instead used two folding types I'd picked up at a thrift store.

Wearing his *Kiss the Cook* apron with pink satin ruffles, he stood at the stove and whisked together butter and flour. Then he ladled the drippings from the Dutch oven in which cooked the beef, potatoes, carrots and celery.

"Need any help?" I asked, hoping he'd decline the offer. I didn't mind chopping, dicing and slicing but it had been a long day and I was ready for a drink.

"Pot roast is almost ready," he said in his sing-song manner. "They'll be here soon, right?"

"Any—" The doorbell rang. I glanced out the window above the sink and glimpsed Morales' Bronco as it pulled into the driveway behind my Corsica. Opening the door to Quint, I smiled at his reaction to getting hit by scents of Oz's cooking.

"That smells great." Quint shrugged out of his jacket and hooked it over a peg in the hall tree.

Morales entered, draped his coat over the peak on the banister, closed his eyes and sniffed the air like a bloodhound catching a scent. He peeked into the kitchen, where Oz continued making gravy, and tilted his head toward the door. "You get tired of Monakee, I'll hire you."

Oz beamed and let his gaze fall over Morales. "For you, Cowboy, I'd do it for free."

Morales' grin died and I'd swear heat colored his cheeks. He headed for the living room.

Under his breath, Oz said, "Oh Girlfriend, I so love messing with a straight guy's mind."

"You're bad," I said, tried to stifle laughter but the chuckle bubbled up anyway. "How much longer?"

"Twenty, give or take. I have a few modest hors d'oeuvrs," he added with a flip of his wrist toward the counter that opened the kitchen to the living room. He'd set out plates of cheeses, sliced apple, pear and multi-seed crackers.

Oz had set up a card table in the space behind the stairs, next to a broom closet that he'd converted into his private wine cellar. On the table, he'd placed his good china and cloth napkins, as though Quint and Morales were VIP guests. Really, Oz loved entertaining and used even a follow-up meeting as a chance to indulge in one of his passions: cooking.

Curling onto the green linen couch, I nibbled cheese while reading through my notes. Morales and Quint piled small plates with hors d'oeuvrs and joined me in the living room. Quint settled beside me, and Morales opted for the lavender Lay-Z-Boy.

Quint hadn't tracked down the other three climbers, but had left a message for Pratt. I hoped he'd return the call. They all knew they didn't have to speak with us.

Morales hadn't found anything of interest in the Gazette's archives, but he still had several articles on the list I'd given him. I still hadn't gotten the final determination from the park rangers.

"I've got the laptop in the car," Quint said. "We could resume our search here."

"No internet," Oz said, weaving between couch and the old shipping crate that served as a coffee table. He'd removed the snacks from the bar and now set them on the crate.

"Still down?" I shook my head. Usually the cable company was quick to solve problems.

"You know that house in the old section of town? The city's founder built it. You know the one," Oz said.

Dread sank through me. He was referring to the Borden House. The one I loved. The one someone had purchased and was now in the process of destroying. "What about it?"

"Construction crew was digging to replace old pipes, I believe, and cut the cables."

"Any ETA on repairs?" I asked.

"Tomorrow? Really, Girlfriend, a day or two without access to the cyber world isn't going to kill you." He sashayed over to the wine closet, where he'd installed a temperature-controlled cooler, and posed with one hand on the knob. "Wine anyone?"

"Please say you've got something," Morales said to me.

"I dug up a couple things." I flipped through pages.

"Quint? Detective? Drinks?" Oz raised a neatly-shaped brow.

"Merlot," Quint said, and turned his attention to me. "What did you find?"

"Red?" Oz propped his fingers on his hip. "With cheese and fruit?"

"White?" Quint said with a hint of impatience. "Grady," he said to me.

"Yeah," Morales added, leaning toward me and resting his elbows on his knees. "What've you got?"

"I've got a nice crisp chardonnay," Oz chimed in.

As though he'd forgotten his sidebar discussion, Quint furrowed his brow and regarded Oz. "Right. The wine. That'll work."

"Or a blend," Oz added. "I've got a sweet little bottle I picked up in Napa. It's simply delish."

He'd banished white wines shortly after moving in about a year earlier, and only changed his mind when he and his *girls*—the all-male acting guild—went on a wine-seeking mission during the summer. In Napa, he discovered that Pinot Grigio, Riesling and Muscat were not equivalent to profanity.

To Oz, Quint said, "Either," reached over and tapped my notebook.

I flipped through until I found the pages I'd composed before leaving work. "The grand jury slammed the Board of Supervisors for not providing enough funding so the mosquito and vector control district could adequately battle West Nile Virus."

"So?" Morales frowned at me.

"Detective?" Oz interrupted. "Wine or beer?"

"Brew."

"Hannah?"

"Beer's fine." When a bit of silence followed, I glanced at Quint, then Morales, and to Oz. Maybe the interruptions were over, and I could get back to letting them know what I'd uncovered so far.

"Last year, we saw three deaths in Madera County," I said, and tapped my pen against the page. "One was a child. The father came before the board and blasted them."

"Where was the kid from?" Morales asked.

Oz returned and handed Quint a glass. "Go ahead," he said, wiggling his fingers as though he'd magically make Quint enjoy the vino. "Taste. I want to know what you think."

Quint raised his hand, looked about to speak, then closed his eyes and shook his head. He sipped. Stared off into space. Nodded, and grinned.

"You're right. This is very nice." He set the wine on a coaster on the crate. To me, he echoed Morales' question: "Where was the child from?"

Oz returned with two beers he'd ordered online from a microbrewery in Washington State: Scuttlebutt. Wishing he'd allow good old Budweiser in the house, but knowing he'd rant about its absolute lack of character, I sighed and took the icy-cold bottle. Homeport Blonde, it had a yellow S behind a mermaid holding a stein.

"They live in Raymond," I managed, and drank. Clean, crisp, with a faint lemon scent. Not bad.

"And that's . . . " Quint asked.

"Used to be District One, but since the census and redrawing of supervisorial lines, it's now in District Five."

"Grady's district," Morales said, accepting the beer from Oz.

I nodded.

"Anything else?"

Oz perched on the arm of the Lay-Z-Boy. Morales cleared his throat and attempted to ignore his admirer, but the sideways glances told me he was very much aware. "That's not all you found, right?"

"Oakhurst," I said, and took another drink. "The library staff had problems with vagrants hanging around the parking lot." I flipped pages. "They shouted obscenities, exhibited obnoxious behavior, urinated in public, used drugs and alcohol on county property and intimidated staff."

"How many vagrants?" Quint rolled the glass, wet with condensation, between his palms. "This really is good. What is it?" he asked Oz.

Great. Not only was Oz distracting us from discussing details of our investigation, he now had both Morales and Quint's attention, and I no longer did.

"Guys?" I wiggled the notepad, its pages fanning out.

"Sorry," Quint said. "How many?"

"Lunatic," Oz said.

"Excuse me?" I shook my head. "What are you talking about?"

"The wine, Girlfriend. Lunatic white," he said and frowned as though *I'd* been the one to break into *his* conversation. "An Alsatian-style blend with an Italian twist. Has a hint of ripe mangos and star fruit then bursts through the finish with flavors of blood orange and kumquat."

"Really does." Quint nodded. "Where'd you find this?"

"Doesn't matter," I said. "Talk wine over dinner. Now, I'd like to finish."

"Oh, dinner. Better check the gravy," Oz said, and fluttered out of the room, but not before calling over his shoulder, "Luna Vineyards."

"Where were we?" I asked.

Quint swirled the wine, brought the glass to his nose.

"Seriously?" I set the pages aside. Drew a deep breath. Counted to ten, as I'd heard parents did when dealing with particularly disruptive children. Only my child was Oz.

Now that he had left the room, Morales had visibly relaxed. "Vagrants. Oakhurst library."

"Yeah, how many," Quint added.

"Okay." I consulted my scribbles. "Several, but only one really pushed back." I'd gone online, checked the board of supervisors' video archives, and researched the issue. The board of supervisors had addressed the problems last summer. "One of the homeless, Pierson Vance, spoke during the board meeting. He became belligerent, made threats against all of them, who then ordered staff to get security to escort Vance out of the board chambers. They did." I sipped my beer. "Vance threatened to *fix* Grady because he was the supervisor in that district. I don't know what he meant by fix, but it could be a credible threat."

"Know where to find him?" Morales asked.

"Nope, that's your job." I flashed him a smile. "Check with the county lockup, behavioral health—although they might not be able to tell you. Check the Mission and Hope House, there are branches of each in Oakhurst. Oh, and some of the homeless hangs out beneath the bridge when he can't get a bed at the Mission."

Morales nodded, wrote Vance's name on his legal pad and peered at me, silently urging me to continue.

"That's it." I shrugged. "I've got nothing else."

"Maybe it's something the grand jury is still working on?" Quint offered. "Grady or his assistant could have threatened to hand over complaints, whoever they're investigating gets wind of it, and goes after Grady."

Good point. If so, I had a contact that had slipped me information in the past. If anyone found out she had spoken with me, she'd face criminal charges. She had served four years total, on an every-other-year basis, on the grand jury and was currently its foreperson.

"What?" Quint said. "I see those mental gears grinding."

"Confidential. But if I find anything, I'll let you guys know."

Chapter 16

The following morning, I rushed through getting ready for work so I could call my grand jury contact. I didn't dare use my home or cell phones. She could be subject to subpoena should she get caught speaking with me. As press, our calls at the office were confidential and protected under the law. Sure, there had been cases testing the strength of that law, and journalists have ended up in jail to protect their sources. But we lived in a thirty-three thousand population community in the Central Valley. No one was going to buck the system here. What was it that state senator had said?

No one lives in the Central Valley among the tumbleweeds.

Needless to say, that senator didn't win reelection.

When I reached the office, I started to pick up the phone and caught scanner traffic. Urgency in the dispatcher's voice grabbed my attention, adrenaline surging in me like a triple shot espresso. She called for D-2, Morales' second in command, to respond to a one-eighty-seven. Homicide.

Cold, dry wind blasted over me as I hurried to the parking lot. Although it's illegal to use a cell phone while driving, I punched in Quint's number.

Dark clouds brooded, a teaser of rain that would never fall. The wind would carry them to Arizona, where they would release their precious load. Here, the ground around trees had cracked into octagon shapes, webbing the earth and roadways.

Quint answered on the third ring. "You're up early."

"Homicide," I said, and gave him the address on Borden's west side, an upscale neighborhood.

"Meet you there." He hung up.

I dropped the phone into the cup holder and headed along Yosemite Drive, past city hall with its retro, Fifties-style flat-roof architecture.

Near the end of Yosemite, I turned right onto Pine Street and stopped. Police cars, lights revolving in shades of blue and red, blocked the street. Three houses down, a tarp covered what I assumed was a body in a driveway.

Normally I'd find Morales, who would give me the details on what had happened. But with him on leave, I'd need to find his second in command, Badorini.

After locking my purse in the trunk, I pocketed the keys and headed for the yellow caution tape, twisting and flapping in the wind. Hair blew across my face, and, wishing I had thought to get the ponytail holder off the blinker switch, I fingered the strands back and tugged the hood of my Anorak jacket over my head, pulled the front together and zipped up. Cold bit my cheeks, my eyes watered. I blinked, letting the moisture dampen my face and, not for the first time, glad I wasn't one to wear makeup every day. No raccoon look here.

Across the street, a woman clutched her bathrobe at the throat, one hand covering her mouth as if to trap in cries of anguish. This was probably the first time this neighborhood had experienced what happened almost nightly on the town's east side. There, gangs and crime and drugs were the norm. Here, with multi-storied luxury homes, manicured lawns, even burglaries were rare. A homicide was unheard of.

Badorini emerged from the pale blue house. He was a stout man with muscles that spoke of his past as a Marine. White slashed his temples from years of wearing sunglasses. His clothing, impeccable as usual, included a tie and white gold tack. For Morales' second in command, he was almost an exact opposite of his detective sergeant.

Badorini consulted with a uniformed cop, Holmes, a rookie who had been on the force less than a year. The younger officer looked pale, and I wanted to offer comfort, let him know I understood completely. I'll never forget the first time I saw a dead body. It had changed something deep inside me, made me a bit harder, a bit less trusting, and sometimes, having to cope with seeing horrible crimes over the years, a bit darker. It had also taught me to savor each day, each detail of life, treasure the moments because in an instant, it could all change. Go away. There's no guarantee of tomorrow.

Holmes' shoulders stooped as though he were relieved that Badorini would take over. Tall, skinny, clothes hung loose on him and his utility belt looked like it should bring him to the ground because of its weight. Pale and with a spatter of freckles, he looked like a young version of Ron Howard during his Opie days.

Holmes turned away from the body beneath the tarp, around which lay a pool of blood beginning to congeal from the looks of the scummy layer on top. Although I'd seen blood more times than I cared to consider, the sight still created a knot in my stomach. Not so much because of the blood itself, but the loss of life it represented.

He sauntered over and gave me a brittle grin.

"You never get used to it," I said, and patted the sleeve of his jacket. "You do, however, learn to cope."

He nodded. "That's what Badorini said." Holmes glanced over his shoulder and returned his attention to me. "Not sure I'm cut out for the job."

"You are," I said. "I bet even Morales went through what you're facing."

"The Sarge?" Holmes let out a humorless chuckle. "That's hard to imagine."

"It is, but he was human once."

That brought a genuine smile.

"Can you tell me what happened?" I asked, knowing it was the lead detective's place and not the street cop's. But if I could get Holmes to focus on the details of the incident and not the death itself, it might lessen the impact.

"You'll have to wait for Badorini."

I nodded. "In the meantime, maybe one of the neighbors saw something," I said, hinting that he needed to get moving, get his mind back on the job. I tilted my head toward the lady in the bathrobe, barefoot on her expansive, wrap-around porch.

"Right. Talk to the neighbors." He started to walk away, stopped and met my gaze. "Thanks."

He walked off with more confidence, evident in his stride.

A van pulled up to the curb across the street. A newscaster stepped out with camera in tow. They would get sound bites of what had happened to use throughout the day during the various news broadcasts. They hadn't sent a reporter, just the cameraman. The station was out of Fresno, where they saw shootings and stabbings almost daily. Someone lying dead in their driveway was no big deal to them.

Quint parked behind the van. A Prius with the Fresno Bee's logo on the door stopped facing the wrong direction on the far side of the crime scene.

Quint jogged across the street. Once he reached me, he pulled his Nikon out of its case and removed the lens cap.

"Didn't see you on the trail this morning."

"I wanted to make that phone call we talked about last night."

"Did you?"

I shook my head. "This came across the radio as soon as I got to the office." I jotted down the house number. They might not be able to tell us who the victim is, but I could satisfy my own curiosity without using it in the news article. "Did you get any further on your research?"

"Got Roberts on the phone. He's checking his calendar and said he'd get back to me." Quint raised the camera and snapped off several shots.

"How about Wickham and Pratt?"

"Not yet." Clicked off more frames, each followed by a barely audible whirring sound. "And just Pratt. Wickham's good, I don't think we need to bother him."

Not according to my research, but I wasn't going to tell Quint that. Instead, I smiled and filed the issue in a mental folder labeled *follow up*.

Badorini motioned to three men in black suits standing next to the Borden Funeral Home van. They opened the back of the vehicle, pulled out a gurney and set a black body bag on the mattress. They moved forward as four other officers held sheets of plastic to block our view out of respect for the deceased.

Once the body had been loaded into the van, Badorini strode over to where Quint and I waited. The cameraman joined us, and the Bee reporter was left to maneuver his way between vehicles across the street in order to join us.

While the cameraman readied the tool of his trade, Badorini motioned me to one side. I followed and he stopped just short of a row of hedges.

"Where's Sarge?" he asked.

"How should I know?"

Badorini shrugged. "He's not at home. Doesn't take vacations. Has no hobbies, not much of a life outside the job. Which means he's onto something. Usually when he's onto something, you're involved."

"You're good, know that?" I smiled. "He's helping out on a hunch." Using my pen, I pointed to the funeral home van. "What happened here?"

"Appears to be a drive by." Badorini frowned. "Not sure if it's gang related, the victim wasn't involved in any gang that we're aware of."

"Anyone see or hear anything?"

He shook his head. "No one heard a sound, which is odd. These people? They're not like those on the east side. They don't hide and stay out of situations. These people look out for each other."

"Then the shooter used a silencer," I offered.

"That's what I think, too." He held his hand over my notepad. "That's not for publication."

"Okay." I glanced around him. On the driveway, next to the pool of blood, lay three yellow crime scene markers, like miniature A-frame tents, indicating evidence. "Three shots?"

"One to the head, two to the chest. Also not for publication."

"Sounds like a professional hit."

"Or someone good with guns." Badorini shrugged.

"Who was he?"

"She," Badorini corrected. "Name's Ava Moaler."

Chapter 17

I gripped my pen. My mouth went dry as if the wind outside had forced its way past my lips. The knot in my stomach doubled in size and pressure built in my chest. "Grady Spinelli's legislative aid?"

The wind grew colder. My jacket no longer kept out the iciness. Tendrils of cold slithered inside, wrapping me, freezing my core. I peered at the funeral van, just pulling away with Ava's body inside.

"Who would do this?" I asked no one in particular.

Badorini, with a mic now clipped to his lapel, was in the process of giving an interview to Channel 30.

Quint snapped a shot of the interview for tomorrow's edition of the Gazette. Numb both physically and emotionally, I stood by the crime scene tape. If nothing else, the shooting told me one thing: Grady's death had to be related to his work as a Madera County supervisor. I needed to spend more time researching the grand jury reports, and call my contact.

First, Grady falls to his death. Now, someone killed his assistant in an execution-style fashion. Had she been dressed for work? Or had something drawn her outside during the night?

Once Badorini finished, he returned to the hedge where he'd left me. "You look like someone just walked across your grave."

Odd phrase, one I've never really understood. But he was right. The shudder that rippled through me was more ghostly than caused by the cold.

I gestured toward the van. "How was she dressed?"

"Ready for work, had her keys in hand, had just unlocked the car door when someone shot her."

"Don't you think this could be related to Grady's death? I certainly do."

"I know what you're saying, but we don't have any evidence as to who did this and no connection to Spinelli's accident." Badorini breathed deeply, exhaled a slow whistle. Finally he nodded. "Okay. I'll call the national park guys, tell them what happened and see what they think. And tell Morales to call. If he's got something on this, I'll see if the chief will let him work from home."

"He'll be thrilled," I said. "Well, as thrilled as Morales gets."

I left Badorini to his investigation and returned to the newsroom feeling hopeful for the first time since Grady's death. His assistant's killing, while tragic, solidified, in my mind, that Grady's death had been intentional.

Morales had returned to the Gazette's morgue. I entered the dimly lit room and sat on the edge of the table. I gave him the rundown on Moaler, and what Badorini suggested. Morales grinned so broadly, I thought his lips would split.

I left him to his euphoria and returned to my cubicle. The message light blinked on my phone. I jabbed in my password—my deceased brother's date of birth—and waited: one message from Carracci, the District 3 supervisor. He was also my former sheriff's department contact.

"Tag, you're it," he's said, and chuckled. "Call me on my cell. You got that number? Yeah, of course you do that's where you left the message. Geeze. This getting old stuff sucks." Again he chuckled. "Anyway, call me back. I'll leave the phone out so I'll hear it."

Carracci had a way about him that commanded respect, and possessed a humor that often left me laughing until I had a stitch in my side. I entered his number and waited.

"When are you coming to work for me?" he asked as a way of answering.

"When you buy a newspaper," I said.

"No, really, how are you? It's been awhile."

"It has, and I'm good. How are things at the county?"

"Oh, man. Guess you heard about Spinelli?" Carracci sighed into the phone, making a sound like wind through reeds. "Guy's crazy climbing like that. You'd never find me up there, hanging from ropes. Nuts."

"That's what I called about." I drew my leg onto my chair's cushion. On the computer, my Tom Petty and the Heartbreakers screen saver shifted to another photo of Petty. "Do you know of anything Spinelli was working on that might . . ."

"Give someone reason to knock him off?" Carracci finished for me. "Maybe, but I can't talk about it. Closed session."

"Not even a hint?" I bit my thumbnail.

"Nah, Girl, you know I can't. Would if I could, you know me, but I can't."

"Not even a nudge in the right direction?" I knew I was pushing it. Carracci was as tight lipped as Morales, he'd had to be. Cops were cops, whether they worked for the county or local police. "Someone killed his assistant. A drive by shooting sometime early this morning."

"Ava? No, really? Damn, this town's going to hell."

"And I don't believe Spinelli fell. The rangers have gear that could have been tampered with. They're conducting an investigation now."

"I'll tell the other board of supervisors," he said, and not for the first time I wondered why he referred to himself as a *board of supervisor*, and not just *supervisor*. "Tell County Counsel, too."

"If the sheriff's department learns there was a closed session item that could have led to—"

"No one would really kill a guy over some shady actions," Carracci said. "There wasn't enough proof, or so he said. There were a few documents a whistleblower gave to Ava."

"A whistleblower?"

"Yeah, and no I can't tell you who he is," he said.

But he did reveal him as a man and not a woman. All I needed to do was figure out who Ava had been hanging out with. Not an easy task, but not impossible, either.

"Thanks. Don't be a stranger," I said.

"You too. And let me know when you want a real job." He hung up.

I returned the receiver, sat back and bit my thumbnail. One thing was for sure. I wouldn't find what I was looking for in the published grand jury reports.

This was one phone number I never wrote down, for the same reason I didn't call my contact from home. She'd been my own *Deep Throat* for years now, and I'd actually won a couple awards for my investigative reporting thanks to her.

I slipped into the old darkroom, no longer in use. Just as technology had killed the hands-on paste up process in the old composing room, it had taken out the need for chemicals to develop photos from negatives. Now, the room was cluttered with obsolete image enlargers, plastic trays, splicing equipment and a cable strung over deep sinks. The only thing in the room still working was the phone.

The sound in my ear seemed to intensify with each ring. When it switched to the answering machine, I hung up. I'd try later. I never left messages. That, too, could be used as evidence.

Morales spied me coming from the darkroom. He abandoned the morgue and followed me to my cubicle.

"What's in there?" he asked, knowing me well enough to suspect I was up to something.

"A phone and privacy," I said. "Heard back from Carracci." I gave Morales the rundown. "I'm working on finding out about this whistleblower."

"Damn," Morales said and leaned against the doorway of my cubicle. "You got better sources than I do. Any leads?"

"Just that it's a guy." Or had that admission of fact been deliberate? Carracci had been a cop. A good one. He wouldn't let anything slip, even a vague reference to gender. Not when there was an ongoing investigation.

I shrugged, and couldn't help but think that maybe Diane had been right about Grady seeing someone. If so, he'd have been careful to not let anyone see them together, which would make discovering her identity that much harder.

Chapter 18

Back in the newsroom, amid clacking keyboards and the din of voices that floated above the cubicles, I found a purple Post-It adhered to my computer monitor. Our community reporter had a conflict, and the note was a request to cover the update on construction of California's high speed rail system. Madera County had been chosen as the birthplace of the Train to Nowhere, as the project had been dubbed, and our managing editor insisted on front-page coverage of its progress.

I plucked the note. The press conference would begin in about thirty minutes. I glanced at the blue, cloth-covered wall, beyond which was Quint's work station.

"Looks like I'm going to the river for the rail presser," I called out.

Quint stood and propped his arms on top of the cubicle wall. "That train is a waste of taxpayer dollars."

"We're journalists," I said. "We don't get an opinion. Want to come?"

He shook his head. "I've got tons to do here, and we've got art we haven't used from the last press conference."

I left him to find the photo and headed east on Yosemite Drive, toward the edge of town. Wind rattled what few dead leaves still clung to branches of dying oaks. A field that had, three years ago, played host to tomatoes now lay fallow, the earth barren, scraggly weeds that had managed to take hold now dead.

With Borden behind me, I turned toward the Fresno River which coursed through town. Within a mile of city limits I came upon a cluster of cars parked in makeshift rows. Behind rose the monstrosity of concrete, wood, steel rebar, the skeleton of a bridge that would, one day, allow a train to cross the river at a rate of more than two hundred miles per hour. Although not particularly fond of the project, I found the behemoth a marvel of engineering and regarded it with awe every time I saw it. This short span, the first segment of tracks, costs millions. The entire system, once completed, is projected to cost around seventy billion.

Closing the car's door behind me, I slung my purse strap over my head and wore it from shoulder to hip. What the rail authorities would announce today would be the next, north-bound section toward the small city of Chowchilla, where what they've dubbed the Wye would veer toward Los Banos, then northwest to San Jose.

The wind shifted, carried a breeze from the west and, with it, the stench created by thousands of cattle in the County's fifty-plus dairies. I breathed into the crook of my arm, the cloth of my blazer's sleeve serving as a filter to partially diminish the foul odor, and joined the small crowd gathered near a podium, at which stood the chairman of the rail authority. Behind him stood staff, including Yates, in construction hats as though ready to hammer the next nail or pour the next load of concrete.

" . . . design and construction is consistent with the nature of the current scope of work," the chairman, a heavy-set man with bulbous nose, said.

I scratched out the quote and returned my attention to his spiel.

"There is monetary efficiency in adding this work to the existing contract," he continued, "where construction is already underway."

He added that the work would allow the agency to use more of the three-billion share of American Recovery and Reinvestment Act stimulus funding, which had a spend-deadline of September the following year.

The work, he said as I again caught a whiff of cow manure-stained air, will bring this viaduct to the Amtrak station, about a mile longer than the original scope of work.

My eyes watered. The fetid breeze threatened to activate my gag reflex. I drew a shallow breath and headed back toward my car. I'd gotten the gist of what the authority came out to say. I needed to get out of that rancid air.

Three rows from my car I spotted a black Mitsubishi, its owner just leaning into the car. Doug Pratt, one of the men who had climbed El Capitan with Quint and Grady. I waved, hoping to catch his attention. Quint had been trying to call Pratt. We still needed to speak with him regarding anything he may have seen or heard the morning Grady died.

I waved again, probably looking like some neurotic fan at a rock concert, hiding my face while attempting to demonstrate enthusiasm. I thought he'd glanced my way, but he didn't appear to have seen me and climbed into his car, started the engine and pulled straight through the empty space before him.

I hurried into my Corsica, considered following him, catching up to corner him into an interview, but he was gone by the time I backed out, his tires spinning dust into a fog-like cloud that enveloped my car. By the time it cleared, a thin layer of brown coated my windshield.

I twisted the washer on. A few drops speckled the glass, and the wipers turned those into streaks of mud. Part of me wanted to get angry. Another part reasoned it would do no good. So I sat there, exasperated, staring at the streaks and wondering what art of karma was in play.

I didn't have cleaner, nor paper towels. In the console, I found three brown napkins from a fast food joint. A crinkled bottle on the floorboard held a couple inches of water, which would be just enough to muddy the entire windshield. I leaned back in the seat and closed my eyes.

Tapping on the side window sent an electric jolt through me. I peered at Yates, and again thought how rat-like his features were. I pressed the button and the glass slid down. The wind had shifted again. The stench no longer stained the breeze.

"Saw what happened," he said, and motioned in the direction Pratt had gone. "I've got some Windex in the truck. Be right back."

He jogged toward a two-ton type with storage in back, and returned with a bottle of blue liquid and a red towel. I climbed out of the Corsica as he set about clearing the mud from my car.

"Wasn't that Doug Pratt? One of the guys you climbed with?" I asked.

Yates looked off, as though he could see Pratt as he faded in the distance, shifted his attention to me and said, "Yeah."

"What was he doing here?" I straightened. "I mean, it's a press conference. He's not press."

Yates sprayed Windex, mottling the glass. "He has a contract with the rail authority. Concrete, and man they use a ton if it."

"Pays well, I would think." Pratt was driving a brand new, Mitsubishi Eclipse Sypder, the same one he'd driven the day Grady had died. Not a cheap car. "He married?"

"Why?" Yates' face spilt into a grin, but there was nothing humorous about it. With his narrow features, the grin looked eerie and uninviting. "You interested?"

"Just curious. Ink in the blood."

"Divorced, two kids, man she took him to the cleaners." He sprayed, wiped, and moved to the other side. "We grew up together in a foothill community."

"Coarsegold? Oakhurst?"

"Near Coarsegold. Don't let the Oakhurst people hear you call them foothill people," he added, and again flashed that creepy grin. "They're mountain folk." He stepped back and admired his work. "There. Now you can see again."

"Thanks," I said, and opened the driver's side door. "Take care."

"You, too." He backpedaled a safe distance and waited until I passed.

In the rearview mirror, I saw that split, rat-like face mend itself, the grin gone, replaced with a deadpan stare which I found just as chilling.

I didn't care if Quint was buried in work. Next time I have to cover anything to do with the high speed rail, he was coming with me.

Chapter 19

Quint had gone online and purchased round trip tickets to Dallas-Fort Worth airport for early Thursday morning. Our flights would arrive in Texas three hours and two time zones later. That would give us four hours before the service at the First Christian Church on Throckmorton in Fort Worth. Grandpa's family had belonged to the church since shortly after it had been built in 1915. Four generations of Bogette's had gotten married there, and at the end of their lives the church had served as the gathering place for mourners.

My vision blurred. I swiped the tears with the back of my hand, drew a ragged breath and sighed. There'd be enough time to think about Grandpa's passing. Now I needed a distraction, and another, suspicious death would afford me just that. While I had abandoned the search through the grand jury reports, Morales had continued looking at archived newspapers just in case something gave us a clue. We still had the leads of the homeless at the Oakhurst library and the Wes Nile Virus incident. Any could have brought litigation against the county, and all litigation was discussed in closed session.

Both could have involved whistleblowers, too. I'd have to look back and see if we covered these stories, and if so, what the outcomes were. But if they were going to target a supervisor, wouldn't they have done so already?

Frustration settled as an ache in my temples. I set my glasses aside and scrubbed my hands over my face. "The answer's here. I know it is."

After the day crew left the newsroom and the pagination team and pressmen came in, I again holed up in the darkroom and tried my grand jury contact. The space was flanked by long, black Formica counters, deep, twin basins, above which draped the string for hanging photos after developing, equipment and ancient phone.

I sat on the counter, let my heels tap a beat against the cabinet door and dialed one number at a time, my finger striking the metal tab, the vintage rotary-style clicking as it brought the plastic disk back to its original place. The air, tinged with a sulfurous odor, was cooler here surrounded by the newsroom on one side and the press room on the other, with no windows to allow light or the heat it carried.

One ring. Two. Three. Another as I studied the webs that draped from the cork ceiling. Not even the cleaning crew ventured here.

My stomach rumbled. While I'd like to go home, snack on junk and get to sleep early I had practice. We always ran through our set prior to a gig. Hanging up the bulky receiver, I slid from the counter and reached for the doorknob. It twisted, the door opened and Morales stepped inside. He regarded the old equipment.

"Why are you in here?" he asked.

Stifling the irritation that tightened my muscles, I gestured toward the outdated device.

"Using the phone. I didn't want anyone overhearing my conversation." I started to step past him. He stuck out his arm, blocking me. He'd never treated me like one of his suspects before, and uneasiness crept over me. I stepped back. "What are you doing?"

"Holding out on me?" He lowered his arm. "Sonofabitch. I'm sharing all the info I find. Think you'd do the same."

Irritation mutated into anger that burned my cheeks. I returned his glare.

"This is a very sensitive source," I explained. "Some people don't want anyone knowing they're talking to me. Why're you so paranoid?"

"Not paranoid," he grumbled. "Just thought it was odd you're holed up in—what is this, anyway?"

"The old darkroom," I said. His gaze hardened, which I found odd. Something was wrong, and although we're friends I wasn't going to become his verbal punching bag. "What's up?"

He turned toward the newsroom. I grasped his elbow, stopping him.

"What's wrong?" I asked, softening my tone.

He rubbed his eyes and shook his head, but the tightness of his jaw told me he was trapping anger that would soon blister into a nasty burst of poison.

The internal investigation. Had to be it.

"I'll be glad when this bullshit's over," he muttered, crossed to the defunct composition room and through the steel door that led to the parking lot. I followed.

"See you tomorrow?" I asked as he headed for his Bronco.

"Got nothing better to do." He climbed in and drove off.

The door behind me opened and Quint strode out. "Where'd you disappear?"

Was everyone getting paranoid? I crossed to my car. "Just following some leads."

"Dinner?" he suggested. "The Dock?"

I was tempted. The Dock was the best in the Valley. They flew in fresh seafood every morning and the chef was a master. The thought of shrimp scampi morphed into a buttery flavor I could almost taste. But I needed answers, and I wouldn't get them at The Dock.

"I want see if I can figure out who hung around with Ava," I said. "Most of the county employees usually have lunch at Courthouse Café."

"I've never known you to turn down The Dock," he said.

I told him what I'd found out about closed session, and added, "If the person who brought the evidence to the board knew Ava, that could have something to do with the shooting."

"It might not be linked to Grady's death," Quint said.

I nodded. "I know. So, the café?"

"Sure. They're not steak, but they make a decent burger."

Sometimes we walked the three or so blocks to the trolley car someone had carted from San Francisco and hitched to a building. It served those working in the hundred-year-old granite courthouse, one of the few originals still in use. Tonight, though, the air was damp and dreary and heavy with a threat of rain.

We each drove and met in the café's lot. Inside, scents of burgers and bacon frying, of coffee and onions filled the air. I chose a booth beside the row of windows with a view of the park. Quint slid into the seat on the opposite side.

The waiter, who everyone called Nikki although her name was Alexandria, pulled out two menus from the holder beside the long counter and brought them to us.

"Don't usually see you here at night." A willowy mid-Sixties woman, Nikki had deep lines around her mouth from years of smoking and thin lips like those of a lizard.

"What can I do you for, Sweetie?" She winked at Quint.

He grinned and picked up the menu she'd placed on the table.

"You know Ava Moaler, right?" I asked.

"Worked for the county supervisors? So awful what happened to her isn't it?" Nikki patted her chest as though keeping her heart beating. "This crappy little town is overrun with gangs. It's enough to make you want to move and I've been here all my life."

"Ava came in here a lot, didn't she?" I opened the menu, scanned the options and chose a tuna melt with salad instead of fries.

"She did." Nikki wrote down my order. "Every Tuesday the board held meetings, and at least twice the remainder of the week. Nice lady."

"Yeah," I said, recalling Ava's attitude toward me yesterday. Not very nice at all. "Did she have lunch with the same group all the time?"

"Mostly." She peered at Quint. "Ready Doll?"

"Burger with bacon—lots of bacon—and fries."

"To drink?"

"Water," I said. Quint nodded.

"You said mostly?" I prompted.

"The last couple of months, she'd meet a guy. I'd never seen him before. They usually sat in the back corner," Nikki added, jabbing the air with her pencil. "They'd have files. I don't know what they talked about. I remember, though, because they took forever to eat. But they always left a decent tip." Nikki's smile emphasized the tip's generosity.

Matching her smile, I asked, "Do you know what he looks like?" I mentally crossed my fingers.

"Why so much interest?"

"Long story," I said. "So? Tall? Short? Heavy? Thin?" Come on. Give me *something*.

"About your height, you know, not very tall. Thin."

"Anything else? Any distinctive scars or tattoos?"

"He was stooped over, like he might have a curved spine."

"Hair color? Eyes? Age?"

"Probably in his mid-forties. Brown hair, kind of dull eyes. Walked with a shuffle." She shrugged. "Probably because of his back. That help?"

"Helps a lot."

She retreated to the bar, returned with the water and snagged another napkin from a nearby booth. Then she lingered, frowning, as though she wanted to say something but wasn't quite sure what.

I offered a smile. She tried to return the gesture, but instead looked as though she was in pain.

"Are you okay?" I asked.

"I did overhear a little bit," she admitted. "They talked about a cemetery."

Although my pulse quickened with hope, I remained calm. "A cemetery?"

"Something about breaking rules. That's all I got," she said. "Whenever I'd approach, they'd clam up. And that guy? He isn't from around here."

"What makes you think that?" I asked.

"The way he dressed, like he was out of the sixties. Jeans, boots which were usually dusty. He reminded me of people I'd seen in North Fork." She flipped the napkin. Set it on the table. Mopped up a water ring. "Why are you so interested? Is this for one of your stories?"

"Could be." I squeezed the lemon into the water and dropped it onto the bed of ice. "If you see him again, will you give him—" I dug a dog-eared business card from my purse and handed it to her. "Give him this?"

"Sure." Nikki returned to the bar.

I turned to Quint. "How many cemeteries do we have?"

"One in town, out by the Church. One just outside of town, near where they built the new jail." He frowned. "Guess that's it."

"Countywide, how many?" I asked, and counted them off on my fingers. "Chowchilla, the Ranchos, North Fork, Raymond, Manzanita Knolls near Coarsegold, Oakhurst. Right? Just the eight?"

My grand jury source might not be able to tell me what they're investigating, but she could tell me if I was on the right path.

Chapter 20

A golden hue pierced the glass of Courthouse Café and shimmered on water glasses, sparked off tableware and chrome beer taps. A cemetery breaking rules wasn't specific enough for me to form an opinion, but that didn't stop the possibilities from swarming my head. There had been Associated Press stories over the years: A Georgia crematorium where the owner stacked bodies in the woods instead of cremating them or the Rhode Island funeral director who stashed the dead in a garage.

But those were extreme cases. If something like that had happened here, in Madera County, I would have known. I sleep with the scanner on the nightstand, a part of my brain always listening for breaking news.

I didn't even know which cemetery, and although my grand jury contact wouldn't be able to tell me much she might give me a location.

"How many employees does a cemetery have?" I pulled the tomato from my tuna melt, set it aside and licked my finger.

"Guess it depends on population." Quint ate some fries and washed them down with water that had clouded its glass with its iciness. "The two here in Borden would be the largest, so I'd assume they'd have more employees."

My head throbbed at the idea of combing through massive lists of those who handled the dead. I flipped over my napkin to avoid the speck of mayo that had dripped from my sandwich and scribbled notes. "I'll start a list and research after practice."

I tucked the napkin away.

"Heard back from Pratt." A slice of bacon fell from Quint's burger. He picked it off his plate. "He said he'll stop by the office next week. He'll call first."

"How did he sound?" I always picked up on small things in a person's voice or the long pauses that intuitively told me if they could be trusted.

"Like a guy." Quint shrugged. "What's he supposed to sound like?"

The throbbing increased. I started to offer a sarcastic rebuttal, but waved the question aside and ate. Although I'd asked for ranch dressing on the side, I poured the entire contents of the miniature pitcher onto the crisp salad.

"How about the other guy?" I asked around a bite of lettuce.

"Roberts?" Quint shook his head. "Nothing yet, but Pratt did have a number for him. I'll follow up tomorrow."

I rubbed my temple. The throbbing attempted to form a twitch in my eye. I closed them and drew a deep breath. "Can't we get anything done today?"

"We're making progress." He slid his hand over mine. "Process of elimination. We'll get there."

His voice had a soothing effect. I relaxed and ate.

The rain that had threatened earlier in the evening now lashed the windows of Courthouse Café and pasted the glass with dead leaves. Puddles quickly formed in the parking lot. Darkness enveloped the world beyond. The shower wouldn't free us from the drought, but provide just enough to turn the air muggy and layer the flesh with a sticky film. Experts had reported that we'd need eleven trillion gallons over fifteen years, the same amount of water that flows over Niagara Falls in less than two hundred days. This was just a trickle.

Falls. All that water—all that *life*—gone in such a short time, like Grady. Gone in a crash and crack of bone. Wickham had mentioned how short and precious life is when he'd launched into his ad-lib service.

"How about Wickham?" I asked, shifting uncomfortably in preparation for a backlash. Wickham was a suspect in my book, clerical collar or not.

"Thought we decided to rule him out," Quint said. "He's a priest."

"Priests bury people. In cemeteries." I shrugged. "It's a connection worth looking into."

"Staff bury people," Quint countered. He shook his head. "Fine. You want to interrogate a priest, you go right ahead." He set the burger onto the plate and picked up fries. "I'm Catholic. I'm not accusing a priest of anything unless I saw it myself."

"Afraid he'll assign you a hundred Hail Mary's?" I smiled. "Give me his contact information, and I'll call. It's the strongest link we have so far."

After we'd finished dinner, I followed in my beaten Corsica to where Quint temporarily lived with Robin, the bass player for our band, Miles Creek. We'd been hired to play a private party Wednesday night, which would make the flight to Texas a challenge. After practice I intended to further my research.

Holding an edition of that day's Gazette over my head to spare my frizzy hair of rain, I hurried up the sidewalk to the porch, where a light warmed the wicker furniture. I waited until Quint parked and joined me. He keyed open the door and motioned for me to enter.

He hung our coats in the foyer and headed toward his bedroom. I stepped into the living room where the Border collie slept in a large, oval dog bed. Robin had gotten her a collar, black with rhinestones, and she looked recently groomed.

Most of the furniture belonged to Quint, he had collected pieces from different countries he'd visited during his time in the Navy: linen couch and loveseat with brightly-colored pillows from India, heavy wooden stands that I imagined came from Africa, the cherry wood baby grand that lent a touch of color to blend with the pillows. Warm, inviting, but a room that subtly warned one not to prop feet on the coffee table.

Robin saw me and grinned. In black skinny jeans and tee shirt, he always reminded me of a male version of Cat Woman, with the exception of shoulder-length hair and bare feet. He bounded off the couch and gave me a hug.

"Hey, Han. Look what Quint brought home." Robin clapped his hands. The collie immediately came to Robin. "Man, she's great. She's really smart. Plays fetch, too. Kind of crazy over her ball. I got her one at Petco."

Robin didn't drive and had either gotten his grandfather—our publisher and owner of the Gazette—to take him places or he walked. Since his hair and the dog's fur were still damp, I figured he walked.

"She's great on a leash, too." He rubbed the collie's ears. "I don't like Baby for a name, and she really doesn't come to it anyway so I changed it. Hope Quint doesn't mind."

Quint would probably be pleased that he was off the leash where the dog was concerned. "What's her new name?"

"See her eyes?" Robin asked, and tilted the dog's head toward light pooling beneath an antique shade. "Copper like bright new pennies. And me being a Beatles freak, well, I thought, you know, Penny Lane."

"Penny Lane. Love it." I pet the dog. Her fur was soft and warm. She raised a paw and touched my leg as if petting me back. Then she lowered her snout to my shoes, sniffed a few times and a low growl vibrated in her throat. I'd been bitten as a child, and that memory—in all its flesh-ripping detail—came back now, sending a hot surge of panic through me.

"Whoa," I said, stepping away.

"That's weird." Robin again scratched her ears. She stopped growling. "She didn't even do that when they washed her."

"Maybe she doesn't like me?"

"She doesn't like somewhere you've been," Robin said. "She growled at your shoes."

Quint returned and peered at Penny. "You really cleaned her up."

"She's awesome." Robin patted his chest. She jumped up, wrapped her front legs around him, giving him a hug. "Sweetest dog ever. You picked yourself a great pet."

"Tell you what," Quint said, and gave me a sideways glance as though I might object to what he was about to say. "Since you know more about dogs than I do, and since you two seem to have hit it off, why don't you keep her?"

"Really? Dude, that's *awesome*. I named her Penny Lane." Robin grinned. "Thanks, man. I really do like her."

He returned to the living room with the dog.

"Guess you know Robin better than I do," Quint said under his breath. Then to Robin, he asked, "Are the others here yet?"

"In the garage. I'll be there in a minute, gotta get my tennies." Robin padded down the hallway, Penny Lane at his heels.

I followed Quint across the clean, orderly kitchen, no clutter on the counter and only a recently rinsed bowl and spoon in the sink. Probably from Robin's dinner which likely consisted of Captain Crunch. Quint did all the cooking. And while Robin is vegetarian, he isn't such a health nut he would forgo his sugary cereal.

A pecan dining set filled the space beside the kitchen. Beyond lay the garage, which Robin and Quint had styled with egg cartons they'd gotten from a wholesaler stapled to the walls to dampen sound. Old blankets had been nailed over windows, which had a layer of foam rubber between blanket and glass. Last thing we wanted was to disturb the neighbors. They had called the police in the past.

My amber shell drum kit had already been assembled, and now sat on the rug I used to keep the kit from sliding while I played. A pillow had been stuffed into the Ludwig's twenty-six inch bass. Even the leather stick holder had been tied to my large floor tom.

"Thought it would save you time," Quint said, and looped the strap of his cream colored Fender over his head.

Sometimes he really amazed me. I never asked for anything. Didn't have to. He was probably the most considerate man I'd ever met and that left me a bit suspicious. No one could be that perfect. One of these days I'd probably see a side of him that I might not like, but would embrace, anyway. It would make him flawed and more human.

I slid onto my throne, picked up the sticks he'd left propped against the rim of my snare and twirled them between my fingers. Then I tested the snare, the most delicate drum in my kit. Perfect. I shook my head and flashed Quint a smile.

Robin joined us, tennis shoes on but untied and Penny Lane at his side. She curled up on the floor beside his bass stand, but didn't sleep. She kept a watchful eye on us, as though scrutinizing, sizing us up, wondering which she could trust and which she couldn't. Who among us had a scent clinging to them that would raise her hackles and prompt that eerie, throaty growl?

Fine hairs on my arms prickled. I smoothed away the sensation and picked up my drumsticks.

While I played by rote (we'd been doing the same set for years with minor revisions) my mind conjured images of the small, bent man with a large folder beneath that the waitress had mentioned earlier at Courthouse Café. I'd need to know which cemetery was the subject of his conversations with Grady's assistant, Ava, before I'd know where to find the guy.

An image of the yellow tarp used to cover her body filled my mind and the crawling sensation returned to work my arms. I shuddered, almost skipped a beat and focused on playing.

If the supervisors had discussed cemetery issues in closed session, it would have been listed on the agenda. While often vague, such items had to include enough information to give the public a general idea of what would be considered, according to the state's Brown Act, the open meeting law for all governmental entities.

One of my drumsticks slipped. I tripped up, hit a double on third and recovered without skipping a beat. Quint glanced at me. I tilted my head in a *sorry 'bout that* gesture. He resumed strumming.

The agendas. I'd get on Quint's laptop after practice, see if could find anything dealing with a cemetery. He had wireless. I had an old

PC with a connection that wasn't much better than dial up, when it worked.

At ten we quit. The others left, Robin returned to playing with Penny Lane, and I followed Quint toward his bedroom.

"I need your laptop," I explained.

"You don't need an excuse to come into my bedroom," he said, and the color of his eyes softened to that of warm caramel.

I grabbed a handful of his shirt and pulled him close. Leaning my head back, I peered up at him and smiled. "Really. It's your laptop I need. It's you I *want*."

"Always give you what you want," he muttered, and brought his lips to mine. Soft, warm, slightly salty and tasting of bacon.

I returned the kiss in feather-soft strokes that prompted a moan from him. Then I pulled away, ducked around him and headed for his room at the front of the house. He caught me by the waist, spun me around and scooped me up in a bear hug. He carried me inside and dropped me onto his king-sized bed.

"Laptop," I said.

After locking the door, he crawled onto the mattress and straddled my legs. "Blouse."

"Excuse me?" I propped up on my elbows.

"Trade. Laptop for the blouse."

I sat up and slowly unbuttoned my sweater.

He slid the laptop from the dresser and handed it to me.

"Battery's dead," he said, and grinned. "Trade your pants for the charger."

Chapter 21

An hour later, I had the laptop propped on the pillow, the power cord snaking between mattress and headboard and plugged into the wall. Sheet and blanket draping my hips, I lay on my stomach and launched the browser. Then I went to the Madera County Website, selected Board meetings and videos, and typed *Cemetery* in the search engine.

Beside me, Quint held a pencil like one would a cigarette, a habit he'd probably never break although he'd quit smoking a few months earlier. He'd donned a pair of reading glasses and now focused on a book of crossword puzzles. He glanced at me, I at him and something almost disturbing pulsed, only for a moment, in the air between us, like a fast-forward thirty years from now.

He shifted, frowned and returned his attention to the crossword. I, too, frowned, feeling as if a stranger had just peeked into a private cubbyhole of my life. The oddity faded, as did the image, and I turned to the laptop, its battery icon filling, emptying, filling again as the computer drew life from the wall outlet.

On the county's webpage, a list dropped down, red indicating where, in the meeting minutes, the word *cemetery* showed up. There must have been more than fifty, which could take all night.

I selected the most recent and a separate window popped up with the agenda to the right, a black box to the left. Then the black box, which was a video screen, showed the supervisors in session. Grady sat at the far right because the supervisors were seated at the dais in order of district with the exception of the chairman, a position that rotated each year.

I turned up the volume. A woman's voice came from off camera, and then the lens panned out and captured her standing at the podium. She delivered a report on the supervisors' earlier decision to approve the Borden Cemetery District bringing beneath its umbrella several other graveyards in the county. They would now oversee operations in Madera Ranchos, North Fork and Oakhurst.

North Fork and Oakhurst were both in District Five. Grady's district.

What had happened to encourage the county to consolidate the various burial grounds? Who was the woman giving the report?

I referred again to the agenda, where her name appeared along with her title of Cemetery District Director. Below, where the body of the schedule outlined the *who, what* and *why,* was a list of five other names, all board members. Okay. The different cemeteries had their own trustees appointed by the supervisor of record. So there were more than just employees to consider when figuring out who had broken the rules.

At some point, Quint had turned off the bedside lamp and now lay sleeping beside me. The only glow was the bluish wash from the laptop. I launched Google and sent it in search of information on Pratt, Roberts and Wickham. We'd already spoken with Yates.

Roberts, who had reminded me of an Elfin King from the movie version of Tolkien's Lord of the Rings with his cappuccino complexion and amber-colored eyes, had local ties. Fifteen years ago, well before I joined the Gazette, his father had been incarcerated for setting fire to the district attorney's offices adjacent to the courthouse. He'd been a deputy D.A. at the time. Why he tried to burn down the buildings, no one knew and he never said. Speculation was that there was evidence that implicated someone close to him, which he had succeeded in destroying. He had gone to prison, and Roberts moved to Oakhurst.

District Five. I jotted down the connection.

The SEAL, Pratt, had local ties, too. He grew up in the Coarsegold area, a small community called Manzanita Knolls. His uncle was a Vietnam veteran who headed up the local chapter of the Veterans of Foreign War. Pratt's brother was former Air Force, and he had been Navy. His uncle on his mother's side raised him, according to an article that ran in the Sierra Star after Pratt had returned from Iraq.

The priest, Randall Wickham, also living in District Five, was just as Quint claimed. Clean. No dark past, no shady family, nothing.

How did they tie in with a cemetery and the board of supervisors' closed session items?

I returned to the county web page and the list I'd found earlier. Appointments to the Borden Cemetery District, but on the regular calendar. Next, another routine item. As was the third, fourth, and fifth. Instead of opening each separately, I read the brief descriptions. None of them seemed controversial. Toward the bottom I found a closed session item from three weeks ago. Pending litigation, *County of Madera vs Mountain Area Cemetery District.*

Why would the County sue a cemetery district? What were its trustees or employees doing? Since it was in the mountains it could connect to Roberts, Pratt and the priest. Did it include more than one burial ground? Perhaps, but it would have only one governing body.

At two Wednesday morning, I turned off the laptop and set it on the headboard. Then I curled up beneath the blankets as close to Quint as possible without waking him. His body had warmed the sheets, and that warmed me.

Sleep eluded me while the words I'd read twisted lazily, forming possibilities and scenarios in my exhausted mind. Sometime later, I dozed off only to wake as pale streaks of sunlight bled through the gap between blinds and windowsill.

I slid my hand over the sheets, peeked through one partially opened lid. A pillow with a slight depression was all that remained of him.

Stretching, I sat up and caught a whiff of freshly brewed coffee. Chilly air brought gooseflesh prickling my arms. I considered snuggling beneath the covers, but tossed them back and crawled out of bed.

A couple of months ago, Quint had cleared out a dresser drawer for my clothes, a space for my toothbrush and hung a rack in the shower for shampoo and conditioner. I showered, dressed in jeans and tank top, over which I added a cardigan suitable for the office, and joined him in the kitchen. Scrambled eggs, bacon, toast and orange juice. He'd make some lady a great man-wife one day.

I drove to the office feeling optimistic despite the fact I hadn't uncovered anything to tell me who the man with the bent back was, or how a cemetery district connected to Grady and Ava's deaths. Maybe it was the lack of sleep.

I had shoved my writing pad into my purse, and now dug around receipts from Save Mart and Starbucks and found the notebook. In the darkroom, I called Carracci. Although he'd already said he wouldn't— *couldn't*—tell me anything about closed session, there was a journalism trick I'd resorted to a couple times. I didn't believe in lying, and I'm rotten at it so I didn't even try. Instead, I let someone believe I knew more than I really did.

Carracci answered.

"It's the cemetery district," I said, "and it's a pretty big mess."

"Who told you?" Carracci demanded.

Gotcha. "You know I can't reveal my source."

"How much do you know?"

"Enough that it would make the County look pretty bad for not staying on top of things." I cringed, hoping I wasn't taking my ruse too far. A delicate line, it could snap and leave me holding a tattered piece of nothing.

"Are you going to print it?" Carracci sighed, which came out as a groan. "The lawsuit, it's a ploy. We're not suing them. We put that on the agenda so we can talk about the issues without anyone accusing us of Brown Act violations. What we plan to do is appoint ourselves as the Trustees and hand the operations over to Borden Cemetery District."

So the graveyard in question wasn't one of those the supervisors had already placed in Borden's care.

"That makes sense," I said. "Especially in light of what they're doing."

"Yeah, and it's gone on way too long," he said. "If we had done this when we first suspected them of embezzlement, we would have saved that district hundreds of thousands. Maybe millions. We don't know how much."

Embezzlement. This was better than I had hoped. Bigger than I had hoped. This could be the type of story that got picked up by the Associated Press, and I closed my eyes, imagined my byline in the New York Times.

"You still there?" Carracci's voice dispelled the image.

"Yep, I'm here." I bit the cap of my Paper Mate. "Why did you guys wait so long?"

"We only learned about it a couple weeks ago. The grand jury was investigating, but word got out that they were and . . . Wait, if you know about the money why don't you know about everything else?"

"My source didn't have this information." Which was true enough. My source was Quint's computer. "Word got out and the GJ had to wrap up their investigation before they finished?"

"Yeah, that's what happened. Report isn't out yet, but we expect it within the next few days. It's gonna make us look like idiots."

A few days. That didn't leave me long to get the rest of the story so I'd scoop the other newspapers. Like the Fresno Bee, a much larger paper. I loved breaking news before the Bee, forcing them to follow my lead. Talk about a rush.

"What now?" I asked.

"We're going to appoint ourselves," Carracci said, "once the report comes out. We also have a person from the area that has collected documents that prove the trustees allowed staff to rip off the citizens."

"How?" I crossed my fingers. I was stepping into strict confidential matters and he may not be willing to follow.

"Nah, I've said too much already. This is off the record, every word."

"Absolutely." Until I confirmed everything on my own.

"Look, I gotta go. If you need anything more, wait for the report. It won't show everything, but enough." He paused and cleared his throat. "You could also look at public records in the Auditor's office."

Carracci hung up, his final words filling my head. Find and follow the paper trail.

By the time I returned to the newsroom, the staff had filtered in and now worked on whatever their beats brought them for tomorrow's edition.

When Morales and Quint arrived, I led them into the morgue and filled them in on what I'd learned. I also told them that three climbers, Roberts, Pratt and Wickham, all had ties to District Five.

"We need to speak with them," I said, "and we need to find this whistleblower."

Chapter 22

After I spoke with Carracci, it hadn't been difficult to figure out which cemetery was under investigation. Of the three in District Five, two had already been taken over by the Borden folks. That left one near Coarsegold, Manzanita Knolls.

According to the website, their board met every other week. Their next meeting would take place in a few hours. I had plenty of time to drive up and check out the facilities first.

I headed east out of Borden and into the fields that had once nourished fruit and nut trees, acres of cotton, corn and tomatoes, fields that were now barren. Although it had rained the night before, it looked as if water hadn't touched the parched earth in decades, leaving the ground cracked, the scarce wind kicking up dust devils.

The fallowed land gave way to rolling hills that usually looked golden but now, were brittle and dead. Oaks that had stood more than fifty years had gone brown and died. Before long, scraggly, water-starved pines dotted the hillsides, adding, as the saying went, insult to injury. A twinge of sadness weighted on me. But knowing the rains would return compensated a bit.

In a lawn of dying grass next to a two-story brick home, a man in jeans and tee shirt strode from one fence line to the next, thin copper rods in his hands, the art of water witching. I didn't understand the process, but had been told it was a science and not mystical divination. Dowsing rods had been used throughout history to find not only underground water sources, gemstones, ores and old gravesites as well.

A weather-faded sign announced the direction to the cemetery. I slowed and eased onto the highway's shoulder and turned right onto the narrow, gravel road. The gates to the cemetery stood open. Single-lane ribbons of asphalt, cracked and sporting potholes as large as dinner plates, wove between plots of land sectioned off by chains threaded through iron loops atop stubby concrete pylons. I pulled into an uneven turnout and parked.

Although the drought had left its mark here as elsewhere, tufts of green sprouted from the base of old headstones, weather-blackened and with barely legible inscriptions. They must have been a hundred years old. The newer graves were marked with flat slabs of granite, easier for mowing purposes. Even those had crabgrass growing over the edges and partially obscured the names engraved into the stones.

A building constructed of native rock nestled among a grove of pines. Two doors offered entrance: one marked *Restrooms*, the other, *Office*.

Between the two signs, a glass-fronted shadow box displayed announcements for upcoming events: the September Eleventh memorial just days away and the Veteran's Day ceremony. The program for the meeting scheduled for later today used the same corner thumbtack as the Veteran's poster.

The door, paint peeling in some spots, rusted bolts in others, creaked open and a bullish woman in her mid-thirties stomped outside. She hiked up the neckline of her too-small spandex shirt and crinkled her nose at me. Her hair had been cut blunt as though she'd taken scissors and chopped just to get it out of her way. She raked her fingers through the strands several times, pausing to scratch, and continuing as though to rid herself of the sensation of something crawling on her scalp. Scabbed-over wounds on her arms lent testimony to the scratching habit of a methamphetamine user.

A rush of anxiety set my heart into a triple beat. I drew long, slow breaths and forced a smile.

A foot taller than me and several pounds heavier, she wore faded jeans tucked into the tops of baby-blue and black western-style ankle boots that looked like part of a child's Halloween costume. I must have startled her because she trembled, dropped her pen and stared like I was an apparition that had clawed its way up from a nearby grave.

She shook again, apparently regained composure, and squatted to retrieve the ink pen the way one would when peeing in the woods, exposing her tramp stamp above her dingy thong. Not a fleur-de-lis, nothing so marginally classy if a tramp stamp could by any definition be classy, but the Harley Davidson logo although I doubted she'd ever been on a bike.

She straightened, hitched up the back of her jeans and spun around to face me.

"What are you doing?" she demanded in a manner that reflected a lifetime of confrontations.

The pounding in my chest slowed marginally. I reached into my purse, found the cell phone on the bottom and curled my hand around it. "Reading the agenda."

She narrowed her eyes, glassy and jaundiced looking, and scanned me from head to toe to head again as if something in my posture or stance or hair color should reveal the mysteries that rode the current of smack in her brain. Finally she asked, "Who are you?"

"Hannah Monakee with the Borden Gazette. And you are?"

"You need to leave," she said, and curled her lip like a rabid dog. "You're friends with that nosey bastard, Harland, aren't you? I know what's going on. We fired that fat fuck because he was a lazy—"

Her aggressiveness gave me a start. I held up my hand and shook my head. "I'm not engaging in an argument, and I don't know who Harland is."

"Like fuck you don't, you skanky whore." She puffed out her chest the way a Valley Quail does when showing its masculinity. Only she just managed to cause the hem of her shirt to hike up, revealing shiny ropes of pregnancy scars. "Harlan sent you. This is just like him. He was fired for harassment, Bitch, and ain't nuthin you or no one else says is gonna change it."

I wanted to hit her. No, really, I wanted to slam my fist into her scabby-skinned face, but doing so would only anger her further and I wasn't one to stoop to such antics. But as a wordsmith, language was the tool of my trade. I smiled in an attempt to extinguish the frenzy she was working herself into.

"Who was his alleged victim?" I asked.

Again the rabid-dog snarl. "What does that mean?" She folded her arms beneath her breasts.

"Alleged?" I raised my brows. "An accusation yet to be proven. When someone says you did something, but they don't have evidence you really did."

"Oh, he did it all right. He harassed me, got right in my face and yelled at me and called me a stupid bitch. That's why he's gone, and he needed to go." Fingers through hair. Again. And a third time. She stretched her mouth, worked her jaw, and tilted her head as though wanting to rub her ear against her shoulder but not quite making it.

"What's Harland's last name?" I asked.

"As if you don't know," she said, and sniffed a loud, wet sound that prompted a knot to form in my stomach. "You're probably sleeping with the hard-dick motherfucker."

Her words struck me like a slap to the face. I opened my mouth to reply, but closed it. I'd learned a long time ago not to engage some types of people, and she was definitely one of them. Unreasonable, aggressive and an explosive personality. Instead I breathed deeply and considered the source.

"I don't know him. That's why I'm asking. If you don't want to tell me, that's fine. I'll ask around." I turned and started to leave and paused, looking at her over my shoulder. "Who keeps records here?"

"That would be me," she said, and jabbed her thumb to her chest. "I'm the office manager and secretary for the president."

President? Not even the board of supervisors assigned themselves such a high position. Their figurehead was *chairman*.

"Who is your *president?*" I asked.

"Ask Harland." She stepped backward into the office and slammed the door.

I headed toward my car, and stopped. Hairs prickled the back of my neck, and I suddenly felt I wasn't safe here or anywhere near Madam Secretary. I shot a glance back at the building. Curtains fluttered in the office window. Phone clamped to her ear, her mouth coiled into that uncomely snarl, the office clerk was likely reporting my visit.

Who was on the other end, listening to her venom?

Chapter 23

Although common sense told me to get the hell out of the Manzanita Knolls cemetery with its tweaker-crazy office clerk, curiosity—the imp that thrived on ink and poisoned the blood of any good reporter—grabbed common sense in a chokehold and shut him up. I had twenty minutes to kill before the meeting would start at, according to the agenda I'd done little more than glimpse, the local VFW hall. I intended to be there, tweaker be damned.

I opened my car's door, sat on the driver's seat and called Quint. I let him know what happened, and added, "I'm going to their board meeting. Maybe I'll get a lead on the whistleblower's identity."

Long silence, followed by him clearing his throat. "I'll never tell you what to do, I'm not your keeper, don't want to be. But I don't want you getting hurt, Babe. Where is the meeting?"

I told him and he rang off, promising to meet me in thirty minutes. I slipped the cell in my purse, drew my legs into the car and scanned the plots around me. Behind the office-slash-restroom stood a large workshop made of corrugated steel and weathered redwood posts. Three men in dingy blue and black uniforms watched from the dimness of the shed.

I put common sense back in that chokehold and strode across the graveyard, hoping the men would be more cooperative than the office manager. If not, Quint was aware of the situation. If I didn't show up at the VFW, he'd know where to recover my body.

The men inside the workshop formed a quasi-huddle, appeared to discuss something, then one of them, short-cropped hair trapped beneath a San Francisco 49ers cap he probably didn't wear while graveside services were underway, strolled toward me. He wiped his hands on a red cloth. The patch above his left breast pocket revealed his name as Andrew.

"Can I help you?" he asked. He had a chipped tooth just left of center.

"Do you know someone named Harland?" I asked.

Andrew stared at me, shifted his gaze to the office and drew his brows into a hard line. "He used to work here."

"Did he retire?" I asked, knowing he hadn't. The way Ms. Tweaker referred to him, he was fired.

"No. The board members let him go." Andrew shifted his weight, bit his lower lip, and wiped his hands again, worrying the cloth the way a Catholic would his Rosary. "They fired him."

"Do you know why?"

"Who are you?" He glanced at the office as though expecting the beast within to burst out.

"I'm a reporter with the Borden Gazette," I said. "I'm investigating some allegations regarding the cemetery district."

"You don't want to do that." Although the breeze was chilly, sweat beaded above his upper lip. Andrew tucked the cloth in his hip pocket. "They ruin people. Make 'em go away. They lied about Harland, said all kinds of stuff because he wouldn't . . ." He swiped his hand across his mouth.

Make them go away? Had they made *Grady* go away? And *Ava?* Shivers speckled my spine. I forced my expression to remain stoic. I didn't want Andrew catching on that his words had chilled me.

"Do you know where I can find Harland?" I found an old receipt and poised my pen over it.

Andrew pulled out his cell, searched through his address book and rattled off a phone number. "Not sure he'll talk to you. He's already filed a lawsuit for wrongful termination."

I jotted the numbers down and slipped the receipt into my back pocket. If I'd put it in my purse, I'd lose it in the black hole that seemed to suck up everything I needed.

Andrew straightened, peered past me and muttered, "Shit."

I turned just as a black Dodge truck pulled into the cemetery and screeched to a stop next to the office. A squat, barrel-chested man marched toward us. From the way he strutted, like a bulldog dog in a pack of poodles, he probably suffered a Napoleon complex.

"Who's that?" I asked, my voice low so the approaching human tornado wouldn't hear.

"One of the trustees." Andrew pulled out his cloth, wiped his hands again although no dirt or grease remained.

Napoleon stopped two feet in front of me, invading my personal space in an obvious attempt to intimidate me. On the outside I smiled and nodded. Inside, my ribs ached from the pounding of my heart. My palms grew damp. I tucked them into my jacket pockets.

"Who are you?" he demanded.

"I'm—"

"What the hell you doing here?" He tilted his head in attempt to peer down his nose at me, only he wasn't much taller and only succeeded in looking like he had a kink in his neck. "You got no business here, Missy."

"It's a public cemetery," I said. "I'm working—"

"Not what the office manager said." Napoleon crossed his short, thick arms over his chest and bowed his back. "Said you're harassing her. I'll call the goddamn sheriff and have you dragged outta here."

"Seriously? Harassment? I'd only asked a couple questions and she accused me of knowing someone named Harland," I countered, and realized—too late—I'd have been better off keeping my mouth shut. These people are mentally unstable, and I wished I'd listened to Quint, left and waited for him instead of trying to get more information.

Napoleon's face reddened, taking on a burgundy hue. His gaze hardened, two orbs of petrified hickory. "Harland? He the one who sent you?"

"I told you I don't know him," I said, and sighed. Why attempt to reason with this guy? He was obviously a hothead with a short fuse.

"If you don't know him then why the hell are you here?"

"Researching a story."

"What, you some kind of reporter?" The hardness of his gaze melted, just a bit, but enough to let me know he was capable of feeling fear.

"Hannah Monakee with the Borden Gazette." I briefly considered offering my hand, but curled my fingers against my palm instead. "I understand the grand jury is on the verge of—"

"They're a bunch of goddamn lairs," he snapped. "Who sent you?"

"I told you—"

"What right do you have, coming out here and harassing our workers?"

"I'm not—"

"You got no business here, Missy," he roared.

"Do you seriously want answers," I snapped back, "or do you just want to hear yourself talk?"

Shut up, my mind screamed, but the anger—at his attitude, his intimidation tactics, the way he bullied me—set fire to my own fuse.

He stiffened, widened his eyes and snorted like a bull getting ready to charge.

"I have every right to be here," I said. "Back off and conduct yourself in a professional manner. I'd like to leave."

Anger again hardened his gaze, but he pressed his lips into a tight line and retreated a step.

Forcing myself to walk at a normal pace, I headed for my car. Once inside, my hands trembled so badly I dropped my keys. That guy was more than crazy. My intuitive side—the reporter in me who had covered enough homicide trials to recognize the traits of killers—told me this guy was dangerous.

Had I just painted a target on my back?

Chapter 24

Anxiety over my encounter with the graveyard Napoleon produced a headache by the time I drove up state Route 41 and into the village of Manzanita Knolls. I rubbed my temple next to my eye that had acquired a twitch.

"I need a vacation," I muttered. "Soon as I clear Quint's reputation. The ocean. Monterey. Maybe visit my friend in Morro Bay."

Wooden structures reminiscent of buildings of the old west housed a market and café, gold panning tourist stop with windmill and water wheel, and the Historic Village with plaster teepee and skeletons of rusted field plows. Among the buildings were shops selling rocks, antiques, handcrafted items and a coffee hut featuring its own special roasts. Beyond the buildings, mountain slopes rose high enough so that the low-lying clouds swallowed their peaks.

A gravel driveway between the market and Robert's Frosty, with its sign sporting a giant image of a soft-serve cone, led to the VFW hall on a rise overlooking the hamburger stand. Granite boulders circled a flowerbed that lacked plants. Instead, three flagpoles sprouted from the circle of stones to display the state and nation's flags, and the symbol honoring those missing in action.

The building itself was single-story cinderblock with flat roof and recessed doorways. A half-moon drive in front led to a gravel lot on the far side. I parked next to the handicap slot, closest to the driveway, so I wouldn't get blocked in. I liked to keep my option for a quick departure open.

Within minutes, people arrived. Napoleon, the staff I'd spoken with—Tweaker and Andrew—went into the building. I started to get out of my car, stopped and decided to wait for Quint. I didn't like admitting I couldn't handle situations on my own, nor did I like the idea of taking advantage of the fact my boyfriend is ex-Navy SEAL to deter people from giving me trouble, but after the morning I'd had it seemed wise to wait.

Ten minutes later, Quint parked his Range Rover on the lot's far side. Once he got out, I followed suit and met him by the curved drive.

"Sounds like you've rattled some nerves. Again," he added and grinned.

"Napoleon and the office manager. Real charmers. Come on," I added, and headed for the VFW hall. "I want to sit in on their meeting."

While we walked I filled Quint in on my encounter with Little Big Man. By attending the meeting, I hoped to gain a lead we could follow that would reveal just what these people were supposed to be doing, and how it connected to Grady. If, in fact, there was a connection.

Quint fell in step beside me. "Roberts and Wickham are coming by at about noon so Morales can talk with them."

"What about Pratt?" I reached for the doorknob. Quint grasped it first, opened and motioned me inside.

"He said he'd call." Quint waited for me to enter and stepped in behind me.

Inside, the dim air smelled of mold. The box-like room was old and stark. Photos on the walls, of various sizes and in mismatched frames, showed events dating back to the Fifties. Some had been hand hung in straight lines across the walls, while others had been nailed above and below, as if placed by people of different heights. Some were of members in uniform marching in parades, others of celebrations and award ceremonies.

Long tables were lined up to one side, while those the board members used as their dais were arranged in a square so half the trustees had their backs to the constituents.

I sat in a folding chair a few feet from the door. Napoleon stalked toward me, and a hammering sensation like a dying bird flapping its wings filled my chest. He glared at me and I half expected him to wrap his sausage-like fingers over my throat and stifle the life out of me.

Swallowing down the surge of panic, I lifted my chin, a small gesture of confidence I didn't feel. Normally, I was good at raising my shields to deflect anger, an art I'd found necessary as a crime reporter. Families of suspects had cornered me in parking lots, confronted me in the courthouse hallways, gone to the newspaper office and ranted at me in front of our publisher. I'd developed something of a thick skin. That thick skin wasn't protecting me now, though. This wasn't a killer's father, but a lunatic with short-man syndrome and somehow, that seemed decidedly worse.

Quint stepped up to Napoleon, peered down at the man and said, "Excuse me."

Napoleon craned his neck and his eyes widened. He stepped back, allowing enough room for Quint to slide past and settle in the chair next to me.

Ha, you bully. Like to see you come at me now.

Napoleon retreated to the block of tables, sat, folded his short, thick arms over his barrel chest and huffed as though delivering an insult.

"I'm glad you're here," I whispered to Quint. "I think he may have pissed himself a little."

Quint grinned and turned his attention to the agenda he'd gotten from the podium, which wasn't a program but a list, one through five, with single or two-word descriptors of what the board would discuss. None were marked as action items, and nothing distinguished them between open session and closed session. Must be the work of their tweaker office manager, who had settled in a chair beside a man who had to be pushing ninety. She tugged the neckline of her shirt, ran her fingers through her hair, spread papers in front of her and positioned a notepad on which I assumed she'd record minutes. The relic next to her peeked down her blouse and a wry grin crept over his leathery features, a grin that sent hairs prickling at the back of my neck. Creepy.

I peered at the agenda in Quint's hand. Across the top were the director's names: Niff Nesmeth, President; Ken Bosley, Vice President; Norm Sonneck, Treasurer; Lois Walker and Vanessa Klair.

First item was the minutes of the previous meeting. "I'll accept a motion to approve." Niff glanced at his cohorts.

"I object," Andrew said, removing his hat. He worked the 49ers cap as he had the red cloth when I'd spoken with him at the cemetery.

"You don't get to have a say," Napoleon injected. "You're not a trustee."

"It's not everything that happened," Andrew said.

"What's not accurate?" Niff asked in a nasally tone that made his words blur together.

Andrew jabbed his finger in the air toward Napoleon. "All the stuff Sonneck said about me. That I'm not doing my job and I'm insubordinate." Andrew gripped the meeting minutes in his fist and shook them toward Sonneck. "I answered those claims. I told him what really happened and none of that's in here."

"We don't have to tell everything. Minutes are just a summary," Sonneck said, puffing out his chest.

"This is a summary of what *didn't* happened. You can amend them to show what you said, but not my response?" Andrew shook his head, obviously dumbfounded. "That's not right."

"We don't have to put everything in there. The law says so."

"Wow," I whispered to Quint, who looked just as dumbfounded as Andrew. "Can't trust their minutes to tell us what may have happened."

"Aren't they governed by the Brown Act?" he asked, referring to the state's bible on open meeting laws.

I nodded. "We're going to need one of them to tell us what's been going on, if any of them are capable of telling the truth."

"Good luck," Quint said, and returned his attention to the proceedings.

The tweaker office manager, whose name, Tracy, appeared on the minutes as the person who had prepared them, sneered at Andrew. He'd be the next to get fired.

"I write them as I'm told," she said. "I didn't do nothing wrong."

Exonerating herself before she's accused. Sounded like she had a guilty conscience. If she had one at all.

"I move we approve the minutes as written," Sonneck said. The others agreed, with the exception of one.

"Talk about rubber-stamp trustees," Quint said.

I studied the lone no vote, a woman in her mid-thirties. Her long blond hair had silvery streaks. The color complimented her strong features, adding a visual measure of wisdom not found in those around her.

She glanced at me, eyes widening slightly as if she had no idea I'd been in the room. Then she smiled, a slight gesture no one would have caught except me. I added her to my mental list of those I wanted to speak with.

Next item was the reimbursement to one of the trustees in the amount of seven thousand dollars. The woman who had smiled at me raised her hand.

"Now, Vanessa," Niff said in a scolding manner, one a father might use with an obstinate child. "This is a standard procedure, there's nothing to discuss. We just need to approve it."

"There's no backup, Bubba," she said.

Bubba? As if the name Niff wasn't punishment enough. I shifted in the hard metal chair, wishing I could stand, walk, and stretch. Although it had only been minutes since the meeting started, I already felt as if I'd been sitting for hours.

"This is how we've always done things," he said. "I got the papers at home."

"It should be here," she said, flipping through the thin stack of documents on the table before her. ""There's no backup for a single item on the agenda."

"Do I have a motion?" Bubba said, directing his question to the other three trustees.

"Where's the receipt for what you bought?" Vanessa asked. "We can't approve reimbursement without proper documentation. How do I even know you bought this for the cemetery?"

"We don't need your approval," he said, and a smug grin twisted his features into something akin to a troll. "A motion?"

"I so move," Sonneck said.

"Second," the elderly woman I assumed was Lois Walker said. She looked at Vanessa as if offering a silent apology.

Vanessa looked back as if in shock. And she probably was. I was.

"You guys—this is *wrong*."

"All in favor?"

A chorus of *Ayes*, followed by her *No*.

"I've been advised by my attorney not to sign anything unless I see the invoices." She sat back and folded her arms. Not in the same manner as Sonneck, but with rebellious determination.

For expenditures, they needed a four fifths vote. They could approve items without her signature.

She took the warrant, drew a line and handed it back. "That's all you're getting until you provide backup."

Tweaker Tracy gripped her pen and took minutes with such aggression I thought she'd dig through the notebook's page. And there was something more going on, something that dawned on me with the same revulsion as walking into spider webs: Bubba was pushing ninety while she was in her thirties. What turned my stomach was the way she leaned toward Bubba, tugging her shirt down so she showed more cleavage. The disturbing way she rested her hand on his thigh.

Quint must have noticed, too. He poked me with his elbow, getting my attention, and glanced at Bubba and Tracy.

Bubba brought forward the next on the itinerary, the payout of vacation time scheduled for October.

"She," Vanessa said, and jabbed her finger toward Tracy, "only earns six hours a month." She passed out photocopies, a stack for each director. "These are copies of her time cards, and it clearly shows she's taken three times the vacation she was due. Now she's claiming she has a full years' worth and wants to get paid out?"

"She keeps track of her own time," Bubba said. "She didn't take vacation, I gave her those days off. She's got this coming to her."

Vanessa stared at the others. "I'm not agreeing to this. You are stealing from the people of the district. You're stealing from the *dead*."

"She didn't take off," Bubba snapped. "I don't know where you got your information, though I'd guess Harland Clarke," Bubba chortled. "Clarke's a digrunted employee that we rightly fired." He glared at Vanessa. "Sign the warrant."

"I won't." She drew a line through the space intended for her signature. "I've read the Brown Act, I've read the cemetery rules and regulations. This is unethical. It's *theft*."

"I'm not believing this," I said, keeping my tone low. "Where is the oversight?"

"I don't know." Quint frowned. "Is this what you've been dealing with?"

I nodded.

"No wonder you looked rattled. Steer clear of these folks, okay? Promise me? Because they're crazy."

I agreed. I didn't want to get mixed up in their drama. It's probably what Grady caught onto. And Grady was dead.

The trustees continued with their meeting, approving—against Vanessa's consent—the purchase of equipment obtained without prior board approval, and the hiring of an attorney, although the contract had been signed and dated two weeks ago.

"I've seen enough." I slipped past Quint.

He stood and followed me to the door. Sonneck watched us leave, but with Quint next to me I didn't feel as threatened as I had earlier.

"What's with that stubby little guy? I mean, damn, Monkey. If looks could kill."

"Earlier at the cemetery, I called him out and I don't think he appreciated it. I bruised his ego."

"Dangerous move. Someone like that could try to even the score." Quint slid his arms around me. "I'd hate to kick his ass, but I will. Might even enjoy it."

"Friend with benefits," I said, and slipped my arms around his waist. I smiled up at him. "I like the benefits."

He laughed and hugged me. Then let me go. "Meet me at the office? We still have time to make it back before Roberts and Wickham get there."

I nodded while glancing at the VFW hall. Tracy stood at the door and appeared to study Quint's car. She jotted in her notepad. Probably license plate information.

Did they have someone on the inside of law enforcement to run plates for them? If so, I intended to find out.

Chapter 25

My headache lingered as I drove along state Route 41 toward the 145 cut off to Borden. The odd, antagonistic exchange from the Mountain Area Cemetery meeting ricocheted in my mind as though desperately seeking a link to reason and logic. Two questions were most baffling: how did the trustees gain such control, and why wasn't there oversight? As soon as I reached the office, I'd put pen to paper and try to organize my thoughts. Coffee would dull the pain in my temples. Then I'd go to the Government Center and visit the auditor's office. Maybe he could help find the money trail.

I came up behind a Toyota, its driver cruising at forty in a fifty-five zone. Irritation added to the pain in my head. I palmed the horn. Honking only made him drive slower. I checked oncoming traffic, pulled into the opposite lane and passed. Five minutes later, a John Deer tractor took up the entire lane and half of the other as it crept along. It pulled into the lot at the Twenty-Two Mile House, a gas station and convenience store. I gunned the engine, leading the charge for the line of cars behind me to gain speed and pass before the tractor reached the end of the lot and returned to the state highway.

Carracci had said the board of supervisors should have taken steps long ago to stop the cemetery district trustees. Why hadn't they? Because of the grand jury investigation?

Or had they intimidated someone. Grady? And when he made his move to take over, they killed him?

That was a far stretch, even for me, and would have been too complicated for a bunch of ignorant hillbillies. I doubted they were capable of arranging death by falling from the face of El Capitan. They'd be more likely to cause an accident while hunting wild hogs.

In the newsroom, I sagged into the wobbly chair in my cubicle. The stress of the morning had drained me. After liberating quarters from the bottom of my purse, I headed for the sludge machine in the break room.

A new black Keurig and carousel holder of single-serve K-cups had replaced the sludge maker. Nice. All I needed was a mug, and had several on my desk that I used for pen and paper clips.

I dumped the contents from one that sported a layer of dust, washed it with a paper towel and hand soap, and selected an espresso roast from the holder. In under a minute, I sipped freshly brewed coffee. I could get used to this. Beside the carousel was a cup with coins, an honor system to offset costs. I dropped in my quarters.

Mug cradled in both hands, I carried it back to my desk. Sitting, I looked around at the years of clutter. Maybe I'd spend some time this weekend clearing things out. Suddenly, I felt claustrophobic.

Instead of checking emails and voice messages, I sat and savored the brew as I mulled over that morning's events. I wanted to speak with Vanessa as well as Harland. She seemed to be the only trustee with any common sense.

I'd written down all their names. From the shelf above my desk, where the digital police scanner picked up traffic between dispatch and the field officers, I found a phone book. A year old, but I doubted anyone had moved into the area just to sit on a cemetery board.

Under Klair, I found Vanessa's number and added it to my notes. She and the other trustees were probably still in session. I'd wait until this afternoon before calling.

Since I had more than an hour before the two climbers would arrive, I finished the coffee and headed for the county government center. Clouds the color of gunmetal edged in from the northwest, remnants of the storm that had hit Washington State earlier in the week and which ABC's weather lady said would dump rain here and possibly snow at the higher elevations. I didn't mind getting their leftovers.

The government center was relatively new, having been built months prior to the economic recession we were just now shaking off. The ground floor hosted three departments and the board chambers, a massive improvement over the former meeting space. Four floors of steel and granite rose like a giant box with what appeared to be a helipad on top, but which really housed the massive air conditioning units.

I climbed the stairs to the second floor. Polished steel letters sat atop a bar suspended above the department doors like gray birds perched on thick wires. TAX COLLECTOR/TREASURER. Across the open space where stairs and elevators deposited their loads, another sign: AUDITOR/CONTROLLER.

Beyond glass, staff answered phones, worked on computers, exchanged pleasantries. It reminded me of the newsroom, minus the profanity.

I asked for whoever handled special districts. The auditor himself came to the counter. I showed him my press credentials and he waved me toward a door that was security locked. A click and the door opened into a white-walled room with oak conference table and a dozen leather chairs. The room's brightness amplified the needles of pain in my head.

"Lester Wallstone." The auditor, all six foot five of him and thin as an anorexic, motioned toward a chair. I sat and he settled at the table's end. He'd won the public office in the June Primary. Normally, the seated auditor would step down the following January. Upon learning the results—Wallstone had won by a landslide—the former auditor slipped into the building just after midnight, sent a letter of resignation via email to each county supervisor, cleared out her office and left. The board took action to place Wallstone in the position early instead of leave the work to an already overburdened staff.

"You may call me Les. How can I help you?"

Referring to my list didn't help. I wasn't sure where to start.

"What is the district you're interested in?" he asked.

I told him, and his toothy grin faded. "Not sure I can say much, they're the subject of an investigation."

"Grand jury. I'm aware." The air conditioner kicked in with a whisper. Cool air spiraled down, lifted the corner of my notepad's top page. I pinned it down with my finger. "Where do they get their money? I know they sell plots, but that can't bring in enough to pay utilities, staff, whatever other costs there are."

Les clasped his hands and bounced them lightly on top of the conference table. "They sell gravesites, mausoleum spaces, niches for cremated remains. This covers the utilities, wages, office supplies and equipment."

"What if their backhoe breaks down?" I didn't know how much one would cost, but it had to be more than selling slots for the dead could cover.

"Any equipment for maintaining the grounds, mowers, the grave diggers, items like that are purchased using the returns from the endowment money."

"Endowment?"

"Yes," Les said, and again bounced his clasped hands. "It's a bit complex. When cemetery districts were created, they were each given a principal amount, call it seed money, which they would have a trustee invest for them."

"Trustee? Like one of the board members?" That would make it simple to embezzle if one of them had control over the *seed money*.

"No, they either have their endowment care trust fund with the regulatory authority—in this case, the County—or an investment firm of their choice."

Air from the overhead vent diminished. I lifted my finger. The page remained still. "How much money would this endowment be?"

"Depends on the cemetery. The initial amount would be at least a million, if my understanding of such special districts is correct. That amount is added to by a fee charged each time a burial space is sold. And people can donate to the fund for specific purposes, say, if they want plants around their grave. The donated amount would maintain those plants."

Manzanita Knolls had been around for a long time, a lot of graves had been sold over the years. Their endowment could be several million by now.

"So this seed money, it's invested? No one can use it?"

"The district board members cannot withdraw the principal of the endowment, but can use the income earned to cover costs of maintaining the cemetery, repairs, replacing landscaping, memorials, roads, walkways, irrigation systems, buildings, and related overhead. You see," he added, released his hands and splayed his fingers as though working out kinks, "these endowments were created to make sure cemeteries would always be taken care of, whether they're full or not."

While recording the information, in the back of my mind I found myself trying to figure out how one of the trustees could get his—or her—greedy hands on the money. A million, or millions, just sitting there.

"The Manzanita Knolls district," I said, finished my sentence on paper, and asked, "Do you have records here of that account?"

"We have some records, but as far as the endowment is concerned I've been told their board removed those funds from the County coffers several years ago and appointed someone from an investment firm to oversee the account. They transfer the money made on the principal over to an account with us, and when they present us with warrants—invoices—signed by the district board members, we cut checks. The sales of all plots, etc., those funds come here, as well, and we have the same process for payroll and utilities."

"But you would have audits, correct? Don't they have to file financial statements?"

"Let me see if I can get an answer for you. One moment." Les pushed back his chair and stood, leaving the conference room door ajar as he stepped into the hallway off which were several small offices. He poked his head into one and spoke in a voice too low for me to hear.

I leaned back and stretched. I had neglected my run this morning and now wished I'd taken the time for at least a two-miler. My muscles felt tight, and that only fed the headache. I searched among the clutter of pens, gum wrappers, receipts and lip gloss in my purse, found the bottle of Motrin and dry-swallowed two caplets. Four-hundred milligrams should kick some serious headache butt.

Les returned with a woman who reminded me of a teacher I'd had in elementary school. Not a particularly nice one, either, and the stern expression on this employees face told me she had the same temperament.

She regarded me over the rims of her tortoise shell frames, set the file she'd brought with her on the table and eased into a chair across from me.

"All this interest in Manzanita Knolls," she muttered, flipping through pages. "First a young man, then a lady, then the grand jury. Now you." She lifted her gaze and regarded me as one would a rodent. "Just who are you?"

"Hannah Monakee," I said.

"Ah, yes. I recognize the name. You're that reporter from the Fresno Bee."

"Borden Gazette." I didn't want to be associated with our rival newspaper to the south. It was bigger. We were better.

"I'm Wilma." She returned to her file, shook her head. "You want to know about the audits? We don't do them. They claim to have hired an independent CPA. Yet, they are about five years behind. We've sent them notices, added penalties, and they call and tell us they're working on it."

"At what point does someone take action?" I asked.

She raised her penciled brows, neither of which still had actual hair, and I waited for fire to spit from her gaze. "Taking action would require a considerable amount of time, both with this office and that of County Counsel. That's a lot of taxpayer's dollars to battle a cemetery district that won't submit its audits."

In other words, requests were easier and cheaper to send. Early on, the district trustees learned they could get away with neglecting the reports. A standoff that favored the trustees year after year, warning after warning.

"You handle payroll, correct?" I asked, hoping the switch in topics would dampen her carefully controlled rage. There had been question regarding the validity of vacation time payouts. If they cut the checks, they'd have to have some records.

"We issue checks based on the warrants they bring us," she said. "The trustees sign them, so we have their authority to draw funds from the account."

"If there's something fishy about the warrants," Les injected, "we wouldn't know. I plan, however, to put some checks and balances in place once this mess—whatever the grand jury expects to find—is straightened out."

"So you don't have their time cards, correct?"

"That is correct. Just the warrants," she said, "requesting payroll, vacation time, sick leave, vacation payout at the end of their fiscal year, and Christmas bonuses."

"Bonuses?" I straightened. "That's a gift of public funds."

"And highly illegal," Les added.

"I only did as I was told," she said, reminding me of Tweaker Tracy—*I write them as I'm told.*

Was this woman, who admittedly hadn't reported the fact the trustees weren't submitting their paperwork and weren't abiding by the laws governing such districts, somehow involved? She should know the laws against gifts of public funds, the need for oversight that had been placed in her charge. This didn't add up. And I didn't like it when things didn't add up.

"I'd like copies of these warrants." This time I raised my brows—completely composed of natural hair—and added, "For the past five years. I'll wait."

She clutched her files against her breast and strode out of the conference room.

"Don't know what to make of that one," Les said, his voice at a conspiratorial low. "I'm still getting to know the staff, some are great, others aren't worth the dust collecting on their computer keyboards. But that one. I just don't know."

I peered through the window that separated the conference room from the hall, where the offices were located. She stood just inside her doorway, glancing back at me, phone to her ear and I could almost imagine her talking to Sonneck or Tracy or Bubba Niff. A young lady in tight skirt and loose-fitting blouse cinched with a wide belt took a stack of papers from Wilma and headed further down the hall. Moments later, the distinct sound of a copy machine zip-hummed its way through the warrants.

"After this is over," I said to Les. "Whatever the supervisors decide, give me an exclusive? I'm not taking many notes right now."

He nodded. "I'll be glad to."

"Have you met these people?" I shifted my weight. The chairs were new and hadn't been broken in yet, and the leather squeaked.

"Just those who come in with the warrants, their treasurer and office manager," Les said and this time his grin wasn't toothy but crooked. "Quite a pair."

"They're all like that. Except one. There's a chance she has her head on straight. Two of them didn't speak so I have no idea what they're like. All but one, Vanessa, rubber stamped everything put before them." I bit my thumbnail.

"Be careful," Les said, and leaned forward. "The girl? Tracy? She's got family who are large supporters of local politicians. And they have money. They'll cause problems for anyone who touches her. And the short, stubby guy? Their treasurer?"

"Yeah. Real sweetheart."

"Struts his stuff like a rooster. He's got relatives with criminal records."

The word *criminal* struck my aching brain like a baseball-bat wielding gangbanger. "Really?"

He nodded a slow, deliberate motion. "I'm from Oakhurst, and people know what others are doing in a small town. Ask around. Someone should be able to tell you."

Chapter 26

The day had gone cold. Gray clouds that had lingered to the north now blanketed the city and the air smelled earthy with the teaser of rain. I carried the oversize manila envelope thick with five years' worth of warrants from the Manzanita Knolls cemetery into my cubicle and settled on the wobbly chair.

A clue lay inside those pages. I just knew it. The prospect of finding a lead, another piece in the homicide-investigation puzzle prompted my heart to beat a bit quicker, my mind to become a bit sharper.

I slid the stack from the envelope and set them on the stained desk calendar, which I still hadn't changed to the current month.

"Toss it later," I muttered. Now, I wanted to start delving into the financial expenses of the cemetery district's past.

The pages held the scent of fresh ink. Not like the newspaper coming off the presses, but that warm smell of hot toner. I thumbed the edge of the stack, watched scribbles flicker like the film of an old silent movie. Then I ran my palm over the top sheet, worked my thumb beneath and started to lift the page.

Quint poked his head around my cubicle wall, apparently checking if I'd returned and, upon seeing I had, perched on the edge of my desk.

"Morales called. Since the chief gave him permission to work this case, he called the park rangers. They're at the station now with Wickham and Roberts," Quint said. He tapped one finger against the stack of warrants and added, "What did you learn at the Auditor's office?"

"I'll fill you in later." Giving the copied sheets a wistful glance, I stood. "Guess Morales wants us there?"

"He didn't say." He stood and motioned toward his workstation. "I've got tons to do. Let me know what you find out, okay?"

"Will do." I grabbed my jacket and retreated to the parking lot.

The police department was relatively new, a state of the art building with fiber optics that provided each division the latest technology. It still smelled of fresh paint and leather. In the detectives' division, I found Morales in the computer room watching the monitor which showed the interrogation room.

The camera hidden in a fake thermostat captured Roberts, the amber-eyed Elfin King. He appeared gritty. His red flannel shirt was rumpled, as did his faded jeans, as though he'd slept in them not once, but several nights. For the first time I noticed his gaze had a keenness that made me feel like he not only looked at people, but could see into their souls and knew their dirty little secrets. Gooseflesh rippled up my arms, down my back, and I resisted the urge to hug myself, warm away the chills.

A man with shaved head shiny with lotion so his dome reflected the overhead lights entered the division and sank into a chair next to Morales' office. Morales strode down the hall before the row of open cubicles, approached the man in shirt, tie, slacks and Birkenstock-style sandals with socks, a yuppie gone wrong.

"Chang," Morales said, and extended his arm.

Chang looked up from the file he'd been reading and raised brows at Morales. "Been a long time."

Morales shook Chang's hand. "Sure has." To me, Morales said, "we worked together in Compton."

"Really?" I gave Chang a nod. "Nice to meet you."

"Same here." He flashed me a smile.

"After I left L.A., he took a job with the parks service, and has been in Yosemite the past few months. Should have stopped by."

"If you're half as busy as I am, it's understandable." To me, Chang asked, "What department are you with?"

"Hannah Monakee, Borden Gazette."

He looked at Morales as if he'd lost his mind. "You brought a reporter in here?"

"She's okay. Anything off the record stays off."

"You were there when Spinelli died," Chang said. "I read your statement." He blanched and shook his head. "How's his wife doing?"

"She's up north with her brother." I glanced past him where Wickham had just walked into the department. He wore black, the sign of his faith announced by way of the small, white square in his band collar. He clutched a rosary in one hand, worried the beads and I wondered if he was mentally praying.

"Let me get him into another room," Chang said, and bowed slightly as a way to excuse him. He ushered Wickham into an interrogation room next to the one where Roberts continued to wait.

I returned to the monitoring room, where two screens showed the suspects fidgeting nervously, Wickham with his beads and Roberts with a thread hanging from his flannel shirt.

Morales settled at the table across from Roberts just as Quint stepped inside and regarded the monitors.

"Has he started yet?" He glanced at the only chair and leaned against the doorway.

"Thought you had tons of work." I sat and shifted my attention from one screen to the other.

"I do, but I can't focus. Not with this going on. Did I miss anything?"

"They're just getting started."

On the screen, Morales set a folder and digital recorder in the center of the table, recited the date and time and drummed his fingers against each other, creating a steeple.

"What's that?" Roberts tilted back, letting his chair rest on its hind legs.

"Few details about your past. Benjamin Roberts, right?" Morales lifted his gaze and watched Roberts, whose leg set into a nervous jig. He nodded. "You have relatives living in eastern Madera County?"

"Sure. Why? Something wrong with one of them?"

"No," Morales said, quit with the fingers steeple. "Mind telling me who?"

"Uncles, aunts, cousins, my dad's still living in Manzanita Knolls. Mom passed away last year. I mean," Roberts shrugged. "What do you want to know? What's this about?"

"Grady Spinelli's death."

"That was an accident." Roberts let the chair clatter to all four legs. "The NPS guys. They said it was an accident."

"How well did you know Grady?" Morales asked.

"Pretty well, we'd climbed before, he and a buddy of his that works at the prison. It was that Rydell guy, his equipment failed. *That's* what killed him."

Quint's back went rigid, a subtle movement most wouldn't notice. But I did, and I knew what it meant. Tension had poured into his body. His jaw line paled, his gaze hardened. The loss of his friend was too fresh, and the accusation cut him deeply.

"Did you see anyone near Rydell's camp, possibly accessing his car?"

Roberts shook his head. "Hate to say so, but I'd been drinking quite a bit. I almost bailed on the climb."

"You've got some history." Morales opened the file on the table near the recorder and tapped his finger on something within the report. "Assault conviction. You like violence, Roberts?"

"No," he said. A blend of anger and fear charged his expression. As quickly as the emotions had surfaced, he smothered them and folded his arms.

"Like beating women?"

"My ex-wife is a liar," he snapped. "I didn't do a damned thing."

"I know," Morales said in a quasi-soothing tone. "No one in prison is guilty. Right? All of you were framed."

"She lied. Those bruises on her? The bitch did it herself. I wanted a divorce. She didn't. She got her friends to back her up because she wanted our kid. I haven't seen him since before I got locked up."

"Says you served less than a year. Get out early for good behavior?"

"Yeah, asshole. I did."

"On probation?"

"Got a couple years, that ended six months ago." He stared at the table, and I wondered how many such surfaces he'd stared at in the past to avoid eye contact, avoid the shame he must feel, avoid a confrontation that could launch him into the type of rage that had landed him behind bars.

"How did you learn about the climb?" Morales asked. "Who invited you?"

"Grady."

"How well do you know Wickham? Did you invite him on the climb?"

"No." Roberts peered around as though looking for something that should have been adhered to the wall. Avoiding eye contact. Interesting. I bit my thumbnail.

"I thought Rydell brought him," Roberts added.

The headache I'd had earlier returned and needled my temples. I removed my glasses and rubbed my eyes. Then I drew circles on the sheet of paper, added names to each and tried to connect them by who knew whom. Quint and Grady had met Pratt on a trail, and they talked about climbing El Cap. Roberts knew Grady, and that's how he came to join the others. Wickham knew Pratt through church.

Yates. I wrote out his name and drew three lines beneath.

"How do you know Yates?" Morales asked. His voice sounded tinny through the three-inch-square speakers plugged into the computer.

"Never met him," Roberts said.

"I thought Yates was with Roberts," Quint said, pulling my attention from the screen.

"Maybe Wickham knows Yates," I suggested. "The NPS ranger is in the other interrogation room with Wickham now."

"Any way we can dial into that?" Quint asked.

"Not sure how this works," I said, gesturing toward the electronics and wires. "But it's being recorded. I'm sure Morales will let us watch."

Quint nodded and returned his attention to the screen. I, too, watched as the camera caught Roberts' face just past the back of Morales' head.

"Know the name of that other guy, the one who works at the prison?" Morales asked.

Roberts squinted, as though he could read the name in the air. Then he shook his head. "Can't remember."

"Know what he looks like? What he drives?"

"They always came together in Grady's Dodge."

I had a contact at the prison, and a guard who was a big wall climber wouldn't be too difficult to find. If they were like Quint, they had photos of themselves with friends dangling from outcroppings thousands of feet above the ground. If I could find this guard, I could see if he connects to Yates. If not, I'd plan to speak with him, and this time it wouldn't be at Borden Books and Bagels. This time, Morales would be conducting the interview in the cramped interrogation room where Roberts now sat.

Chapter 27

After releasing Roberts, Morales switched cameras so Quint and I could watch the other interrogation room. Inside, just past the back of Chang's bald head, the camera captured Wickham. He clutched a rosary in one hand, working the beads as one would when reciting the Rosary, and I wondered if he prayed now.

He shifted uncomfortably and kept his attention on the floor, where a speck of dust about the size of a pencil eraser swayed, driven by the gentle current of the air conditioner. He worried his beads.

"How did you get in on the climb?" Chang asked. He'd opened a spiral-topped notepad and held the yellow pencil ready.

"Pratt. He mentioned that a group was planning to climb El Cap, and they needed another man for two, three-man ropes."

"Where'd you meet Pratt?"

"He sometimes attends church. He has family in the mountain area."

"What about Yates? What can you tell me about him?"

Wickham shrugged and pocketed his rosary. "I know of him, but no, I'd never spoken with him prior to the climb. I think Rydell invited him."

Morales had taken Quint's spot in the doorway, and now Quint gripped the back of the chair I was perched on. I reached over my shoulder and gripped his hand.

"Apparently, none of us knew him," he said. "How'd he know about the climb?"

"Maybe he knew Grady?" I suggested. "Who can we ask?"

"Diane isn't in any shape," he said. "If he knew Grady, and Grady climbed with someone with the prison . . . I don't know. Longshot."

Maybe. But definitely worth looking into.

The interview with Wickham had wound down. I made the notes, gathered my things and followed Quint to the parking lot.

"I don't feel like we've gotten anywhere," he said.

"These things take time. Meet you back at the office?"

He nodded, waited until I was buckled into my aging car, and left.

Back at the office, the stack of warrants enticed me. I wanted to snatch them up, get into my car, drive home where I could get a beer, put up my feet and focus solely on them. But first I needed to figure out how Yates had come to be with the other climbers.

Inside the semi-privacy of my cubicle, I wiggled my mouse, brought my computer out of its slumber and opened my Outlook contact list. Officer Ed Grimes, the media liaison for Central California Women's Prison in the northern portion of Madera County, had become a friend and trusted me well enough to talk shop. I could sit for hours listening to his stories from the big houses he'd worked, including Pelican Bay and Corcoran, where he'd dealt with Charlie Manson during a parole hearing. From what Grimes said, Manson played the madman role quite nicely. Crazy, Grimes had said, no doubt about that, and about as evil as any human could be. But the wild-eyed persona was an act for the media.

My call went to Grimes' voicemail. Hope sank with my enthusiasm, leaving room for the dull ache to return to my temples. I left a message and hung up. The light on my phone blinked an announcement that I'd missed calls, so I punched in my password and poised a pen above a stack of Computer Aided Dispatch sheets I'd picked up the week before.

The first call was from the sheriff's PIO with an update on the copper wire thefts from an elementary school. They'd made an arrest, and she would send me an email with the details. She was good about giving me a heads up so I could save space in the newspaper's A section.

The second was a hang up, and I wondered if it had been the man I'd given my card to this morning at the cemetery. If so, I figured he'd call back.

The third was Vanessa, the rebel trustee. She had left her cell number. I penned it on a sticky note and adhered to my computer monitor. Then I dialed. She picked up immediately.

"You're the reporter, right?"

Hope resurged like a swell of heat. I gripped the handset tighter. "Guilty as charged. You're the *draw-A-line* lady, right?"

"That's me. I need to speak with you. Where's your office?"

I gave her the address and she said she'd stop by after lunch. I held onto that swell of hope, even allowing a smile to touch my lips. Maybe, finally, this case was coming together.

I glanced at the clock on the lower left corner of my computer screen. Today lunch would consist of a candy bar from the vending machine and another cup of coffee. Newsrooms ran on two stimulants:

Caffeine and nicotine. Since I didn't smoke, I doubled up on the caffeine.

While waiting for Vanessa to arrive, I organized my thoughts in a Word document, outlined what I'd learned from the auditor, including the bonuses and vacation time the trustees had given the employees. I needed to see the time cards, which were probably inside the cemetery office. I could drive back up the hill, ask to see them. But I seriously doubted they'd let me even though they were paid with public funds and the time cards would be public documents.

I reached for the copies from the auditor's office. My phone rang. I diverted my hand, picked up the receiver and started to introduce myself when a woman verbally slammed into me.

"Hello, Miss Hannah Monakee. News reporter Hannah Monakee. Stick your nose in where it doesn't belong Hannah Monakee," she said. "I know who you are. Oh, we *all* know who you are, I've read the garbage you print about people in our county and it's just that— *garbage.*"

A trembling seeded itself deep inside me, flared with a rush of heat that burned my cheeks. "Who is this?"

"Danielle Bosley. Trustee for the Mountain Area Cemetery District. And you better watch your back, Missy, do you hear me? What were you doing at the cemetery, anyway?"

"I was—"

"You don't even live in this area. You had no business coming up here. You and your buddy, Vanessa, are scheming to get Harland his job back. Well it's not going to work. We've contacted our attorney."

"I don't know—," I said.

"Liar," Bosley snapped. "I know you all went to school together, you guys hang out and drink and hell, you're probably sleeping with— "

"Lady," I shot back, not even trying to strain the anger from my tone. "I don't know who you are, but you are out of line. I'm hanging up."

"Don't you dare hang up on me," she screamed. "You're a public servant, and I can talk to you any way I want."

"No, I am not a public servant," I countered.

"My tax dollars pay for your wages, Missy."

I slammed the receiver, hoping it left a painful ringing in her ear. Drawing a cleansing breath, I leaned back and tried to calm my nerves, which felt like an over-loosened snare, rattling in a tinny manner.

Apparently having heard me raise my voice, reporters in neighboring cubicles peered in at me, asked "You okay?" and offered to get me water. I nodded, waved away the offer and closed my eyes.

Quint pushed past the others and slid onto the chair beside my desk. "What was that about?"

"Cemetery district trustee, one of the two who didn't talk this morning. She's vocal now and as nuts as the guy with little-man syndrome." I scrubbed my hands over my face. How was I supposed to reason with these people? "They think I'm friends with the trustee who refused to sign papers and some guy they fired. I don't know these people."

"I know you don't." He rubbed my shoulders. "Let it go, Babe. They can't touch you. I doubt they'll drive down to the Valley just to rattle your cage. Let's get out of here. Get some lunch."

"No time. The lady they're saying is my drinking buddy will be here around one."

"Thought I was your drinking buddy." Quint offered a grin. "I'll pick up some burgers and bring them back. Fries?"

What the heck. It wasn't like I was some health nut, anyway. And a salad wasn't going to console me. I nodded.

The warrants. They'd distract me, and just then I needed a distraction. The phone rang. I ignored it, withdrew the stack of papers from the envelope, propped my feet against the edge of my desk and rested the pages on my legs.

In the eighteen minutes it took Quint to get our lunch, my phone rang another seven times. I let the calls go to voicemail. As a rule, we don't use caller ID in order to protect the privacy of those calling in news tips. I'd check the messages before I left for the day and return calls as needed. I didn't want another verbal assault from Bosley.

I'd tried to focus on the warrants, but my headache had gone from dull to sharp. When Quint arrived with the scent of food, I set the stack aside and cleared a space on my desk. He sat in the plastic and chrome chair and sorted out the contents of the white bag.

I folded back the wrapper from my burger and ate, savoring the blended taste of mustard, pickles, beef and onion.

"We fly out after the gig tomorrow." He delved into his cheeseburger. "Want to stay over?"

"I haven't even packed." I pulled fries from the packet.

"I have."

"That doesn't surprise me." I rubbed my neck muscles, which had gone rock solid. "Why don't you stay with me tonight? That way I can pack, and we can leave from there."

"You're fifteen minutes closer. Okay."

We continued eating in silence. Halfway through my lunch, the inner-office intercom buzzed, and the receptionist let me know Vanessa had arrived.

Quint gathered his half-eaten burger and remaining fries, stood, planted a kiss on my forehead and retreated to his workstation.

I walked the long hall that separated the newsroom from the advertising department, from which the break room branched off, and took a right to the front office. The blond lady in designer jeans and *Bebe* zippered jacket waited on the other side of the glass.

Opening the door that locked from the inside, I motioned for her to follow me, and headed back toward the newsroom.

"I'm Hannah Monakee," I said, "but I guess you already know that."

"Yep. I'm Vanessa Klair."

I glanced into the break room, the coffee maker, the selection of flavors.

"What some coffee?" I asked.

"I'd love some."

The room was dimly lit, the glow from the soda vending machine washing the air a pale blue.

"How long have you been on the cemetery board?"

"A few months." She chose French vanilla, used a paper cup from the stack next to the machine, and brewed.

"That's it?" I chose espresso.

"I've known Harland most of my life," she said, blew across the top of her coffee and sipped. "What they did to him is wrong. Is there any cream and sugar?"

I pulled open a drawer, where our sports editor kept his stash of C&H and small tubs of half and half. She plucked up two sugar packets and one creamer.

"That's the guy they fired, right? The one I've been accused— twice now—of sleeping with." I led her to my cubicle.

She sat in the chair Quint had vacated, set her cup on the desk calendar and looked around. Tucking her hands between her knees, she seemed to draw in on herself. That sealed it. I needed to clean my workspace.

"Have you spoken with Harland?" she asked.

"Not yet. I did get his number." I pulled it from my back pocket. With all that had gone on, I'd forgotten I had it. The slip of paper probably would have wound up in a billion pieces in the washing machine.

"Know why they fired him?" The paper cup was still too hot. I transferred the contents into my Borden PD mug, sipped and closed my eyes.

"The office staff, I refused to call her a manager because all she does is answer phones and make mistakes by selling the same hillside niche to two different people. Anyway, she claimed Harland was harassing her. And he wasn't. He wrote her up for wearing cutoffs and sports bra."

"To work?"

Vanessa nodded. "We had a funeral going on that day, too. There she was, outside, knocking down spider webs when he told her to go home."

"What did she do?"

"Starting cussing. Loud. The family burying their loved one turned and looked, they shouldn't have to deal with that." She retrieved her cup and lowered her gaze. "I've lost family. They're buried in that cemetery. It's hard enough without a crazy woman shouting during a time of mourning."

"I know. I've lost family, too," I said, and for a moment my throat constricted and an image of Grandpa filled my mind. I breathed deeply, rubbed my temple against the pain that wouldn't leave my head or my heart.

"He took the problem to the board, but they sided with her. Some of the trustees wanted him gone and used that situation to fire him. She's obnoxious. It's hard to have a conversation with her."

"That's for sure." I sat at my desk, glanced at the blinking light. The small window beside the voicemail indicator showed I now had eleven messages. "I had a run in with her this morning before your board meeting. She's got quite the mouth."

"You don't know the half of it. You were at the meeting. You saw how they run things. What those guys are doing is illegal, you can't get reimbursed for something when you don't have proof you bought it."

"Do you have documents?" I never take anyone's word unless supported by backup.

She studied me, her eyes slightly narrowed, her head tilted. Sizing me up. Deciding if she can trust me. Finally, she nodded. "I have them. Another person gave them to me. He's the one who went to the supervisors' staff person, and they called the grand jury. His grandfather was a trustee, but he died in the middle of his term. He collected evidence of stuff they've been doing for years. He kept everything in a folder. He told his grandson about the folder a few days before he passed away."

"Died how?" I hoped we didn't have a third questionable death. Grady and his assistant, Ava, were enough.

"He was sick." She flipped her hair over her shoulder, sat back and drank. "He gave me copies of some of the paperwork before I was appointed. He and I know each other, too. We went to school together."

"So you get on the board to see for yourself what's going on and you confirmed what he'd told you." Good move. Only, she and her source could become targets. "You said *some* of the documents. He didn't give you all of them?"

"He couldn't. He said if anyone got hold of those papers, the trustees would be charged with felonies. All of its criminal behavior, but whatever he kept from me was huge." She nodded to emphasize her words and brushed her hair back over her shoulder again. "Now, the supervisor died in an accident, I saw on the news where his assistant was shot. I'm the one who encouraged my source to speak with Ava. He and she went to the Supervisor. Now they're dead."

"I have Borden's detective sergeant working on this with me. He's in contact with the National Park Service. Would you be willing to speak with him?"

"You bet I would," she said. "I have seven family members buried up there. My son is buried there. I want to see that district run right, and the cemetery taken care of. If I have to bring down every one of them to accomplish that, I will."

Wow. My pulse quickened. I matched its beat with my pen against my notepad.

Maybe we'd finally gotten a break.

Chapter 28

For the first time since Grady's death, the spark of hope stayed intact. Just a tiny speck, but one I believed Vanessa's insight would nourish into a blazing fire. If a connection existed between the cemetery district and what I firmly believed was murder, she might be able to provide us with that information.

Morales had returned to the morgue, where the bound volumes of newspapers dating back more than a hundred years were kept. I had intended to bring him to my cubicle, hadn't realized Vanessa followed me until I reached the morgue.

I opened the door. Morales looked up and raised a brow, which disappeared beneath his shaggy hair. He straightened and looked Vanessa over. Then he actually smiled. I hadn't seen him smile in months.

When he stood, his windbreaker shifted revealing the firearm holstered to his side. Not his department-issued Glock, but a snub nose .38 Colt. For some reason, I hadn't considered he'd carry a gun from his small collection, and I was glad he had. I felt comforted knowing he was armed.

"Vanessa Klair," I said by way of introduction. "The cemetery district trustee I told you about."

She offered her hand in a professional manner, yet something about her stance, the look in her eyes and her coy smile almost made me want to break out in the old *Fiddler on the Roof* number "Matchmaker." Who would have thought?

She shifted her attention from him to the file on the table with Robert's name. Her smile faded.

"Why are you investigating Roberts?"

"You know him?" I asked.

"His grandfather is the *president*," she said, adding emphasis to show how ridiculous it sounded. "And he and I don't get along."

"I'll look into *president grandpa*." Morales motioned for Vanessa to sit. She chose the chair at the head of the table. Morales settled beside her. There was an electric surge between them, one I knew all too well. I'd felt it many times between Quint and me.

"How do you know Roberts?" Morales asked her.

"Small community. Everyone knows everyone," she said. "At least those of us who have lived here most of our lives."

"What do you know about him?" I settled in a chair at the table.

"He married Penelope Jenkins in a huge wedding. *Everyone* was there. Five months later they had a kid. That's when he got in trouble for domestic violence and spent time in prison."

"Forget the background check," Morales said. "Should've called you."

She smiled back. "Call any time."

Get a room, I wanted to say but kept my thoughts to myself. "Anything else?"

She looked from Morales to me, and leaned back in her chair. "There were a couple of assaults, but the charges were dropped. That was back in high school."

"Think someone could get him to . . ." I let the unspoken question hang in the air. I didn't know her, and the last thing I wanted was her thinking I was making unfounded accusations. Calling Roberts a killer could come back to bite me in a lethal way.

"Beat up someone?" She tilted her head as though carefully considering the question. Then she nodded. "Yeah, I think he would."

Morales tapped the table, appeared ready to speak, paused and asked. "Think he'd kill someone?"

"Like the Supervisor?" She shifted her gaze from Morales to me. "Is that what this is about? You don't believe Supervisor Spinelli died by accident?"

"We're exploring the possibility," I said.

"Oh my God." Vanessa leaned back as though she'd been physically struck and touched her fingers to her lips. "Someone murdered him?"

"We don't know that for sure," Morales said, "but yeah, it's possible."

The air in the room grew heavy as though the overhead fan no longer circulated. I understood the numbness she must have been feeling. I'd felt that way myself after seeing Grady's body strike the granite ledge.

Tears wet her lashes. She opened her purse, larger than mine, and rummaged around.

Morales peered at me. "Tissue?"

I hurried and snagged a box of Puffs from a coworker's desk.

Vanessa tore three free, clutched two and used one to dry her eyes. Her mascara blackened the space beneath her lower lashes.

"This isn't public information." I set the box on the table. "We're still trying to figure out who did this."

"Roberts is a possibility," she said. "Who else was with them?"

"Other than my boyfriend, Quint, there's Wickham, Antoine Yates and Doug Pratt."

She tilted her head in that contemplative manner again. "I don't think I know Pratt or Yates. But the other guy, he's a priest, right?"

"Yeah. Catholic church in Oakhurst," Morales said.

Vanessa waved her hand as though dispelling the notion that Wickham could have had anything to do with Supervisor Spinelli's death. "I know the priest. No way could he have killed anyone."

"Sure about that?" I asked. He wasn't cleared in my opinion.

"Positive. I know him. He went to school with my brother."

I sat next to Morales and folded my arms on top of the table. "Those documents you mentioned? Dealing with the cemetery district? I'd like to see them."

"They're in my trunk." She stood.

I pushed away from the table and motioned her to follow. "Are you parked in the lot?"

She nodded. I led her through the newsroom and old composing room with its hint of solvent clinging to the old wooden paste-up tables, through the heavy steel door and into the side lot. She approached a silver Corvette, probably from the sixties and in mint condition, popped the truck and pulled out two expandable file folders, each about five inches thick.

"This is everything Ni—" She stopped short. "My source gave me, and everything I've collected since then."

My reporter's intuition perked up at the partial name. Ni—Nicholas? Nico? Niles? I licked my lips, an effort to keep from asking. She'd withheld the name for a reason.

If her source's relative had been a trustee, and his name had been included in the records, I would find the whistleblower's identity. A couple quick Google searches was all it would take.

We returned to find Morales pacing before the floor to ceiling cabinets. When she set the files on the table, he immediately claimed the folders, pulled out pages and files within files, and a calendar on which Vanessa had documented everything since she'd come onto the board.

"The grounds crew," she said, and pulled out documents from the auditor's office, the same warrants I'd gotten copies of that morning, showing each employees' pay scale. "They make about five dollars an hour less than the office staff yet they've been there more than twenty years."

"How long has the office staff been there?" I asked.

Vanessa flipped a folder onto the table. The label showed the name Tracy Parkston.

"Parkston? As in the lawyer?" I asked.

"That's her uncle. Her father has beef cattle and a dairy." Vanessa propped her elbow on the chair's arm. "Why? Do you know him?"

"The attorney, yes, unfortunately." Parkston had filed a lawsuit against the newspaper for a story I'd written almost a year ago. Since then, he's strung out the case by filing one motion after another and we still hadn't gone to trial. He wanted me to name my sources, and that's information I'll never give up. He'd handled several trust accounts and had been skimming off the interest. The district attorney's office has been building a case against him. Maybe it was a defective family gene if Tracy was, in fact, stealing from the cemetery district.

I swiped my hand over my mouth stifling a groan. Now I knew what we were up against. Parkston Farms were big-time ranchers in the Central Valley. Worth millions. Millions upon millions. No wonder Tracy got away with tweaking on the job.

Morales fanned out the copies of weekly time sheets Tracy had filled out. There had to be at least two years' worth. Attached to each of December's cards were warrants showing payouts of vacation time, although she'd taken time off. The trustees had paid her twice.

I dragged the file from in front of Morales and turned the page to read the numbers. "She claimed seventy two hours and was paid out."

"She took off two weeks off in April, another in May, and she accrues six hours a month," Vanessa explained.

"I'm not good at math, but I don't think six hours a month equals three weeks' worth of time."

"It's seventy two hours per year," Vanessa said. "She claimed, in the first half of the year, one hundred twenty hours." She found that summer's time sheets. "Here, she claimed the doctor took her off the job on stress-related illness, and she exhausted her sick time. Following that, because she was pregnant, she was placed on half-days for the final three months. Each day, she claimed four hours vacation time. The trustees know what she's doing. They sign off on the warrant for her paycheck. That's why I won't sign."

"Smart move," Morales said. He reclaimed the file. "How long has this been going on?"

"I don't know. The only records I have are those of the former trustee, and what I've collected." She pulled out a separate folder. "This is where they approved items after they signed contracts or made purchases."

"Shady," Morales said, "but nothing I'm interested in."

"But they aren't complying with the Brown Act," Vanessa said.

"And that's not criminal, at least not that I know of. Money," he said. "Got any more proof of misappropriations?"

"Plenty." She pulled another from the expandable folder and opened. "For the past two years, they have submitted claims for reimbursement but they won't give receipts. And here," she said, sliding one sheet from the stack, "is one of the trustee's tax returns— Don't ask how I got this, I'll have to lie. Anyway," she said, and used the back of her hand to push her long hair behind her shoulder. "They're using the receipts on their personal taxes as deductions to keep from having to pay."

"So they do have receipts," I said. "They're not claiming money that isn't owed them. They're just not turning in those receipts."

"Exactly. And sometimes they turn in receipts, only no work had been done."

"Example?" I asked.

"There's a claim for repairs on the grave digger, and it wasn't broken, so that's about three thousand unaccounted for." Spreading the contents of another folder on the table, she tapped the warrant to reimburse Norm Sonneck five thousand dollars for new office furniture. "There's no new furniture in that office. It's threadbare and old. It hasn't been replaced since Reagan was president."

Morales shot me a perplexed look.

"One of the trustees," I said. "He tried to bully me today at the cemetery."

"He came at you?" Vanessa gripped her file so tightly, her knuckles whitened and the page wrinkled. "You're on his radar now. Please be careful."

"He can't be that bad," I said. "True, he's a complete nut job, but . . ."

"You wonder if Supervisor Spinelli's death was murder?" she asked. "If there's anyone on that board who's capable of violence, it's Sonneck."

Chapter 29

We sat in the morgue, which had become silent as its namesake. I regarded Morales and Vanessa with a blend of curiosity and frustration. I didn't feel like we were getting anywhere. I stood, paced, and returned to the table.

"With bulldogs like Sonneck and Bosley guarding the bank accounts, the auditor should work with the district attorney to get a search warrant for the books. If Tracy is in charge of the books, that could be where she's getting her drug money. Right?"

"What's that?" Morales asked.

"With the way the trustees rubber stamp the warrants, she could present anything and they would sign it. She takes it to the county office and she's got a couple thousand in her pocket," I said.

A sour knot rose in my throat. I swallowed it back. Was any of this reason to kill Grady?

"I'd like to speak with this Sonneck character," Morales said to Vanessa. "Know where to find him?"

"I'll give you his address, his home phone, his cell phone." She handed Morales a piece of paper. "That's all the trustees' contact information."

"I'll make a copy," I offered and took the page.

While they spoke, I stepped out of the morgue, made the copy, and returned with a new file folder where I'd collect information for our investigation.

"I'd like copies of those time cards," Morales said, "the receipts, anything dealing with money."

I took those out and made copies, returned, and Morales already had another stack. I'd become his personal secretary.

"I need to make a call," I said, eyeing the growing mound of evidence. "Copy machine's right outside the door. I don't think anyone will mind if you use it. I have the former superintendent's cell number."

"Harland?" Vanessa asked. "He's a good guy. He's made his share of mistakes, but no one wrote him up, not a single time, and that was small stuff, anyway. Then they claim he's harassing Tracy and fired him. Her word against his and there wasn't a bit of truth to it. He's suing."

"How many lawsuits they got against them?" Morales asked.

"Just the one as far as I know."

To me, Morales said, "let me know what Harland says."

In my cubicle, the message light blinked. The window at the top of the phone showed I had an additional two messages.

I tapped in Harland's cell number. He answered halfway through the second ring.

"Andrew said you'd call," he said by way of answering. Caller ID. "Guess you got a taste of what I went through the last ten years."

"How long had you worked for the cemetery district?" I asked.

"Almost forty years. I was going to retire when I hit sixty five." Harland had a gravelly voice, like someone who had smoked too many Camels, the no filter type. "Now, I lost everything because one person's lies and the newer board members buying those lies."

"Newer?" I picked up a pen, flipped to a clean page in my notebook. "Which ones?"

"The one who came after you today, Sonneck, he's only been on the board five years and he's been on my back every day of it." He coughed as though telling me I was right. "Bosley came on the board around the same time."

"The rest of them have been on the board how long?"

Harland sighed a smoker's sigh, one laced with congestion and the hint of a wheeze. "The other lady, she's okay but not very bright. She came on a couple years ago, when Ray Larson died."

The whistleblower's grandfather. I wrote the name down and, beside it, scribbled a star. "Did he have any family?"

"Oh, sure. Two daughters, Melba and Hazel, and three grandsons, Nigel, Parson and Trinton."

Vanessa had started to say a name. What had it been?

She had started to say *Nigel*.

"Still there?" Harland asked.

"Just thinking." I bit my thumbnail. "How aggressive are these people? Are they capable of violence?"

"Like pit bulls on chickens." Another cough, almost hacking. "Bubba seems mild and all, but he's poison. He sets it up and lets others fight and take the fall. He's been a trustee for about twenty years."

Did they stay until they died? "Does he have relatives?"

"He's got some nephews, but no kids of his own."

"What do you know about the office clerk and vacation?"

Harland scoffed. "She takes off any time she wants, and gets paid out at the end of the year. She's been doing that since she was hired."

"Why does she get away with it? What's wrong with these trustees?" I couldn't help but wonder if the office clerk was sleeping with one—or more—of them, but they were so much older.

"Want to know what I think?"

"Yes, I do."

"There's money missing. They know it. They don't know what to do, so they keep everyone else away and cover it up." Hacking. He cleared his throat. "And the way she hangs on Bubba gives me the creeps. He's old enough to be her grandfather."

I swallowed hard. "Do you think . . ."

"Oh, I *know*. That's the real reason they fired me. I caught them."

The mental picture his words conjured was enough to make me feel sick. I'd need to take bleach and a pumice stone to my brain in order to rid myself of that image.

"Maybe not outright sex," he added. "Hand job, blow job. Stuff like that. Hell, Bubba would have a heart attack and die if they actually had sex."

I thanked him for his time, he said I could call again if I needed, and rang off. Leaning back in my chair, I stared at the ceiling with its rectangular light fixtures that had always reminded me of my grandmother's old metal ice trays.

My brain was overcrowded with the craziness of these mountain folks. Not all of those who lived in the foothills and mountains were like this small handful. I knew and respected a lot of them. These people, however small an exception, were something I'd expect to find in the Thirties, living in the back woods someplace.

Someone tapped the metal frame of my cubicle. I turned and saw my publisher standing in the entrance to my workstation.

Tall, lean, in his mid-seventies, Leslie Vargas looked like he'd just stepped off a fashion show runway. He wore Armani like a well-chiseled model. Even his salt and pepper hair didn't make him look old, but dignified.

I motioned toward the only other chair in my cubicle and invited him to sit. He scanned my space, and I half expected him to recite multiple OSHA violations. The three-foot stack of old newspapers being one of them.

"Is this about the dog?" I asked. Robin was Vargas' grandson. "Quint will help take care of her."

Vargas smiled, shook his head and sat. "No, this is not about the dog. But that's one of the best things to happen to Robin in a long time. He loves that dog." The merriment left Vargas' eyes. He rested his arms on his thighs, clasped his hands and leaned forward. Finally he lifted his gaze and regarded me with furrowed brows.

"I received a phone call. Actually, three phone calls. The rest I'm letting go to voicemail. Want to explain what you're working on?"

"Let me guess. Her name's Bosley."

Vargas nodded.

"I have calls, too. Haven't checked my voicemail yet, but I'm pretty sure those are from her." I tilted my head at the blinking light.

He gestured toward the phone. "May I hear them?"

"Sure." I punched the speaker button, entered Richard's date of birth.

The first message was from Badorini, so I skipped to the second. That was from my contact with the highway patrol. Skipped.

Third was Bosley, her whiny voice that dripped with hatred telling me I was wrong, wrong, wrong, that they were going to sue me for harassing the office manager, I needed to stay out of Manzanita Knolls and away from Tracy, and that she hoped I ate crow for dinner, choked on it and died.

The next two were also from her. In the last, she bashed me because I hadn't returned her calls. Really? Was she that blind to her own actions? Why would I talk to her again? She was nuts. I wasn't.

"I just met these people today," I told Vargas.

"That must have been when she gave up and called me." Vargas rubbed his palms together. "She claims you and another trustee, Vanessa, went to school together, party together, and you're both fornicating with the former superintendent."

"Seriously?" In the span of six hours, I'd gotten a reputation as a slut. A hot ball of anger tightened my chest. I breathed deeply, that cleansing breath that Robin claims chases away negative emotions. This time, it only made me dizzy. "Vanessa is in the morgue right now with Morales, he's interviewing her on this very subject—the cemetery trustees, not fornication. I met her this morning. Actually, no, I didn't meet her, I saw her. I met her when she came to the office about an hour ago."

I told him about the misappropriation of public funds, the gifts of public funds, the huge paychecks some of the trustees gave themselves without invoices to prove they had spent the money. I also told him about the grand jury and its investigation, adding that once the report was released, I would have one hell of a story.

Vargas smiled, clapped his hands together and I knew he believed me and the issue was closed. He stood. "Don't worry about this Bosley woman. And when you have time . . . " he waved his arm, indicating my cubicle. "Tidy up, okay?"

"Sure."

I saved the messages so I could play them for Morales and, should Bosley make good on her threat to sue, for our company attorney. Then I played the rest. Badorini had the CADs ready. I glanced around at the stacks of paper, which were beginning to look like a fortress.

I spent the next thirty minutes reducing the clutter and filling the recycle bin. With everything on my desk back in proper places, the computer and monitor dusted, the calendar turned to the appropriate month, I lost the sense of peace doing mindless tasks generates and faced the dilemma of how to deal with the mountain crazies.

Ignore them? Somehow I didn't think that would work. Confront them? These types couldn't be reasoned with. The best thing to do would be dig deep, find the dirt on these guys and write a well-crafted article busting their little scheme wide open.

That scheme was only the summit of the mountain, like the top of El Capitan. What were the three-thousand-feet beneath that summit?

The endowment was the real money. Who had access? Which investment firm had been appointed to oversee the funds?

Next to Nigel's name with the scribbled star, I added the questions. Now, I needed to figure out how I'd get the answers.

Chapter 30

Down the corridor that marked the maze between cubicles, our community reporter's radio, always tuned to sounds from the Thirties, Forties and Fifties played Johnny Mathis' "Chances Are." His voice, like liquid honey, soothed my raw nerves. I breathed deeply, exhaled slowly.

"Okay, Google. Let's see what you've got on Tracy Parkston."

That was one of two topics I wanted to investigate further before the end of the day. The other was endowments.

The computer screen flickered. Lights overhead first dimmed than winked out, leaving the room in complete darkness.

"Damn." Not only couldn't I see, I couldn't continue my research unless I went home, and it wasn't even two o'clock. Even if I had a fully charged laptop, with the servers down I couldn't connect to wifi.

"Anyone have a flashlight?" I called out. Quint did, but he was out on assignment and I wasn't sure where he kept it.

"No," a reporter shouted from across the room.

"Not me," another responded.

Figured. The majority of us hadn't learned survival skills as Quint had. I should get a list of *in-case-of* items I could keep in my desk. Flashlight included.

After having cleaned up my cubicle, I wasn't sure I could find my way out. I'd grown accustomed to the clutter—the paper fort I'd created. I'd probably fall over a chair or something. But I couldn't sit in the dark. I'd have to risk a bruised shin.

Extending my arms before me like a blind person trying to keep from running into something, I felt for the wall behind my desk. My hip banged against its corner and pain flared up my side. I sucked in a breath, muttered, "damn-it," and move farther right. I found the cloth of the cubicle and ran my fingers along the fabric until I felt the metal that framed the entrance.

The inky blackness pressed in on me, creating a weight in my chest. I paused in the hallway, not knowing if there was someone in front of me. Or behind. For that matter, anywhere near and suddenly I felt claustrophobic. Hairs prickled on my arms. I have never liked total darkness. Now I remembered why. As a child I had been convinced that a monster lurked beneath my bed, waiting for me to touch my feet to the floor so it could reach out, wrap its claw-like hand around my ankle and yank me into a world of its creation. And why was I thinking of this now? Scaring myself, that's all I was doing. There hadn't been anything under the bed, and there's nothing in the darkness now. And if I kept telling myself that, maybe I'd believe it.

I tried to shove the childhood fear from my mind, but shivered anyway.

"Get a grip," I muttered.

"You say something?" A voice from the darkness.

I ignored him. Ahead and to the left, pale yellow seeped from the community reporter's cubicle. Candles weren't allowed and she loved candles so, for her birthday, I had gotten her the battery-powered type that gave the illusion of flickering flames. Too bad I hadn't thought to get some for myself. I made another mental note and tacked it amid with the clutter in my head.

I slipped into Quint's cubicle. Here, I knew where everything was. He was a creature of habit, very neat, which made us something of an odd couple. Where would he keep a flashlight? I touched the back of his chair, the top of the computer's monitor, the overhead shelve with slide-up door. I started right to left, feeling my way inside the cabinet. My fingers struck a box, inside which felt like pens.

I pulled out the chair and sat. If I were Quint, I'd have the light within reach. He's taller, his arms longer than mine, but I reached up anyway, raised off the chair, and in the left-hand side of the overhead bin touched the flashlight. I removed it from the shelf and thumbed the button.

Nothing.

From somewhere in the room came a crash, followed by a string of expletives that ended with "*shit.*"

I unscrewed the end, felt inside for batteries. None. He kept them separate so they wouldn't drain as quickly.

On the same shelf, directly behind where I'd found the flashlight, were the size D Eveready. Flat side down? I dropped the batteries inside, returned the cap and again thumbed the button. A stream of light cut through the darkness.

Applause filled the newsroom.

"Way to go, Hannah," shouted the same someone who had muttered profanities.

I strolled to the door that opened to the street and propped it so sunlight, albeit muted due to the storm, cast shades of gray into the department. The other reporters approached like moths drawn to light.

Morales and Vanessa emerged from the morgue and, aided by the penlight he carried clipped to his keychain, made their way through the newsroom.

"Years of drought and now we get just enough rain to kill the power," he grumbled. "Need some widows in here."

"We had windows," I said, and sat on the edge of the nearest desk that wasn't trapped inside a cubicle. "Too many drive-by shootings. The former owner had them all plastered over."

"Speaking of drive-bys." He leaned against the wall next to the open door. "Ava was shot with a nine millimeter. Interesting striations, from what Badorini said. If we find a weapon it'll be easy to match."

I didn't think that would happen. Whoever shot her, presumably the same person who'd rigged Grady's fall, wasn't stupid. He'd carefully planned Grady's death. Had used a silencer—an assumption I'd bet a week's pay on—to kill Ava. That took a special type of intelligence to plan and execute. No, we weren't dealing with the average killer. This guy had smarts. Which meant it wasn't one of the cemetery district trustees.

Cold poured in through the opened door. On the sidewalk, fat raindrops splashed the concrete. Thunder rumbled, but it was too gloomy to have seen the preceding lightning. The cold seeped into my legs, chilling my feet and I knew I'd never get them warm until I got home and into a hot shower.

From the far side of the newsroom came sounds of a door opening, closing, and then footsteps. A gray form at first like a spectral entity taking shape as he came closer, Quint emerged from the blackness.

"Guess I should call and find out what's going on." I slid off the desk, turned on the flashlight and found my cubicle. Phone lines were on a different system, and didn't go down because of a power outage. Vargas had considered going totally digital. Good thing he hadn't.

I called Pacific Gas and Electric, whose call volume was high and a five-minute wait turned into seventeen. A transformer had blown. No idea how long it would take to repair. Which meant overtime because, regardless of the outage we had a paper to publish. Grabbing my purse and coat, I reported the news to the group by the street side door.

"I'm going to check it out," I said, working my arms through my coat's sleeves.

"I'll get the camera." Quint took the flashlight, which turned into a yellowish cone in the darkness. He returned with his Nikon, handed the light to Morales and we stepped into the storm. He'd parked in the lot at the buildings other side, so we walked around. Already puddles had formed and water ran in a thin stream along the gutter.

The rain fell heavier. The wind had grown colder. I shivered and zipped my coat. My breath hung in the air. I hurried toward his SUV.

"Where are we headed?" he asked, keying open the passenger side of the Range Rover.

Climbing in, I gave him the address, only three blocks away. On the floorboard was a week-old edition of the Gazette, dusted with dirt. A hammer lay half hidden beneath the passenger seat. I searched the cab and found a sliver of what appeared to be drywall on the carpet in back.

Once settled in the driver's seat, he started the engine and set the wiper blades into silent action, swiping away what had become sheets of rain.

"And you were worried about a little dog hair?" I gestured toward the dirt.

He glanced over the floor. "Doing a project for a friend. It'll clean."

"Yeah. That's what I said about the dog hair."

"And it cleaned." He flashed me a grin.

I powered the window down an inch and breathed deeply, savoring the musky scent I hadn't enjoyed in longer than I could recall just then. Rivulets formed in the gutter. A glossy sheet settled over the road.

Three minutes later, we reached the blown transformer. Quint climbed out. I stayed inside, trying to get warm. Setting on the ground beside an abandoned storefront, sparks flew from the metal box. It emitted growling sounds, rumbled like a plane during takeoff. Quint snapped off several shots, climbed back into the car and reached into the back seat for the roll of paper towels.

"Coming down hard." He tore off a couple sheets and used them to dry his face and hair. "How long before P G and E arrives?"

"They're on their way."

"I'd like to get shots of them making repairs."

"We could wait," I suggested. "It's not like we'll get any work done at the office."

Quint studied the side mirror, and if I didn't know better I'd accuse him of being vain. Then he leaned back and tapped his fingers against the steering wheel.

"What's wrong?" I asked.

"Blue Mercedes." He turned in the seat and peered through the back tinted window. "I've seen that car three times today."

"Someone's following you?" A surge of panic filled me, and I stomped it down. But the thought of someone tracking Quint's moves made me decidedly uncomfortable. Months earlier, I'd been stalked by a psycho who had tried to kill me.

He opened the door, stepped out and headed for the car.

It jerked away from the curb, pulled a U-turn and sped off. Its license plates, both front and back, had been removed. It had tinted windows, so I couldn't see who was inside.

"That's not good," I said when Quint crawled back into the Rover. "Any idea who it is?"

"Nope." He resumed blotting rain from his hair. Then he slid his cell from his jacket pocket and punched in a number. "There's a newer model blue Mercedes headed north on Sycamore, and it has no plates. After that drive by shooting, I thought I should call it in."

He hung up.

We resumed waiting, both of us sneaking glances at the side mirrors in case the Mercedes returned. Fifteen minutes later, the baby blue PG&E truck arrived followed by a flatbed with a new transformer. Quint got his action shots and the names of the workers for his cutline.

Lightning brightened clouds to the west, followed by the low growl of thunder. Rain ticked the glass, a steady rhythm I could also put to music. Wavy lines distorted the outside world and, for a moment, everything seemed peaceful.

He returned, grabbed the paper towels and again used them to blot moisture from his hair.

"The library has computers. If they're on a separate grid, we could keep researching," I said.

"Good idea." He headed for the center of town.

The Madera County library was housed in a sixty-year-old building that had been patched and repaired so many times the brick no longer matched, its mortar cracked and age weary, some windows were double paned while others were old and dingy. It stood across the street from the government center, huddled in the shadow of its monolithic parent like an unsightly child. Gray strips ran along the edges of all the windows, an alarm system that drove the police crazy. Every time there was a strong wind at night, the gusts buffeted the glass and set off the alarm.

I climbed the steps behind Quint. His legs being longer, he reached the door while I still had several steps to go. Warmth enveloped me. The drone of rain quieted as the door closed behind me.

Past the counter fashioned in a large square that also served as the employees' desk, and behind the staircase and tucked in the far corner stood a row of desks with computers. Only one was available, so I claimed it by settling in the seat.

Quint pulled up a chair beside me.

"You're up to something," I whispered.

"What makes you say that?"

I clasped his hand, turned it over and caressed the cuts on the pads of his fingers, his knuckles, the blackened spot on his thumbnail. "How did all this happen?"

He shrugged, but the hint of a grin gave him away.

"Climbing. Really tears up the hands."

"Excuse me," a woman behind me said.

I turned toward the voice.

"You need to register before using the computers." She was small, thin, almost birdlike. She was also the assistant librarian and had worked for the county as long as I could remember. She had to be in her seventies. "You also need your library card to log in."

Looking at Quint, I hoped he'd have a card with him. Mine was in the jewelry box on top of my dresser where it had been the last five years. With technology at my fingertips, I'd quit using the library. Now, I couldn't even access that technology.

"You don't have your card?" he asked.

I shook my head. "You?"

"Nope." He stood, returned the chair to its proper place and raked his fingers through his hair.

"I'll get a new one," I said, and followed the librarian back to the wooden counter. Fifteen minutes and ten dollars later, I returned to find someone else using the computer. Now, they were all in use.

Frustration burned a path though my chest. Briefly, I closed my eyes and breathed deeply. "Any suggestions?"

"My place?" Quint suggested. He lived farther from the Gazette than I did, and hopefully wasn't on the same grid as the newspaper.

Wind lashed the car with rain. The Gingko tree in the front yard of Robin's house had gone bright yellow. The gusts tore leaves from its limbs and scattered them across the lawn. The maple had gone fiery orange, and the pecan wore a cloak of red and brown. Fall had come early this year, as had cold temperatures and rain. I wasn't complaining.

Inside, Penny Lane greeted us with tail wagging. I reached down, carefully, and rubbed her ears. I still wasn't sure why she'd growled at me, and didn't want to push my luck. She touched her nose to my palm as if to assure me she had no intention of harming me.

Quint strode down the hall. I stepped into the kitchen. A hint of Lysol from a recent scrubbing, sink so clean it almost glowed, counters cleared except the coffee maker and basket filled with fresh pears, grapes and persimmons. I pinched off a small cluster of grapes. Beneath a magnet, a souvenir from Monterey Bay Aquarium that showed otters cracking abalone, was a note from Robin. He was babysitting next door.

Quint returned with his laptop. We settled at the pecan wood dining table. Penny curled on the floor beside us. He booted up and slid the computer toward me.

I launched Google, typed in *Tracy Parkston* and *Borden, CA*. Her Facebook page came up. She hadn't made use of security blocks, which allowed complete access. There I found more examples of her vulgar nature. She had written, in very colorful language, accusations about Vanessa, Harland and now, me. The photos she posted were mostly of her children, who appeared unkempt. The little girl wore a food-stained shirt and had ratty hair. More images were selfies or mirror shots that showed in the background a house in disarray. No, that wasn't quite accurate. Her house was filthy.

She had thirty-six friends. Didn't list where, or if, she had graduated high school. A group photograph that looked like it had been taken at one of the trustee's homes showed the former board, before Vanessa, at a Christmas party. Sonneck didn't even smile when celebrating. The room in the background was neat, clean and orderly. Frames on the wall held photos of Sonneck and a woman, probably his wife; family of three I figured was his son, daughter in-law and grandchild; men, probably in their thirties, wearing the sand colored uniforms of the military and the same men in what I called Navy crackerjacks and what Quint had informed me were working uniforms used while in non-office environments, like at sea. One of them looked familiar. I'd almost swear it was Pratt.

Penny bolted to her feet and let loose a string of sharp barks, the pitch sending needles of pain through my head and setting my nerves afire. Claws scratching the tiled floor, she ran into the entryway and growled at the door.

"What's wrong with her?" I asked.

Quint turned, parted the blinds with his fingers and peered out the window. "The Mercedes. It's back."

Chapter 31

I peered over Quint's shoulder as he again parted the blinds and looked outside. The Mercedes with tinted glass idled at the curb two houses away, too far to see who sat behind the wheel. A sudden chill fell through me. I rubbed my arms, but the coldness was too deep to warm. Penny Lane had come to Quint's side as if she knew whoever sat in the blue car intended to harm him. She no longer barked, but issued soft whines. He stroked her head.

I called Morales on his cell and told him about the suspicious visitor and the fact Quint had seen the vehicle three times already.

"No plates," I said. "Quint called it in earlier."

"Be right there," Morales said. "Stay inside. Don't let them know you saw them."

"Will do." I rang off and returned to the computer.

Quint left with Penny and returned to the dining table. He set his handgun, a Sig Sauer he'd gotten while enlisted in the Navy, on the microwave.

"You have your gun?" he asked.

"It's in my nightstand."

"I didn't teach you to shoot so you could leave it at home," he said.

Heat prickled my cheeks. I knew he'd be disappointed when learning I didn't carry the weapon. "I don't like guns. Where's the dog?"

"Spare room," he said and sighed, obviously not ready to abandon the gun topic. "She's a good watch dog."

"I didn't even hear a car," I said. "Think she senses things? Maybe she's sensitive to sounds?"

"She's a cattle dog," Quint said, and I figured he'd already gone online and researched the breed. "Smartest of all dogs. Where most understand about a hundred words Border collies respond to three times as many. They're loyal, too."

"You think she knows you're not safe?"

He leaned against the counter and folded his arms, a frown creasing his brow. "Why me?"

A fist of fear gripped me. I stroked the back of his hand. "I haven't noticed anyone following me."

"I was on the climb." He sat, stretched out his legs, crossed his ankles and laced his fingers behind his head as if someone stalking him was normal.

"We must have rattled a nerve with our investigation." I didn't have the opportunity to finish lunch, and it was nearing dinner time. Fruit would hold me over. I stood, chose a pear with just a hint of a blush and moved to the sink. "We just have to figure out what nerve."

Returning my attention to the computer, I searched Bob Roberts. There were a gazillion people with his name, and weeding through all the Google hits would take time.

We still hadn't heard from Pratt. I searched his name. He, too, had a Facebook page, as did most everyone now days. I didn't. No time, and besides, what would I put on there?

His page mostly showed him with different women, photos of him in his Ferrari, a Corvette, and a Tesla. He'd graduated high school in Oakhurst and now worked for a financial firm in Fresno.

In the spare room, Penny Lane barked. The distinct *whoop-whoop* of a patrol car's siren sounded outside. I peered out the window above the sink. Quint joined me.

"Morales got him," I said, and relief lifted a weight I hadn't been aware of carrying.

Although I should stay out of the way and leave the police work to Morales, I needed to know who had been stalking Quint. I darted out into the drizzle, the remnants of the earlier storm, and crossed the street. He caught up with me and we stood on the sidewalk a few yards away.

Morales' Bronco angled in front of the Mercedes and a patrol vehicle blocked the back. He stepped back from the driver's side window. The door opened, and a man got out. He straightened as much as his bent spine would allow.

Goosebumps rose on my arms. I opened my mouth to ask the questions tumbling in my mind as I recognized the whistleblower, the man the waitress in Courthouse Café had described as meeting with Grady's legislative aid.

"Why the hell are you stalking Quint?"

Of all the characters involved, he was the last I suspected. Once the shock subsided and heat spread through my chest, I stepped closer.

"Answer me," I said.

Quint slid his hand over my shoulder, gripped slightly, his silent plea that I not get involved. "Morales has this."

Heat rose inside me to burn my face. "I want an answer. Now."

"I was trying to decide if I could trust him." The whistleblower glanced at Quint and inched his hand toward me, uncurling his fingers. "Nigel Lee."

The drizzle wet the dust on his boots. His jeans jacket, lined with sewn-in hoodie, quickly absorbed the moisture. His features reflected both pain and determination, evident in the lines between his brows, the hard set of his jaw. I regarded the proffered hand, extended mine and gripped firmly.

"Hannah—"

"Monakee," he finished. "And you're Quint Rydell. I've wanted to contact you for weeks."

"Why didn't you?" Quint asked.

"Ava and Supervisor Spinelli," Nigel said. "They asked me to keep quiet. They wanted to wait and see what a grand jury investigation would uncover. If I'd come to you, Supervisor Spinelli might not be dead."

"We don't know that," Quint said, but an edge to his voice led me to believe he felt that maybe, Nigel was right.

"We'd like to talk with you now," I suggested. "Do you have time?"

"I've got plenty of time. My files are in the trunk." He retreated to the rear of the car.

Morales spoke with the patrol officer, who reversed the vehicle, pulled a U-turn and left. He stepped down off the sidewalk and gestured at Nigel. "Seems harmless."

I nodded. "He's probably scared. I would be if I had information someone had gotten killed over. Whoever tampered with the climbing gear, whoever killed Grady, must not know this guy is involved."

"If that's the case, we need to make sure no one finds out." Morales strode to his Bronco, parked askew so the black car couldn't drive away. He retrieved his cell from the cup holder.

Nigel returned with a backpack slung over his shoulder. "Do you think it's safe to talk here?"

"I think so," Quint said.

I wasn't so sure. I scanned the street, but I didn't live here and wouldn't notice if something was out of the ordinary, anyway. "Maybe we should meet someplace out of town."

"Like Manzanita Knolls?" Quint laughed. "If someone is watching us, they're going to no matter where we are."

I scowled at him, hoping my anger registered. "Fine. Let's talk inside."

"Sorry, Babe," he whispered. My anger *had* registered. "That was uncalled for. Guess this whole mess is really wearing on me."

I understood. It was taking a toll on me, too. "We'll get this figured out."

He nodded and strode across the street. Morales moved his Bronco to curbside in front of Robin's house. Nigel and I followed. I eyed the backpack, heavy with promise, and resisted the urge to lick my lips. Finally, we may be getting someplace with this investigation.

Chapter 32

In the kitchen, Quint prepared a pot of coffee. While it brewed, we gathered around the pecan wood dining table, its polished surface reflecting the overhead light and issuing a warm, golden glow. I closed the laptop and set it on the counter. I didn't know Nigel Lee. Until I did, until I felt I could trust him, I wouldn't share particulars about our investigation.

Nigel set the backpack on a chair, unzipped and pulled folders from its depths. Each neatly labeled. All pertaining to the cemetery board.

I selected one and leafed through the pages. "Looks like you know Vanessa."

"I gave her some. She collected other documents on her own. These were part of my grandfather's files."

He handed me a thin stack of papers. Before I could take them, Morales snatched them from Nigel's fingers.

"What's this?"

"Statements from the investment firm," Nigel said, giving me an apologetic grimace as though Morales taking the items had somehow been Nigel's fault. "I also have this." He handed me the document. "It's the warrant signed by all the trustees except my grandfather. This was shortly before he died."

I peered over Nigel's shoulder. All but one signature line had been filled in. "What is it for?" I asked.

"This allowed for the transfer of the endowment out of the county auditor's department and into an investment firm."

"Central Valley Securities," I said, reading from the warrant. "Investment, financial consultants. So that's where the money is now?"

"Maybe." He settled in a chair and held out his hand toward Morales, who scowled and handed the stack of paper back to Nigel. He thumbed through the sheets, pulled several free and spread them out on the table. "They aren't originals. Not even the district has originals. They're all copies."

I picked up a sheet. A faint line marked the page just below the cemetery district's address. The imperfection reminded me of, back in the days of paste-up and darkrooms, when I didn't quite roll the waxed strips of copy onto the grid sheet as well as I should have and the edge left a shadow when printed. Another page had a similar line near the account number.

My pulse quickened and I grinned. "Someone generated false documents."

Bits of the puzzle started to fall into place. We weren't talking about a thousand here and there from the income earned off the principle amount. Whoever made these documents was covering up what was really going on with the endowment, and I'd bet a week's pay that was the heart of the embezzlement case. Someone had gotten their hands on the millions.

The row of numbers on another statement caught my attention, and I picked it up. The last three digits were out of order. "How many accounts does the district have with this firm?"

"Just the one."

I drew my foot onto the chair, rested my chin on my knee and bit my thumbnail, a position that, for whatever reason, aides me in the thought process. Now, that process was dedicated to finding a link between the cemetery board members, an investment firm and the four climbers.

"This," I said, sliding the statement across the table to Morales, "is a different number."

Quint brought mugs to the table and set the pot on a trivet. Morales poured himself a cup.

"Anyone want water?" Quint asked.

I nodded, as did Nigel. From the refrigerator, Quint brought bottles and passed them out.

I uncapped mine and drank, savoring its coldness. "Any time money is moved, there has to be some paperwork, right?"

Nigel removed more files from his backpack, glanced at Morales and handed the pages to me. I immediately recognized the warrants; they were similar to those I'd gotten from the auditor's office.

"Their secretary generates these at the request of the board," Nigel said. "You won't find copies of any of these in the cemetery office. I've looked."

I almost asked how he'd gotten inside, and bit my lip. I'd been known to find an unlocked door. In one case a secluded dumpster. How investigators came about their information was often something we would, as the saying goes, take to the grave.

The forms were for transfers. I shuffled through them, seventeen in all, and the transfer amounts varied from five-thousand to five-hundred-thousand, transferred into three different accounts, a high-stakes shell game.

"Know who tells the secretary to draw up these warrants?" Morales unscrewed the water bottle, drank half its contents and set the uncapped bottle on the table. I wanted to reach over, secure it, while in my mind the container tipped, poured over the precious evidence and destroyed everything.

"Tracy. I have no idea who gives her direction." Nigel sipped from the bottle. "This is what Grady was killed over. I'd also shown his assistant all of this, and now they're dead."

Quint cleared his throat, stood and sauntered toward the living room. He'd been dealing with his friend's death in the only way he knew how: quiet reserve. Mass would be later in the evening, and graveside tomorrow, which he'd miss because of Grandpa's funeral in Texas. Too much death. I breathed deeply, a ragged breath that I hadn't intended. I, too, handled sorrow in my own peculiar way and that included not drawing attention to my pain but cradling it in silence. Only those closest to me had ever seen me cry.

Morales' cell rang. He retreated to the living room and answered.

Quint returned and sat beside me.

"Sonneck is the treasurer, correct?" I asked Nigel. He nodded. "So he's the one telling Tracy to draw up the warrants?"

"That I don't know," he said, and sipped again. "It could be any of them."

True. None of them, except Vanessa, read anything before they signed. With such inattention, even I could wipe out their bank accounts. I checked the dates. These transactions were over the past six months.

Morales returned and pocketed his cell. A grin spread across his face.

"I'm going to the office with all the evidence. Chang's meeting me. You wanna come?"

"Do you need to ask?" I peered at Quint. "You coming?"

"I have assignments," he said. "I can download and process photos here and email them to the office. Meet you there after?"

I nodded. "Nigel?"

Morales shook his head. "Badorine is sending an officer to get him. We can't risk his safety. If these people really had anything to do with the supervisor's death, and that of his assistant, they could come after him," Morales added, nodding toward Nigel. "You're going into protective custody until we straighten this out."

Nigel fiddled with the water bottle's label, crinkling it. Finally he shrugged. "Don't take too long, okay?"

"We'll do our best." To me, Morales said, "Ready?"

I nodded.

"May I take these?" Morales asked Nigel.

"Sure. I have copies."

Morales gathered up the documents. I slid into my coat and followed him to the curb. Since I'd left my car at the office, I rode with him. The wind had picked up, and the sky took on a greenish hue that made me decidedly uncomfortable. I'd seen that shade in Texas. What had followed was a tornado. But this was central California. While tornados had occurred, they were rare. The last one had taken out half the trees in a park in Chowchilla.

"Climate change," Morales said, as if latching onto my line of thought.

"Probably," I said. "Did the deputy tell you anything?"

"They have members of the cemetery board there and that office manager." Morales stopped at a red light. "They've arrested her several times."

"For?" I prompted.

"Drugs, mostly. One count of embezzlement, but that was reversed when the complainant dropped the charge."

"Embezzlement? And they put her in charge of a cemetery office? What is *wrong* with those people?" I wound my hair, still damp from the rain, into a ponytail. "Wait until you meet her. She's a piece of work."

This time they met at the sheriff's office, an adobe structure built in the Fifties and expanded upon by way of portable buildings. We entered through the lobby, a tight square with three chairs that made the space even tighter and a window with a button attached to its frame. Morales waved at whoever sat beyond the darkened glass. A buzzer sounded and he pushed open the door. I followed into the long hallway with doors every ten feet, both sides, alternating every five. A young deputy escorted us to the detectives' division, a room crammed with four desks, file cabinets, shelves and eight chairs, office style for the deputies, hard plastic with chrome legs for guests.

Chang had taken over a small office normally used by the evidence technician. Since budgets were tight, and their technician retired, the sheriff shared the police's IT.

Light glinted off his dome, shiny with lotion. He looked up as we walked in. "Did you bring the files?"

Morales lifted the two expandable folders he'd gotten from Vanessa and set them and Nigel's warrants on the desk.

"Good. I want to look these over before interviewing the trustees." He led us to a small conference room with a rectangular table and eight chairs, pulled out the folders' contents and started leafing through them. Then he read Vanessa's report, which outline how she came to her conclusions.

"How does this tie to Spinelli's death?" Chang asked.

"His office was investigating allegations of embezzlement," I said.

"What makes you think Supervisor Spinelli's death was intentional?"

I explained about Quint, and his meticulous manner in which he kept, well, *everything*. "He inspects his gear after every climb. If there was something wrong with that rope or cam, he would have tossed it. And, Grady's assistant was gunned down in her driveway. This is a homicide."

"Who is Quint?"

"Photographer with the Gazette," I said. "He and Grady were good friends and often climbed together."

"The county's auditor is checking into their books," Morales added.

"When?"

Morales looked to me for an answer.

"Not sure."

Chang nodded. "I'll give him a call. Right now, lay this out for me, okay? I've got three angry people in the next room waiting to be interviewed."

Chapter 33

Although wanting to join Morales and Chang in the interrogation room, they wouldn't allow it. Not being law enforcement had its drawbacks.

Instead, they parked me in a dimly lit, box-like room with coffee maker, small refrigerator, and a window with one-way glass. A table and chair had been positioned before the glass, and I settled in for what I hoped would be an insightful show.

I still had the stack of warrants I'd gotten from the auditor and set them on the badly-scarred table. Instead of working back, I flipped the ream upside down. Five years had been the longest all but Bubba had been trustees, and he'd probably leave when they buried *him* in Manzanita Knolls. The files were for routine items signed by Bubba and the former board members. A tenth of the way down, the names changed when Sonneck and Bosley had joined.

A wicked grin tried to play my lips. I licked it away and tapped my pen against the page.

"Sonneck, I'd love to learn that you're tangled up in this mess."

According to the documents, one of the first newly seated board's actions was to remove the endowment from the County to an investment firm. Unfortunately, the warrant didn't specify which one. I searched several more documents from the same timeframe and came across the deposit into an account with Central Valley Securities, the name on the statements Nigel had given us.

Tracy Parkston had created the warrants.

I studied the earlier pages. None had her name. She had been hired at the same time Sonneck and Bosley had joined the team.

All I needed to do was figure out her connection with one of them. Or both.

The glass before me lightened. In the room on its far side, the door opened and Morales, Chang, and a ranger with the National Parks Service I didn't recognize entered.

They had escorted Sonneck into the interrogation room. He sat at the end farthest from the door, by design on behalf of Morales I was sure. Sonneck folded his arms over his barrel chest and tilted his head back in attempt to look down his nose, yet again coming across as someone with a kink in his neck. The arrogance oozed from him like sap from a pine.

I set those warrants I'd already read face up on the upside down stack and returned them to the depths of my bag. The show was about to start, and I didn't want to miss one moment. An advantage to viewing and not participating is, I could scrutinize without the suspect knowing, catch the subtle movements and quirks.

"How are you doing today?" Chang asked and sat with his back to the mirror.

"Fine until now." Sonneck puffed up like a rooster.

"We'd like to ask a few questions. Is that okay?"

"Nope."

Morales leaned against the wall beside the door, to the right of the room. "Got something to hide?"

Curling his lip into a sharp frown that reminded me of a Chinook salmon, Sonneck shook his head. "What I got is none of your business. I already called our lawyer. Not sayin' a word 'til he gets here."

And just like that, the show ended. I leaned back, trying not to let disappointment color my mood. If Sonneck had the intelligence to pull the lawyer card, the rest of them would, too.

Chang stood and motioned toward the door. Once Sonneck left, Chang turned to Morales.

"No sense in trying to speak with the others," he said. "They'll just parrot each other until their representation arrives."

"Then we wait." Morales hooked his thumbs in the belt loops of his black Wranglers. "In the meantime we can talk to their office staff. They're here, right?"

"The head groundskeeper and the woman who runs the office are." Chang stepped into the hallway. He returned moments later gripping Tracy by her arm. Apparently, she hadn't wanted to cooperate. I could have warned them. She was anything but cooperative.

She jerked herself free and scowled at him with such hatred I half expected Chang's face to melt. I twitched back, although I knew she couldn't see me.

"Get a grip," I muttered.

Tracy refused to sit when he motioned toward the chair, instead moving in a jig that wasn't quite pacing and wasn't quite bouncing but an odd blend of both. Scratching her arm, she glared at the three men in the room.

"Let me go," she said, "or I'll claim you guys tried to gang rape me."

"What's with the scratching?" Morales asked.

"None of your fuckin' business." She quit, but her nails were already bloodied, her skin smeared where she'd gouged her flesh.

"We'd like to ask you about the supervisor who died," Chang tried.

"Fuck you," she snapped. "I'm not saying a word and you can't make me."

"That's not going to work for you," Chang said. "The attorney works for the trustees. You're not a trustee."

"Then I want to call my uncle," she said, and stretched her mouth, worked her jaw. "He's an attorney. Lance Parkston."

The name chilled my blood. I rubbed my arms. "Figures she'd be related to Parkston."

Morales visibly bristled. They, too, knew Parkston. He sued anytime someone pissed him off. Morales had been the subject of more than one suit, and Parkston's latest had been against the Gazette. And me.

Morales stepped into the hallway, I assumed to get Parkston on the phone.

Tracy leapt toward the door, attempting to grab it before it could close. She missed, drew her arm back and returned to scratching only this time her throat. Long angry lines appeared in her mottled flesh.

"Miss, are you okay?" Chang asked.

"No you fuck head," she said. Again her nails reddened with blood. "You drag me in here because some bitch on the board is making shit up so no, I'm not okay."

"No one has accused you of anything," Chang said. "I was referring to your agitation. Are you under the influence of drugs?"

She paled, shifted her gaze from Chang to the NPS ranger. Morales returned and leaned against the door.

"They're getting in touch with her uncle," he said. "What's going on?"

"She doesn't seem capable of being still, and she's scratching herself raw." To Tracy, Chang said, "You are on probation, Correct?"

"She is. Which gives us the right to drug test her," Morales said.

"You can't make me," she shouted. "You fuck, you dumb fuck cop, you can't make me—I'll lawyer up and sue your ass," she added at a volume that shook the glass in its frame. *"You get me the fuck out of here."*

Chang stood, crossed to an inner office intercom, depressed the button and asked for a female officer.

Tracy developed a tick, stretching one side of her mouth toward her ear, relaxing, stretching again in quick, jerky movements.

A female deputy came to the door and motioned Tracy out of the interrogation room. She stepped away, let her knees buckle as if she wanted to sink to the floor. The deputy gripped her upper arm. I'd seen toddlers behave the same way when launching into a hissy fit. For a moment, I wanted to see the deputy handle the situation the same why my mother had when I'd been a brat. Smack her. Instead, she lifted Tracy back onto her feet.

"Knock it off, or I'll get a couple guys to cuff you and carry you out."

Tracy glared, but her shoulders sagged in resignation.

I leaned back and clenched my teeth until my jaws ached. I tried to relax, but damn, I wanted answers. I drummed my fingers against the table.

"Someone's gotta cave in," I muttered.

These were the most unreasonable people I've seen in a long time, and I've seen a lot of them in my line of work.

"Not very accommodating, is she?" Morales said, more of a statement than a question. "If she's clean, I'll buy you a pitcher of beer."

"If she's clean, I need to retire," Chang said. "If I can't spot a tweaker, I don't need to be on the job."

My cell chimed the guitar and drum intro of "American Girl." I retrieved it from the depths of my purse. I'd gotten a text from Oz.

"G2G ISO—" I knew that one, the cops used it, *In Search Of*— "din-din" was his slang for dinner—"IDK if u need anything. If so, text. TTYL, BRB ur BFF Oz. Really? What the hell does that mean?"

Okay, I got that he's going *ISO* dinner, and if I needed something to text him. Only, I don't text. I don't know the lingo, and what was TTYL? I found his number in my contact list and pushed send. He answered halfway through the first ring.

"Told you to text," he said. "How are you ever going to learn new technology if you don't use it?"

"I don't want to use it," I said, keeping my voice low although I was alone in the room. Something about two-way glass made me feel like *I* was being watched. "I gather you're going to the store?"

"Oh, Girlfriend, you're so last century," he said, and I imagined him rolling his eyes. "So? Din-din? What would you prefer? I was thinking something like pasta with a white wine sauce or perhaps a nice lobster bisque since it has grown chilly and that just sounds so comfy."

"Pasta," I said, knowing he'd cook whatever he wanted. I didn't care for lobster bisque, too much seasoning for my taste. "Or I could grab a burger before the gig."

I'd be at The Dock for the private party anyway, and they made awesome burgers.

"Absolutely not," Oz said, and scoffed. "I think I'll make both. I can put lobster in the wine sauce to pair the two. Oh, and a bottle of Lunatic!" he added and rang off.

I dropped the cell into my bag and tapped on the glass separating me from Morales and the other cops. He left and reappeared beside me in the dimly-lit room.

"About four and a half years ago, Sonneck and Bosley became trustees. About the same time, Tracy started working at the cemetery. That's when they removed the endowment from County control."

"Good work." Morales grinned. "Still say you should've been a cop."

"She's working for one of them," I said. "She draws up the warrants for their signatures. They all sign, no questions asked. Until Vanessa," I added. "Which is why I think someone needs to keep an eye on her. If they—one of them, a hired hand, whoever—killed Grady and Ava, they might come after Vanessa, too."

Morales nodded. "I'll talk to Chang, see if they can spare someone to watch her until we figure this out."

"When you go back in there?"

"Yeah?"

"Pretend you already know Tracy is working for one of the trustees. Ask her how much of a kick-back they're giving her."

"Good technique," he said, and his dark gaze hardened. "Ever use it on me?"

"I'm not telling," I said, and flashed him a smile. I had. More than once. And it had worked beautifully.

He left, reemerged beyond the smoky glass and spoke with Chang, who used his hand-held radio to request a babysitter with a badge for Vanessa.

After delivering the results of the test and determining that Morales wouldn't be buying the beer and Chang wasn't going to hang up his holster, the female deputy asked if she needed to escort Tracy to the county lockup.

"I don't know what she's on, of course," the deputy said, giving Tracy a glance that displayed disgust. "But she's dirty."

"One question first," Morales said, and motioned for Tracy to sit.

The deputy left.

Tracy complied this time, sitting on the chair's edge to avoid resting her back against her cuffed hands. "Are you really going to lock me up?"

"Yes. We are. But," Morales said, and flicked his gaze at the glass then back at her. "If you cooperate, I'll make sure to mention it to the district attorney."

She closed her eyes. Even though cuffed, she still tried to scratch but could only reach her wrists.

"How much is he paying you?" Morales asked.

Her head shot up. She stared at him through wide eyes. Her face paled, as though the meth had soaked up all her blood.

"Hundred? Thousand? More? What's drawing up those warrants worth?"

She shifted her attention between the men.

"D.A.'s a good friend of mine."

Her shoulders sagged and she sighed. "Five hundred each time. I find a note on my desk telling me to make one up giving permission to remove funds from the endowment trust. I do it, they all sign it—no one reads *anything*—and I mail it to the investment firm. After the meeting, the next day, I find five hundred bucks in my desk drawer."

"Are you expecting me to believe you don't know who is leaving the notes?" Planting his fists against the table, he leaned over Tracy and glared down at her. "Do you think I'm that stupid?"

"It's the truth," she said, and her jaw trembled. "I don't know who leaves them. They're left at night."

"Who has keys to the office?" he asked.

"Everyone. All of them." She tugged at the cuffs, twisted, and relaxed. "Did you call my uncle?"

"We did."

"Good. I'm not sayin' another word until he gets here."

Chapter 34

Chang had placed Tracy in another room to wait for her uncle-slash-attorney. They would book her into the county jail after they had another chance to test her memory on which of the trustees were like the cobbler's elves and snuck into the office at night. Instead of making shoes, they were leaving orders that made her an accessory to a felony.

Five-hundred a pop. Over four and a half years, that had probably added up to quite a tidy sum. She'd drawn up seventeen requests for funds in six months. I flipped over one of the reports I'd been reading and jotted down the numbers.

"Eighty-five hundred. Not bad for a few minutes work."

I'd given those seventeen to Morales. She'd sent them directly to the investment firm, Central Valley Securities, and kept copies. Not smart. The orders had come from someone with a key to the cemetery office and that pointed to the trustees. Now I needed to find the connection between them and the securities firm.

Had to be Sonneck or Bosley. Both had come onto the board the same time as Tracy, when the endowment funds were placed with the private investor.

On the far side of the glass, the quiet trustee, Lois Walker, entered the interrogation room. I'd gotten a cup of coffee from the pot on the shelf behind me, sipped and longed for the Keurig. But the brew was hot, warmed my hands as I curled them around the ceramic mug and contained caffeine. The morning had been busy, the hours packed with more activity than the past few days and my mind had gone from sharp to dull. I desperately needed the caffeine.

Walker was a mousy-looking woman, short and round with dingy hair. Her glasses were straight out of the eighties, oversized frames that covered a third of her face yet just as simple and round as she. Her polyester pant suit reminded me of something my grandmother liked to wear, and this woman was probably around the same age. She didn't wear jewelry or makeup. A wallflower, and I imagined her when she was young, sitting on the sidelines at the school dance and watching all the other students enjoy themselves. I could relate. I'd been a scrawny kid, more interested in reading and writing than any social activity.

She sat next to the attorney, who introduced himself as Jerry Anderson. He wore a pinstriped suit he'd probably had since his paralegal days. The cloth looked as worn as he was, and he seemed as comfortable in it as I was my pajamas.

Chang and Morales positioned themselves as they had before, Chang closest to the target, Morales farther way. They were well practiced at good cop/bad cop. Morales was *always* the bad cop.

"Ms. Walker, do you know why you are here today?" Chang asked.

"No," she said, barely above a whisper, so softly I had to lean closer to the speaker to capture the word. "I was just told to be here. So I'm here."

She lifted her head enough to peer at Chang over the rims of her glasses.

"How long have you been a trustee for Manzanita Knolls Cemetery District?"

"Two years."

"The terms are four years, correct?"

She nodded. "I was appointed to finish a term when one of them died."

I shifted in the chair. Its leather seat cracked with age. Propping my elbows on the scarred table, I tilted my head so I could capture the words that seeped into the room.

"You'll probably stay on, seems to be what most of them do."

"No," she whispered, glanced at the attorney, and lowered her gaze. "I don't want to be on the board anymore."

"Why is that?" Chang jotted notes. When she didn't answer, he looked up from the canary yellow pad and raised his brows. "Why don't you want to remain on the board?"

She twisted the straps of her handbag, one that also reflected her age. Its ends resembled an inverted V with brass clasp. I hadn't seen one of those since I was a kid. The straps were well worn; the faux leather had peeled away leaving a brown color as dingy as her hair.

Anderson gave her an encouraging nod as if to say *It's okay. No one is going to hurt you here.*

"It's not what I thought it would be," she said, a bit more courage strengthening her tone. "The way they do things. It's just not right."

"Not right how?" Morales moved from his post beside the door and sat at the table.

"Well, that office person, Tracy. I don't understand why she's there." Lois quit working her purse straps and folded her hands on top of them. "She obviously has a drug problem. You don't dare say anything. The others come to her defense. Except the new girl, Vanessa. I worry about her. I've got her in my prayers every night. She don't take nothing from no one."

"Is Tracy related to one of the trustees?"

"I don't know. I think her uncle, that awful lawyer, might have something on one of them," she added, referring to her fellow board members. "Why else would they keep her? She is rude, insensitive, and I think she's stealing money."

"Oh?" Morales raised his brow. "Do you have proof?"

"No, but I can get some. She keeps copies of everything at the office, and I have a key." She twisted the brass clasp, parted the metal trim and I imagined the hinges creaking as my grandmother's purse had. Lois pulled out a shiny key that looked to have never been used. She handed it to Morales. "Go ahead, take it. I don't want it, didn't want it to begin with. They said I had to have it. But with that girl taking drugs and doing God only knows what else in there, I want no part of it."

"You don't go into the office when she's not there?"

"Lord no. I don't want to get accused of anything, and I'll bet there's plenty wrong in there."

My breath caught. I leaned forward. "Come on," I urged, although I knew she couldn't hear. "Tell us what you know, Lois."

She pulled a lace-trimmed handkerchief from her purse and blotted her eyes.

I sighed and leaned back.

The now-tepid coffee coated my mouth with a burnt taste. I set the mug aside. I needed caffeine, but not that badly. If Lois was telling the truth, that she hadn't used the key, I could rule her out as a suspect. I didn't believe she was behind the embezzlement. That left Bubba, who I also ruled out. If he had been behind the thefts he wouldn't have waited until Sonneck and Bosley came onto the board.

While Bosley was annoying and crazy with all her talk about choking on dead crows, I didn't think she was involved, either. I'd bet on Sonneck. He was crazy in a much darker way.

"You've signed the statements for reimbursement, the warrants, right?"

She nodded. "I have to. When I asked to see receipts, Norm got all upset and told me to shut up and sign them. He said he bought furniture once, got reimbursed about five-thousand dollars but there's no furniture out at that office."

"Why don't you just quit?"

"I do as I'm told," she said, her tone dropping to a whisper. "I already let Supervisor Spinelli's office know I don't want to stay on. I'm going to Montana to live with my daughter. I don't have much longer. Quitting isn't an option. Bubba and Norm want to keep things as they are."

"So they can manipulate her," I said.

I wondered if that plan emerged before or after she'd taken a seat on the district board. Having dealt with Sonneck, I'd say after.

"He acted the same way when I questioned why Tracy should have a debit card. He said she needed it for office supplies, and shouldn't have to come ask us for paper clips and tape." Again Lois glanced at the attorney. "I got the mail," she whispered. "Can I tell you something? It'll make Norm mad, but I need to tell you. I need to tell someone what they're doing."

"Go right ahead," Chang said.

"Wait." Anderson held up his hand. "If what you're going to say will implicate another trustee in a crime, we need to talk first."

The words felt like weights on my limbs. Damn. So close. I drew my legs into the chair. "Come on, Lois," I muttered. "Say it."

"But it *is* a crime." She turned back to Chang. "My heart has been heavy long enough. There's thousands of dollars unaccounted for. Our bookkeeper quit, she said she wasn't going to take the fall for what the trustees are doing. Only, I didn't do anything except sign like Norm and Bubba told me to."

Doing.

Something.

Wrong.

She had opened the door and confirmed what I knew in my gut. I smiled.

"Way to go, Lois."

"You're under duress," Anderson said. "Let's step outside and talk—"

"No." Lois stood. "I'm finished. I quit the cemetery board as of right now. What those people are doing is wrong and I want no part of it."

Thousands missing. They were dumb enough to give Tracy—a meth addict—a debit card. Guess there really isn't a way to fix stupid.

Lois left. The attorney trailed behind.

I hurried out of the viewing room and met them in the hallway. Anderson had stepped into the men's room. Wide eyed, Lois stared at me. She clutched her bag in both hands as if I would try and snag it from her. Then she apparently recognized me, and the tension left her features.

"Ms. Walker?"

She looked me over. "What?"

"I'd like to ask you about Grady Spinelli."

She shifted her weight and seemed to close in on herself, evident in the way she hunched her shoulders. "He's the supervisor who died."

"Yes, and I don't believe it was an accident." I touched my fingers to her arm, a hesitant attempt to help her relax. "He knew about the money, didn't he? That thousands of dollars are unaccounted for?"

Lois nodded. "He knew. He called me two weeks ago. He asked me not to say anything. He said I'd be protected when all of this came out." She looked up. Tears glistened in her eyes. "Now he's dead and there's no one to protect me."

"Protect you from what?"

"The other trustees. They're going to find out I talked, and . . ."

"And what?" I asked.

"Norm Sonneck is not a nice man," she said, "and he knows people who can do things."

My blood ran cold. I rubbed my arms through my blazer sleeves, trying to restore some warmth. "What things?"

She shook her head and stepped backward, as though trying to escape her verbal admission.

"Hurt people?" I asked.

Slowly, she nodded and wiped moisture from her eyes.

Anderson returned and looked from me to Lois. "You didn't say anything incriminating. Did you?"

He cupped her arm and led her down the hall. I returned to the viewing room just as Morales and Chang entered.

"I think the attorney knows something."

"Sounds like it," Morales said.

"Lois is scared. You might have someone watch her," I suggested.

"Good idea." Chang unclipped his iPhone from its holder on his belt and thumbed in a number. "Now, we need to get a search warrant and get all the records from the cemetery office."

"They might have files at their homes," I said. "We should check there, too."

"I'll work on the warrant," Chang said, lifting the phone to his ear, "and give you a call when I have it."

Chapter 35

Morales dropped me off at the Gazette while we waited for Chang to get our permission slip to search the cemetery office. Stepping from the coldness into an almost sweltering newsroom brought a film of perspiration to dampen my skin. I slipped out of my coat and blazer and draped them over the back of my chair.

The power had been restored and everyone worked double time to make deadline. Phones rang and the din of voices filled the room. The message light on my phone flashed. Sitting, I tapped the button and entered my password.

The public information officer with the women's prison had called about a press release—had I gotten her email? My computer screen had died when the power failed and was still dark. I brought it back to life. While it clicked and whirred, I called the PIO. It would take a while before I could check email and I still needed to speak with the correctional officer who had sometimes climbed with Grady.

After she'd given me the details of a fundraiser they were planning for Christmas, I trapped the handset between shoulder and ear. "Do you know any big wall climbers who work at the prison?"

"Yeah, that would be Officer Fisher. He showed me photos of him and the supervisor who died hanging from outcroppings with the valley thousands of feet below. Crazy if you ask me."

"Can you transfer me to his extension?"

"Sure." Click, ring and a man's voice invited me to leave a message. I did.

My computer had finally woken. I found the email and crafted it into a fluff piece for the community page. Then I wrote ten inches of copy on the power outage. It would accompany Quint's art.

I stepped around to his cubicle, expecting to find him there. He hadn't returned and his computer was still off. Using his desk phone, I called his cell and let him know the power had been restored.

"Good. And I've dug up an interesting piece of information on Norm Sonneck," Quint said. "You know how he claims to have been a Vietnam combat veteran?"

I sure did. He'd plastered it on the back of his Jeep and always wore his Veteran ball cap.

"He was a supply clerk at Fort Ord," Quint said. "Not only did he never see combat, he never left California."

Sonneck was so insecure he had lied about his military record? What a sad little man. "Can you go there? Gain access to his records?"

There might be a list of relatives, if the Army required such information.

"The base shut down in Ninety Four," Quint said.

Figured. "Anything else?"

"He got a general discharge for unspecified reasons," Quint said. "Looks like he couldn't hold his temper in the Army, either."

"How did you . . . ."

"You're not the only one with sources," Quint said. "This is off the record, as you say. I wasn't supposed to access his files."

"Wow. My by-the-book man broke a rule. I'm impressed."

"Bent the rule," he said. "See you tonight."

I hung up and returned to my cubicle. With a reporter's notebook propped against my knee, I hooked my feet on the edge of my desk and slumped in the wobbly chair. I'd made a list of the trustees, and now crossed out Lois and Vanessa. I added Tracy and a money sign. Then I jotted Roberts, Wickham, Yates and Pratt.

Other than climbing, what connection did these guys have?

Sonneck had lied about this military service. Bullied Lois. Embezzled money through reimbursements for purchases he'd never made. I needed to look closer at his circle of friends, if he had any. He'd created such a world for himself that, in his mind, demanded respect. Bringing him down would ruin him. Would he kill to keep that secret? Kill to keep the respect he believes he deserves, regardless of the fact it was based on lies?

Tracy Parkston had embezzled thousands, from what Lois had said, and was getting kickbacks to the tune of five-hundred each. But I doubted she was smart enough to try and stop Grady from investigating the thefts. She'd be the type to ruin his credibility and try to destroy him politically with lies and wild accusations. I drew a line through her name.

Bubba. He was a manipulator. Had he gotten someone to tamper with Quint's gear? It would've had to be one of the climbers; they were the only ones with access. He was also Roberts' grandfather. Roberts had a criminal past. Bubba and Tracy had a thing, if not an actual affair. They'd been caught messing around, and the thought prompted a sour knot to form in my stomach. I scribbled a star next to Bubba and Roberts' names.

Yates had been convincing enough I hadn't given him a second thought. I Googled his name, found his Facebook page—was I the only one without a page?—and his affiliations with climbing blogs and news feeds. He offered advice on his own Web site, which was filled with photos of him and his friends on walls all over the world.

The wiggling sensation, one that told me I'd missed something important, worked my memory. The coffee shop. When the barista brought Yates' coffee, he apologized.

Chills prickled my skin. I gripped the pen. "He'd apologized for the loss of Yates' friend. Grady. They *had* known each other."

Had Yates been giving Grady information? As far as I could determine, Yates had no ties to those on the cemetery board. I started to cross out his name and drew a question mark beside it, instead.

Roberts. Wickham. Pratt.

Wickham was a priest. He'd remained very quiet when Chang had questioned him. Perhaps too quiet. Vanessa said she knew Wickham, and he wasn't capable of killing. But I'd learned that all too often the quiet ones have dark, violent sides they don't readily show. I needed to take a harder look at Wickham's background and why he was transferred from San Diego. I circled his name.

Bubba was also a veteran. He'd obviously served prior to Sonneck's tour as a supply clerk at the former military base near Monterey. Roberts probably hadn't served, not taking into account his prior conviction. Unless he had served before he'd been convicted in the domestic violence case. I jotted a note to have Quint check it out. The ink was barely noticeable. I tossed the pen into the trash.

Then there was Pratt. He said he'd call when he would be able to stop by, but hadn't. All I knew of him was that he'd been in the Navy during Desert Storm, he'd been a SEAL, and he was a skilled climber. I circled his name.

My phone rang. I set the notepad on my now-uncluttered desk and answered.

"Officer Fisher here. What can I help you with?"

"Questions," I said, and scooted closer to my desk. I plucked a fresh pen from the coffee mug. "I understand you and Supervisor Spinelli were friends."

Silence. Then a heavy sigh. "Yeah. The best."

"This may sound odd, but did he ever mention feeling threatened by anyone?" I asked. "Someone in the climbing word?"

"No. Why?"

"The sheriff's department has opened a case in conjunction with federal investigators," I said. "We don't believe Grady's death was an accident."

"He was acting strange, now that I think of it," Fisher said. "Uneasy."

"When was the last time you saw him?"

"The prior weekend. My wife and I had dinner with Grady and Diane at The Dock." Another weighted sigh. "I can't believe he's gone. It just doesn't seem real."

"Do you know a lot of the local climbers?" I tapped out a four-four rhythm against the legal pad.

"Some. We usually climbed alone or with my son, a three-man team."

"Do you know Bob Roberts, a priest named Wickham or Doug Pratt?"

"I know Roberts," Fisher said. "He did some time right here, that's when he learned I climbed and where he got interested in climbing. We'd had some short conversations."

"How about the others?" Please give me something to go on, some lead, however tenuous.

"Wickham, I believe he was with a bouldering group I'd gone to a couple years back. I remember because he joked around and wore his priest collar with his climbing clothes. Kind of a nut."

I could see that, although the time I'd met him was a somber occasion. I recalled his pun, and how he'd said Spinelli was climbing the highest peaks in heaven.

I also recalled the way Pratt had knelt to tie his shoe, although it almost looked as if he'd tucked something into one of the boxes Quint and I had our belongings in. What had been in there? What could have drawn Pratt's attention?

Quint's wallet. But he hadn't said anything was missing, and if something had been Quint would have noticed. He was meticulous with *everything*.

His spare car key? They had been in the box, next to the wallet.

"Still there?" Fisher asked.

"Yep, sorry about that. How about Doug Pratt?"

"Nope, never met the guy. Look, I'm back on duty in five. If that's all you need, I've got to go."

"That's all. Thanks for returning my call."

He recited his personal phone number, and added, "Call if you find out anything more. Grady's death, what a loss of a great life. A great friend."

"I will." I hung up.

The floor rumbled. The now lukewarm coffee in my mug rippled the way the water had in Jurassic Park when the T-Rex came after Jeff Goldblum. Only this wasn't a dinosaur of the Jurassic period. It was a dinosaur of a different nature, an old printing press that outdated those used by our competitors.

The documents Nigel had provided showed faint shadows where someone had placed the cemetery district's address over whoever's had been there, making it look like the money was still in the account when, in fact, it had been transferred out.

The culprit had to be an insider. How else could he have generated false statements? If he'd come in with a warrant to withdraw funds, the employees at the investment firm would know that the endowment could not be withdrawn. Where did the climbers work?

Wickham was a priest. Yates, an engineer, worked for the high speed rail project. What about Pratt and Roberts? I couldn't recall.

My head ached from all the reading and hours on the computer. I removed my glasses, rubbed my eyes, added another star beside both of their names and set the pen and notepad aside. I'd ask Morales.

Even though I had another hour on the clock, I wanted to go home, relax before the gig, eat the dinner Oz had promised and hopefully get a couple hours sleep before flying out to Texas. My mind felt like it had been running in overdrive all day, and while the headache had been tamed, if I didn't take a break it would likely return with a vengeance.

I gathered my things, returned the pen to the mug I'd taken it from, and the phone rang. Watching the red light flicker with each annoying sound, I considered not answering. It could be a follow up on a story I'd need to tag onto the end of one I'd already written. It could be a hot news tip. Or it could be Oz, he had an annoying way of informing me of his plans, regardless of whether I wanted to know or not. I closed my eyes, sat at my desk and lifted the receiver.

"Judge signed off," Morales said. "On our way to the cemetery office. Want us to swing by and pick you up?"

Thoughts of relaxing and eating fluttered like lightning bugs trapped in a jar, then winked out. "Sure. When?"

"We're at the curb now."

I hung up, made my way through the building to the front door. Morales' Bronco idled in the no parking zone. Since Chang was in the passenger seat, I climbed into the back, closed the door and buckled in as Morales drove toward Manzanita Knolls.

Chapter 36

I rode in the back seat while Morales drove. He made the trip into the mountains in under twenty minutes, took the narrow road that led to the cemetery too fast and by the time we arrived my tailbone ached and the headache was on the threshold of stepping back into my brain. He stopped, the Bronco's tires spinning up dust, and I climbed out feeling like I'd just stepped off a Tilt-A-Whirl, dizzy and unsteady. Chang looked like he hadn't fared any better, he stumbled out of the passenger seat and swiped moisture from his upper lip.

He'd parked by an untended flowerbed that had been overgrown with the community's namesake, the manzanita's branches a deep maroon, the leaves, what few clung to the shrubs, were small and round, stunted by the lack of water. Rain from the earlier storm had filled the potholes and now provided pools for a sparrow to bathe, a lizard to drink.

At three-thousand feet, the entire graveyard sat high above Manzanita Knolls. Thick forest formed a misshapen ring around the cemetery. Behind the office were tall, gray markers, some of which were more than a hundred years old. Cement angels harkened and prayed. Rod iron gates closed the dead inside crypts. History's resting place.

On the native rock structure that served as both the office and public restrooms, about fifteen feet ahead, a sheet of paper had been taped to the glass-front case, beneath which that day's agenda was still displayed. The page on the glass simply stated *Closed*.

From his jacket pocket, Morales withdrew the key Lois had given him. He unlocked the office, pushed the door open and motioned Chang and me inside.

I flipped on the lights, although it wasn't near dark. Storm clouds still hovered, coloring the room a dingy gray. It felt wrong to be there. Chills climbed the ladder of my spine. Light made the act of entering without anyone present a bit less disturbing.

A steel desk with badly scarred plywood top was positioned to face the door. On top stood a computer monitor, the old boxy type that took up a third of the desk's surface. Behind were a row of file cabinets. On top lay stacks of large, leather-bound books similar to those that held past editions of the Gazette. These had dates on the spines going back more than a hundred years. I lifted the cover on one. Inside, a list of names ran along the left like an accountant's grid that, in rows from left to right, showed where each had been buried and the dates of interment.

Gravel crunched outside. I peered through the barred window, expecting to see a car. Nothing. Morales must have heard it, too, and now stepped close to the door, opened to the outside. He scanned the graveyard, shrugged and crossed to the row of file cabinets.

He yanked open the top drawer. I moved to the far end and started there. Chang chose the middle.

Files were neatly lined up, each with labels stating what lay inside. These were old, long before Tracy came to work. I skipped to the next metal cabinet.

"Fucking mess," Morales grumbled, and I abandoned my search. A mess most likely translated into Tracy's handiwork.

Reaching in front of him, I grasped a handful of files and brought them to the desk. The documents were in no sensible order, just crammed inside, some dog-eared, and others had been shoved down by other pages and were now creased like miniature accordions. I pulled those out and used my palm to flatten the sheets against the plywood.

An hour later, Morales slammed the final drawer shut. None had held any of the warrants signed by the trustees that allowed for the transfer of funds from the endowment trust.

"Fucking waste of time," Morales said.

I rifled through the desk drawers, pulled out the plastic wastebasket and checked there, too. "They've got to be here someplace. She isn't very bright, so she wouldn't have removed them. Most likely she hid them."

While they pulled out furniture and checked behind, I crossed to the bathroom and pulled the chain dangling from the ceiling fixture. The toilet had a black ring, the water lower than the stain. They'd probably placed a brick in the tank, a trick to turn water guzzlers into drought friendly bowls.

Or something was hidden in the tank.

I lifted the lid. Inside, beneath the float, was a gallon-sized Zip Loc bag containing several sheets of paper. After shoving up my coat sleeve, I reached in and grasped the bag by its zippered end.

"Guys?" I said.

They turned and looked.

"Sonofabitch," Morales muttered. "She hid them in the toilet?"

He snagged the Zip Loc from me and set them on the desk.

I peered over his shoulder as he and Chang examined the forged statements and warrants signed by the trustees.

"None of them have dollar amounts," Chang said, "just gives permission for the securities firm to withdraw funds."

"Wow. Rubber stamped them all," I said.

Morales grunted. "We've got what we came for. Let's get out of here."

He straightened and turned toward the doorway. Just as Chang stepped onto the stoop, a subtle sound like a dart striking a bulls-eye came from somewhere outside.

Chang stopped. Turned as his knees buckled and he slid down the doorframe.

A neat, black hole appeared in his forehead, a hole that quickly filled with blood. A trickle of fluid cut a path down his face. He wheezed. Deep in his chest, something rattled. The sound stopped, his body jerked and then stilled.

My breath caught. Panic gripped me, squeezed air from my lungs in a startled cry. Morales' hand came down hard on my shoulder and I crashed to the floor. Then he snagged Chang's leg, pulled the deputy toward him to clear the doorway and locked us inside.

Chapter 37

Chang lay dead on the floor, a growing pool of blood spreading outward from his head. His eyes, staring blankly at nothing, had gone black. Looking at him sent fear rocking my heart, but it was hard to look away, as though I'd become mesmerized by some morbid fascination with death.

I shivered, crouched lower on the cold linoleum floor of the Manzanita Knolls cemetery office. I wanted to speak but couldn't find the strength and groaned instead.

The air had already taken on the metallic scent I'd always associated with autopsy rooms. The clock above the door showed just minutes until five o'clock. Soon the sky would darken, air grow colder.

Morales, three feet away, slid his snub nose from its holster, moved toward the window and sat with his back against the wall, the sill inches above his head.

From outside, silence, just as still and quiet as Chang.

I crawled to the metal desk with its scarred plywood top, walked my fingers along its edge until I found the phone resting in its charger. After thumbing the TALK button, I brought the unit to my ear.

Nothing.

Morales looked at me expectantly, his brows inching beneath his shaggy hair. I shook my head. The unit was digital, and the electricity was still on, which meant someone had cut the lines outside. I set the phone on the desk, slid to my heels and sat.

Whoever was out there, whoever had killed Chang and likely wanted Morales and me dead as well, wasn't in a panic. If he had been, he'd have fired more shots, peppered the building. Instead, he'd waited. Meticulous. Calculating. Waited until he saw his target and brought him down with a single bullet.

"How long do you think he'll be out there?" I whispered, although no one could have overheard me.

"Unknown," Morales said.

"Do you think it's more than one?"

He glared at me. "How the fuck should I know?"

"Try your cell," I suggested, brushing away his brisk attitude. I'd known him a long time, and nothing he said surprised me.

Why had I left my purse in his Bronco? In my purse was my phone. I had no reason to carry a purse into here. I wasn't going to buy a plot. I'd come to find the evidence that now lay in a disorganized heap on the floor. Morales had dropped the documents in order to pull Chang into the room and close the door.

Again I regarded Chang, and shivers returned to walk my spine. His iPhone was clipped to his belt. Swallowing hard to rid myself of the knot tightening my throat, I rolled onto hands and knees and inched toward him.

The growing pool of blood made its way toward his belt. The closer I got, the closer it got and I imagined the warm, tacky fluid greeting my fingers. I stretched out my arm, snagged the phone, holder and all, from his belt and hurried back to the desk.

Once the cell powered up, a box appeared asking for a password. I slumped against the cold steel and fought the urge to chuck the cell against the far wall.

"What's wrong?" Morales moved his phone to the right then left, and I realized he was searching for a signal.

"Password protected."

"Try his badge number."

I glanced at the star clipped to Chang's belt, punched in the numbers and the phone unlocked.

"How'd you know?" I asked.

"It's what I use."

Apparently, it was what all cops used.

Once unlocked, I tapped in Nine-One-One. Static, then a female voice: *What is your emergency?*

More static. Poor reception. I needed to give her our location fast.

"We have an officer down," I said. "We're at—"

Static, then silence.

"Shit," I muttered, and again wanted to throw the damned thing. I tried three more times with no results. The signal was too weak. "Any luck?"

"Sonofabitch can't get a signal. Fucking mountains."

I tucked Chang's cell into my coat pocket. "What now?"

"Wait him out?"

"How will we know when he's gone?" I didn't want a small, round hole in my head.

"He'll leave. Only, we need to get out of here before dark," Morales added. "Otherwise he'll have the advantage."

"He'll be able to see us, and we won't see him," I said.

Morales reached up beside the locked door and flipped the switches. Lights inside and on the stoop went dark. The air grayed. The only glow came from the computer. We didn't have much daytime left. Dark fell quicker in the mountains than on the valley floor.

The clock ticked off seconds, the repetitive sound filled my head like someone tapping on my brain. Using my fingers, I plugged my ears. The sound stopped. Unplugged and the tick-tick-ticking returned even louder.

Twenty minutes later, the sky tinged orange, Morales stood, careful to avoid the window.

"We need to get out of here." He waved his hand before the glass, and I fought the urge to plug my ears again. I didn't want to hear that *phitt* sound, didn't want to watch as a bullet tore through Morales' hand. Didn't want blood spatter to cover me as it had when Grady had fallen.

No gunfire. No shattered bone and flesh. No blood.

Morales stepped over Chang's body and tugged his service weapon from its holster. He handed me the snub nose.

I stared at the gun. I didn't want it. But I knew Morales would insist, so I pinched the revolver's handle between thumb and finger.

"You know how to use it," he said, his attempt to encourage me. "Stay calm. Keep your head clear. Aim and fire."

"Aim and fire. Okay." My hand relaxed around the pistol's grip. I started to stand, but Morales motioned me to remain on the floor. Then he opened the door and peered outside.

"Either he's gone or he's hoping that's what we think," Morales said. "Car's not too far away. Stay on the driver's side, get in back. When I say, keep your head low and run."

"That's fifteen feet," I said. "He can kill me in fifteen feet."

"Run fast."

My palms grew damp, my mouth dry. The rocking sensation returned my chest, and my breathing had slowed. I made my way to Morales and stood on knees that trembled and threatened to send me crashing to the floor.

"Ready?" he asked.

With a glance at Chang's body, the blood that had stopped spreading and now held a thick ring around the pool, I nodded.

Morales flung the door open, said, "Run," and I bolted for the Bronco. His footfalls hammered the ground behind me. Just as I reached the car's fender, something whizzed past my head, followed by that dart-striking-cork sound I'd heard when Chang had been shot.

Once I'd reached the safety of the driver's door, I turned. Morales jerked, went still and fell. Blood covered his face, glistened on his black jacket.

My body trembled. I covered my mouth, but couldn't trap the shrill scream that bubbled up my throat and tore from my lips.

Chapter 38

I choked back more screams. If I didn't do something fast, I'd be lying on the ground, bleeding just like Morales. The air had grayed, and I knew it would be full dark within thirty minutes. I had to get out of the cemetery.

I had to get to the forest where I'd have a better chance of escaping the fate that had taken down Chang and Morales.

The woods were a hundred yards beyond the oldest section of the graveyard. The thumping in my chest intensified. I breathed deeply, rose to a crouching position and darted across the driveway.

The whirring sound of a bullet skimmed the air beside my ear. I ducked behind a tall granite marker, weather-worn and darkened with age, then ran for the next, again taking cover. I huddled there, my breath harsh and clouding the air before me. Scanning the cemetery, I spotted a four-sided monolith that rose seven feet into the air. I bolted and ducked behind it just as a bullet struck the stone, sending shards of rock biting my cheek. My pulse pounded. Heat seared my flesh. I bit my lower lip, stifling a cry, and made a dead run for the tree line.

Thick underbrush snagged my coat. Pine needles created a thick carpet that dampened the sound of my feet hammering the ground, which could work against me if the sniper behind me decided to follow. I didn't dare glance over my shoulder. A second could cost my life. Instead I pushed through the shrubs, darted around trees to get as far away from the shooter as possible.

My lungs burned. My mind raced, thoughts turning toward who could be tracking me down, intent on killing me. Flashes from Facebook pages, snippets of conversations, invaded my head: The shooter had fired on us with the calculating precision of a sniper. Central Valley Securities. Photos in Sonneck's house showing him with his nephew, a man I hadn't recognized before but whose image became sharp now, solidifying into features as real as if he stood before me.

He'd knelt beside the plastic tub holding our belongings shortly before leaving base camp in Yosemite. Quint had loaned him gear for a climb on Chilnualna Falls Road, which I now knew the killer had obtained for a single reason—to compromise and use to kill Grady.

The ground opened up before me. I skidded to a stop inches from the edge of a thousand-foot drop to trees and boulders below. Pebbles ticked as they scattered over the side. I sucked in my breath, which caught and burned in my throat. Reaching out, I tried to find something to grab as I leaned back and knelt. Dizziness tilted the world around me with a sense of vertigo brought on by my crippling fear of heights. I could hike to a large slab of granite and enjoy a view, but not this vertical drop. My body trembled. Sweat trickled down my temples. My heartbeat raced and only evened out when my fingers touched the ground. To my right, the narrow, weed-choked trail vanished. To the left, boulders perched precariously on the cliff's edge leaving me no escape route.

My only choice was to backtrack, run along the cliff until I found a path that would take me to the valley below. In the distance, light glowed beyond a stand of trees. A house. If I could reach it, I might find help.

I turned and started to return to the woods when the dark shape of a man stepped from the grove and into the dying light of day. The retired Navy SEAL. The man who loved fancy, expensive cars and who worked at an investment firm and whose photo had been on the wall in the image taken during the cemetery district's Christmas party.

Doug Pratt raised his weapon.

Chapter 39

Crouched on cold granite, its chill numbing my feet, I stared at the gun clutched in both Pratt's hands, an unusual weapon, and why I focused on it I didn't know. Perhaps because I was shocked he hadn't already put a bullet through my brain. The grip appeared normal, but the barrel resembled a hatchet blade, only black and not as large, and I briefly wondered if this was one of the new weapons I'd heard about, one permanently integrated with a silencer. That thought made me weak in the knees, made me wobble and I collapsed onto the cold stone.

"You son of a bitch."

I expected to hear the weapon's pop, feel the piercing hot lead, but he just stood there keeping the handgun trained on my head.

"Get up."

Slowly, I stood, battling down the surge of fear as I glanced at the edge. Cold wind buffeted me. I widened my stance to keep that wind from pushing me over the cliff and onto the trees and rocks below almost masked by near total darkness. I still had the snub nose in my hand but wasn't going to draw the weapon on him. He'd never let me raise it high enough to pull off a shot. I discretely slipped it into my coat pocket, hoping against hope I'd have an opportunity to catch him off guard and put a slug in his brain.

"Huh uh," he said, dipping the gun's odd barrel toward my pocket. "Take it out. Slowly. Place it on the ground and slide it to me."

My stomach lurched with the sickening assurance of my last hope edging away. I curled my fingers around the gun's cold steel, closed my eyes for a moment and tried to figure out some course of action that would reverse our roles, leave me holding a weapon on him, but there wasn't one. I stepped closer to the cliff, peered down. Not as high as El Capitan, but enough that should I fall I would die. There'd be a good chance no one would ever find my body.

A mild bout of dizziness washed over me. I breathed deeply, suppressing the sensation.

"Do you really think you can get away with this?" I asked.

Eight feet below was a ledge. If I could figure out a way to get down there, maybe I'd live. I let the snub nose drop. It struck the outcropping, spun near the edge and stopped.

Heat from running faded from my body, leaving me cold and trembling. The icy breeze bit my cheeks, and my eyes watered. I blinked, cleared my vision, poked my glasses back in place and regarded Pratt.

"What are you waiting for?" I asked, not that I wanted him to kill me. He hadn't hesitated with Chang or Morales. What made me so different?

"The evidence," he said. "What do you have? Where is it?"

Where were the warrants with his securities company's name? All over the cemetery office floor. The forged statements that the rubber-stamp trustees believed showed the endowment funds to be intact? Chang's office in Yosemite. The cams Pratt had damaged to facilitate Grady's death? Also in Chang's office. Any of these answers would get me killed.

"Where?" Pratt shouted. Despite the frigid temperature, sweat beaded on his forehead.

The dizziness left me lightheaded. I could tell him whatever I wanted. Maybe *there* was the hope. I straightened and glared at him.

"You should've known we would speak to law enforcement," I said. "We wouldn't keep everything to ourselves. Those men you shot? Both cops. The DA has copies of everything."

Pratt seemed to consider this, squaring his shoulders and slowly nodding. "But they don't know it's me."

"They will," I countered, resisting the urge to hold out my hands as if doing so would stop him from shooting me. "It's just a matter of time before they figure it out."

"You figured it out, didn't you?"

I nodded. "You're already facing capital punishment for killing cops," my throat constricted. In my mind I saw Morales on the pothole-riddled driveway in the cemetery, blood splashed over his face and clothes. I cleared my throat and shoved the image aside. "You're going to get the death penalty."

"Then killing you won't make a difference," Pratt said, and a sly grin split his features. "Besides. You're the only one who knows I killed them."

The metallic taste of fear dried my mouth. The thumping in my chest returned, bringing on the rocking motions I'd felt before. My arms trembled, legs threatened to buckle and I became acutely aware of every sound, every sight, and every brush of air against my skin. I stepped closer to the cliff.

The shelf where the gun had landed was barely visible. If I was going to jump, I needed to do it now.

Chapter 40

Although I could miss and fall to my death as Grady had from El Capitan, the ledge eight feet down the cliff was my only course of action. If I didn't move fast Pratt would kill me. Fear tightened its hold, spreading sweat over my skin despite the coldness that grew icier by the minute. I stared at the gun, its small black hole that would unleash the bullet that would end my life.

Again I peered down, over the edge, toward the three-foot wide, five-foot long outcropping of granite and then the blackness beyond.

I breathed deeply.

Exhaled slowly.

I had no option.

I stepped off the cliff.

Air rushed by me, creating a roar that filled my head.

The ledge seemed to jump up to meet me, my feet slapped the granite, I tottered, spread my arms, slammed against the rock and clawed for something to stop my downward momentum.

I gripped jagged stone, the razor fine cusps sliced into my fingers. Pain flooded my body and I smothered a scream. I rolled over, leaned against the minimal safety of the sheer wall. My breaths, harsh and deep, hung in plumes before me. Cold from the stone seeped into my legs. Sitting, I looked around but darkness had fallen. All I could see were glints of moonlight on smooth rock. Then another glimmer, metal, at the far side of the shelf. I scooped up the snub nose revolver.

Above, Pratt had gotten to the edge and now peered down at me. He started to raise his arm, and I knew if I didn't fire first I'd be dead. Stretching out my arms, I aimed and fired, striking his hand that held the gun. A second shot lodged in his shoulder, knocking him off balance. He tottered, his feet slipped from under him and he careened toward me.

He struck the outcropping, grasped the far edge, his body going over and slapping the stone wall beneath him. Then he pulled himself partially onto the ledge, reached out and grasped my ankle. He yanked, using me to save himself, pulled so hard tendons burned. I screamed, tried to raise my free leg and kick, but I'd dug my heel in a crack and to lift it could allow his weight to pull us both down.

"If I'm dying, so are you, Bitch," he said, his voice gravelly with the attempt to choke back pain. Then he grinned, and my blood turned to ice.

I gripped the thirty-eight in both hands as I'd been taught. Raised the barrel. Sighted the space between his brows. The trembling in my hands ceased. A wall rose in my mind, severing my fear. Although I was about to do something almost too horrible to acknowledge, a sense of peace so complete and so dreadful filled me I wondered if this was how serial killers felt, detached yet driven.

I fired. The report rang in my ears. A black hole, just as neat and round as if made by an ice pick, appeared in Pratt's forehead. Blood, bone and brain matter burst from the back of his head with an audible crack. His eyes went black and expressionless, as had his features. His body jerked, first forward than back and his grip on my leg loosened sending him free falling into inky blackness.

The control I'd felt once I'd decided to shoot and kill Pratt now faded, leaving me sick and weak. I laid on my back, forcing myself to take slow, even breaths while two words flashed like neon lights in my mind: What now?

How was I supposed to get off the ledge?

I stood, but I couldn't look down. Instead I looked up. Eight feet. I could manage that. I leaned against the cold stone and closed my eyes. I had dropped eight feet over the side in order to save my life. I could do this. I ran my hands over the rough cliff side, searching for handholds that could support my weight.

A humming in the distance grew closer and morphed into the distinct flap-flap of helicopter blades. Above, footfalls drew close and stopped. I peered up just as a flashlight beam bore down, blinding me.

"Lieutenant Chang?" A man called out, and I knew that voice, would know it anywhere. Quint had led the county's Search and Rescue team to find the fallen deputy, the few words I'd gotten across to dispatch before losing the signal.

"Quint?" I shouted.

"Hannah?" followed by, "oh, shit," and then, "hang on, Babe. I'll be right there."

I reached into my coat pocket and touched Chang's iPhone. I hadn't considered it would have GPS, but most phones did and I thanked the powers of the universe and Steve Jobs that Chang's was one of them.

*   *   *

Although Quint had wanted me to get medical attention, he accompanied me back to the cemetery where I found Morales sitting in his Bronco bathed by the car's ceiling light. He'd found some paper towels and now held them to his head, but it looked as though the bleeding had stopped. Relief struck a blow to my chest, robbing me of breath, and I couldn't stop the tears from filling my eyes. Choking on a sob, I stumbled toward him.

"You're alive," I said, choking back tears.

He looked up as I approached and stepped into the light's fringes. I read the same sense of release in his eyes. He slid off the driver's seat, reached out and hugged me. I returned his embrace, stood there, basking in the knowledge that we had survived.

"The way you fell, I thought you were dead."

"Grazed me hard enough to knock me out," he muttered and released his hold. "Glad you're okay. Where'd you go?"

"Pratt," I said. "He came after me."

"Where is he now?"

"Dead." I pulled Morales' snub nose from my coat pocket and handed it to him.

He took the weapon and secured it in his holster. Then he studied me. "You okay?"

I shuddered, closed my eyes and nodded although I would never again be okay. I'd taken a man's life. I'd always have that blood on my hands. What bothered me more was the almost serene manner in which I'd killed Pratt. That sense of divide within me, the stranger I didn't know existed taking over and firing the gun.

Morales gripped my shoulders. I peered at him, knowing he understood. "You did what you had to, Hannah. Remember that."

Again I nodded, but I knew something inside of me had changed forever.

Chapter 41

I drew my legs onto the couch and pulled the afghan up to cover them. A mug of chi tea sent fragrant ribbons of steam into the air. From upstairs drifted Oz's voice, Mr. Hopalong Heartbreak from the musical Urban Cowboy—*Oh I picked a doozy, he's a real piece of work.*

I curled my hands around the cup, letting its heat warm my fingers. If I had made it to Texas, I'd be getting ready for Grandpa's funeral service, but after explaining everything to the National Park rangers and sheriff's deputies, Quint and I had missed our flights. I was with them in spirit, though, and Grandma said she understood.

I'd called my editor to let him know I'd be taking a couple days off, which was fine as long as I wrote the story about what had happened at the cemetery and emailed it to him. I'd spent the morning working on it and had shipped it off twenty minutes ago.

Now, I just wanted to relax. I sipped the tea and let its peppery flavors rest on my tongue. Closed my eyes. Tried to shrug off the stress of the past several days. The doorbell rang. I waited to see if Oz would come skipping downstairs, but he didn't so I tossed back the blanket and padded across the living room.

Quint stood on the porch with a subtle grin that only I would notice, one that suggested he needed to tell me something but struggled with just how he would. Nothing bad, the soft shade of his hazel eyes assured me.

"You feel up for a drive?" he asked.

"Now?"

"It won't take long. There's something I need to show you."

"Can't you bring it here?" I glanced back at the sofa, the mug releasing trails in the air.

"It won't fit in the car. Come on, Babe," he said, sliding his hands around my waist. "Thirty minutes at the most. Then I'll bring you back and we'll watch a movie."

He flashed me a grin. The color of his eyes softened to that of warm caramel, a trick he knew I couldn't resist. I sighed. "Let me get some shoes."

Quint stepped inside and closed the door. Instead of sitting in the kitchen or on the lavender La-Z-Boy, he remained in the entry. I climbed the stairs as quickly as my tired, bruised body allowed, pulled on my jogging shoes, grabbed my coat and called out to Oz that I was leaving. Then I returned and Quint led me to his car. Not the Range Rover, but the vintage Mustang he rarely drove any more.

The rain we'd had earlier in the week had scoured the air, which now smelled sweet and fresh. The storm had stripped the trees leaving bare branches to shiver in the wind. He drove south on Sycamore where branches that had formed a canopy now looked moth-eaten, the lack of foliage allowing glimpses of the brooding sky.

"They arrested Sonneck," I said. "He was the one leaving notes whenever Pratt wanted more money. Pratt was his nephew, and he threatened to expose Sonneck."

"Expose what?" Quint slowed and parked at the curb outside the Borden house.

"Same thing you found, that he'd never served anywhere except stateside. That he'd been living a lie for thirty plus years."

"Blackmail?" Quint shook his head. "His own family?"

"Yep. I should have known it was Pratt when you told the NPS ranger that you'd loaned him some of your gear prior to the El Cap climb."

"Yeah, that should have been a red flag for me, too." He grinned. "Come on. I have something to show you."

He got out, came around the hood and opened the passenger door. The work crew I'd seen during my run days ago, which felt like weeks, busied themselves replacing the roof and gingerbread trim.

"What are you doing?" I stepped into the debris-scattered gutter and onto the sidewalk.

He clasped my hand and urged me to walk with him, across the lawn and up the steps to the wrap-around porch.

"We can't be here," I said, keeping my tone low so the workers wouldn't hear.

"Yes we can." Quint selected a key on the carabiner he used as a keychain and plugged it into the deadbolt, the only thing I'd seen so far that didn't keep with the house's original style.

"*You* bought the house?" Shock struck me like a snowball in the face.

"Yeah, call me crazy," he said, pushing the door wide and gesturing for me to enter. "A contractor wanted to level it and build apartments."

I ran my palm over the smooth, walnut banister, several of its balusters blond wood where they'd been replaced, as were some of the risers and treads. Stained glass in the bay window had been replaced or scrubbed clean, their beauty restored. In the living room, with a fireplace of intricately carved wood, about thirty votive candles glowed. A bouquet of daisies, my favorite flower, lay on a barstool, the only piece of furniture.

"You're bringing her back to life." I spun around, taking in all the work he'd done, and work yet to do.

"I know how much you love this old place." He slid his arms around my waist and pulled me close. I closed my eyes, breathing in his scents, those of sandalwood soap and coffee. He brought his lips close to my ear. "Once finished, it'll be a great place for a wedding."

I leaned back and peered up at him. "Quint Rydell, are you trying to tell me something?"

"Trying to ask you something." He reached into a pocket of his jacket. Then he held a small, velvet box that looked to be as old as the house. He opened it and lifted a ring, just as beautiful, amber-colored diamond flanked by two, slightly smaller clear stones and set in platinum. Heaviness settled in my chest, a blend of fear, anxiousness and excitement leaving me lightheaded.

"Hannah? You okay?" He cupped my face in his palm, providing the link back to reality I so desperately needed.

Staring at the ring, I nodded and exhaled a breath I hadn't been aware of holding. "It's beautiful."

His grin broadened. "Glad you like it. It's been in the family since my ancestor had it made in early eighteen hundreds."

"It's too much," I said.

"Nothing's too much for you, Babe." He brushed his lips over mine. "So? Going to marry me?"

Marry him. Become his wife, he my husband, God those words sounded foreign and frightening and wonderful. I looked around the room, the candles, the flowers, the partial restoration and slid my hands over his chest.

"Yes," I said, and flashed him a smile. "After all, you come with the house."

THE END